Ω

Published by
PEACHTREE PUBLISHERS
1700 Chattahoochee Avenue
Atlanta, Georgia 30318-2112
www.peachtree-online.com

Text © 2013 by Melissa Keil

First published in Australia in 2013 by Hardie Grant Egmont.
First United States version published in 2013 by Peachtree Publishers.

Jacket design by Nicola Carmack
Interior design by Melanie McMahon Ives
Title hand lettered by Kyle Brooks

Printed in June 2013 in the United States of America by RR Donnelley & Sons in
Harrisonburg, Viriginia
10 9 8 7 6 5 4 3 2 1
First Edition

Library of Congress Cataloging-in-Publication Data

Keil, Melissa.
  Life in outer space / by Melissa Keil.
    pages cm
  Summary: Sixteen-year-old Sam Kinnison is perfectly happy as a game-playing,
movie-obsessed geek until beautiful, friendly, and impossible to ignore Camilla Carter
starts him wondering if he has been watching all the wrong movies.
  ISBN: 978-1-56145-742-7 / 1-56145-742-6
  [1. Interpersonal relations—Fiction. 2. Friendship—Fiction. 3. High schools—Fic-
tion. 4. Schools—Fiction. 5. Gays—Fiction. 6. Australia—Fiction.] I. Title.
  PZ7.K25187Lif 2013
  [Fic]—dc23

Life in Outer Space

MELISSA KEIL

PEACHTREE
ATLANTA

1

A sort of dance scene with a sketchy Humphrey Bogart

I start this Monday by falling flat on my arse. A normal guy might think his day could only improve from here. I seriously doubt this is going to be the case. I hear laughter and clapping. Someone cheers.

Above me, a giant sign hangs precariously from the corridor ceiling: a pink and purple, glitter-encrusted symbol of doom, handmade by the Spring Dance Committee.

Justin Zigoni takes a flying leap over me and slaps the sign with his hand. A shower of glitter descends from the ceiling and a piece lodges itself in my eyeball.

I close my eyes.

I wonder if it's possible to induce a fatal stroke?

Justin cheers again, and pumps his fists above his head. A crowd has formed around him—a swarm of nonspecific girls, and some guys who all seem to be wearing the same shoes. Assorted Vessels of Wank, gathering their day's supply of glee from my arse-planting like squirrels storing nuts.

If there was an award for the world's best high school cliché, Justin Zigoni would not only win, but they'd name the award after him as well. He would, most probably, gain permanent induction into the High School Arse-Hat Hall of Fame.

Judging by the look of pure smug on Justin's face, I'm assuming he was responsible for what passes for wit at Bowen Lakes Secondary: tipping a bottle of cleaning wax on the floor right in front of my locker.

"Nice trip, Sammy?" Justin calls. The Vessels of Wank and their various minions laugh.

No one calls me Sammy. My mother occasionally throws a "Samuel," but I am, and have always been, just Sam. Sammy is a name for five-year-olds and game show hosts and Shiny Happy People.

I am, definitely, not a Sammy.

Mike is peering down at me with semiconcern. Semi, because a) my best friend's face rarely shows more than semi-anything, and b) Mike knows that displaying anything more will only lead to additional torment when I do, eventually, stand. I remain frozen for approximately nine more seconds until Mike holds out a hand and yanks me to my feet.

Adrian appears beside me, glaring down the corridor. He has his about-to-open-a-can-of-whoop-arse face on.

Objectively, Adrian Radley has zero cans of whoop-arse to open. I fear that this day is about to go from bad to epic-level suckage.

Mike gathers the muesli bars that have spilled from my hoodie pocket. Then he adjusts his glasses and faces Justin with a frown.

"You're a knob, Justin," Mike murmurs.

"What's that, gay-boy?" Justin says, hand to his ear like he's deaf and not just stupid.

Justin does not know Mike is gay. No one knows Mike is gay, apart from me, Adrian, and Allison. Since I have no means of responding without outing my best friend, I make the logical decision not to react.

Adrian, however, has other ideas. Adrian barrels past, and it's only a last minute survival reflex that makes me reach out and grab him by the hood of his sweatshirt.

"Control the Troll, Sammy," Justin says. He's still laughing, but it's the laugh that movie supervillains do, right before they release the radioactive sharks.

Adrian barely comes up to my armpit. He has recently developed a layer of fuzz that stretches from ear to ear across the bottom part of his chin, which he refuses to shave. He has not cut his curly hair in years. He is very slightly overweight. I can see how, to people ill-informed about mythical cave dwellers, Adrian might be considered some-what troll-adjacent. Adrian has been known as the Troll since year eight. I'm not even sure if he minds anymore.

"It's okay, Adrian," I mutter.

Adrian's face has turned purple. I suspect he is about to launch into a rant peppered with *Star Trek* references, but Mike distracts him with a muesli bar, and then with gathering my books, which are scattered across the corridor.

Justin smirks. "Seriously, if this loser factory was awarding Losers of the Year, you boys would be up for a Loser Grammy or something."

The statement makes no sense, but it doesn't matter to the Vessels. They laugh. I fantasize about Leatherface from *Texas Chainsaw Massacre* making an appearance in the school corridor. Then the bell rings, and Justin hip-and-shoulders me as he passes. I am taller than him, but he belongs to a more enhanced male genus. I allow myself to be shoved into the lockers.

The guys follow him, glaring at us. The girls disperse, giggling.

Adrian and Mike appear at my side. I straighten my hoodie. "Have I mentioned I hate my life?"

Mike sighs. "Frequently." He looks at me blankly. "Ready for English?"

"I could so take that guy," Adrian growls.

"Yeah," says Mike. "And then we could take you to the emergency room. Rein it in."

We stand where we are for nineteen seconds, a silent agreement to wait for the length of time it will take the

Vessels to reach our English classroom. We don't look at each other. But when an appropriate interval of time has passed, we start to walk together.

✳

I have never been a fan of Bowen Lakes Secondary. If my life were a screenplay, BLS is nothing more than the slug line above the first scene. But lately, it feels like events have been conspiring to turn my vague antipathy into full-blown, resolute detestation.

Zigoni's knob-jockey-ness has taken on new life this year. Maybe he fell into a vat of some kind of knob-jockey supervillain juice over the summer vacation. Or maybe his three functioning brain cells are just extra bored.

In addition—despite the fact that the Spring Dance is nine months away—the Spring Dance Committee has turned the entire school into a fortress of glitter and pink.

Our walls, once papered with art projects and posters warning about STDs, now hold a sea of Spring Dance detritus. Collages of faces in various lip-joined poses have appeared everywhere, while movie posters have been bastardized in unforgivable ways. I am yet to be convinced that the "Glamour of Old Hollywood" can be replicated on poster paper with art supplies from Target.

The chess club's pin board is covered with a *Casablanca* poster. Humphrey Bogart and Ingrid Bergman have been replaced by the faces of Justin Zigoni and Sharni Vane, Sharni's vacuous eyes gazing into Justin's vacant ones. I have been contemplating whether old school mustache-and-horns vandalism is too good for them.

If the Spring Dance Committee stabbed me in the nuts with a blunt pencil, it would be marginally less painful than the selection of this theme. I tend to avoid movies that have anything to do with high school, dancing, or any combination of the above. However—if pressed—my top five all-time greatest movie school dance scenes are:

1.   The prom scene from *Carrie*. Chick goes ape and blows up her school with her brain. How could it not top the list?

2.   The prom scene from the original *Buffy the Vampire Slayer*, for similar reasons as the above, minus explosive ESP but with the addition of bloodsucking vampires.

3.   The prom scenes from *Prom Night*, if only for the vague hope that our own end-of-year dance will be graced by a rampaging serial killer.

4.   The dance scene from the end of the original *Footloose*, only watched as part of the Extremely Gay Weekend.* It makes the list for sheer lameness, and also because not a single guy in it possessed any sort of rhythmic ability, which is something I can relate to.

* This is not what it sounds like.

5. The graduation scene from *Grease*—a carnival that ends with a flying car. I believe the flying car is symbolic of a journey to the afterlife, which means that Sandy and Danny were probably shoved off the Ferris wheel, or maybe that someone put the muscle-man mallet to proper use. There was only one appropriate end for the smug, semi-brain-damaged jock.

Mike says it's possible I missed the whole point of *Grease* as, apparently, I am dead inside. I choose to take that as a compliment.

✳

Mike and I have English together now, but Adrian has math with Mrs. Chow. He walks us to our classroom anyway, even though he'll have to backtrack and will therefore be late.

Mike shuffles unhurriedly to my left, and Adrian shuffles slowly to my right. Mike adjusts his glasses again, and then flicks my arm casually. Glitter drizzles from my sleeve. Adrian clears his throat and runs a hand through his hair. I do the same; another pink and purple glitter shower rains over the linoleum floor.

It is the closest I will ever come to coordinated movement with the other human beings.

Suffice to say, I am not going to the Spring Dance.

F irst period. English. I hunker down in my usual seat, third row from the front. Mike is beside me, expressionless and silent, as is his MO in any public setting. With his brown hair and brown clothes, Mike blends in to most backgrounds. I'm half expecting him to develop the ability to change skin color as well, like a cuttlefish.

On my other side, Allison Winfield is doodling on her notebook with a chewed-on Hello Kitty pencil. She looks sideways at me and grimaces. She grimaces a lot. I don't always understand why. But in spite of the Hello Kitty, I know that a habitual grimacer is one of my people.

Allison is my only female friend. She has the wispiest blonde hair I've ever seen, which is constantly statically attached to her face. She's one of those girls who might hit puberty at twenty-five, if she's lucky.

Mike is constantly hinting that in terms of girl potential, Allison is as good as I'm likely to get. I dunno. I've tried, experimentally, picturing her shirtless; I suspect she looks like me when I was twelve. I am happy to report that this does nothing whatsoever for me.

Allison is chewing on her hair. Mike has shoved two pencils under his lip like tusks and is staring vacantly at the clock above the whiteboard. On his other side, Victor Cho has assumed his standard position, head down on his folder. He will be asleep and drooling in two point four minutes.

Mr. Nicholas's head is buried in his drawer, and the volume of the class is steadily increasing as the clock ticks. Mr. Nicholas is okay, if a bit earnest. He lives in a uniform of jeans and vintage jackets, and I know he's a fan of classic horror movies because I've seen him a couple of times at the Astor Theater, which makes him slightly cooler than every other teacher at this school.

I'm normally pretty keen on English, but the latest Zigoni incident has left me in zero mood for *Macbeth*. I flick to a blank page in my exercise book. I begin an intricate sketch of the Fortress of Solitude from the original *Superman* movie, which, if I time it correctly, should take me the rest of the class to complete.

There is a knock on the classroom door.

The door opens.

Our assistant principal Mr. Faville enters, clearing his nose on his handkerchief in one noisy, gluggy blow. He looks at the contents for longer than is necessary, then squashes the handkerchief and shoves it into his pocket.

He is followed by a girl.

In movies—not art-house movies made in people's backyards, but Hollywood movies where significant events are signposted for the clueless—there are certain tropes that let you know when something is about to change.

If life was a movie, this is what should have happened when the door opened that Monday morning:

The music should have swelled—pianos and violins. Maybe a cello.

A breeze should have blown through the room, bringing with it a flurry of leaves, probably in slow motion.

The entire male population of the room—minus Mike because he's gay, and me because I'm dead inside—should have shot cartoon hearts out of their chests, à la Pepé Le Pew whenever he saw that chick cat.

But this is not what happens. Instead, the noise in the classroom wavers and dies.

Mr. Faville hurries over for a hushed conversation with Mr. Nicholas. Mr. Faville nods at Mr. Nicholas, and nods at the girl, and nods at the class, then hurries out of the room again without saying a word.

I have no interest in anything that happens at this school. I am, however, a fairly decent observer, like one of those scientists who spend their days staring at microscopic fungus. A new girl means fresh meat, a possible reshuffling of the social order, and maybe three lunchtimes' worth of drama that I will somehow hear about regardless of how uninterested I am. All pointless, but possibly fodder for future screenplays.

I drop my pen on my Superman sketch. I poise my mental pencil over my mental social scorecard.

Mr. Nicholas leans against his desk. The class is silent. The girl waits.

She is wearing a yellow dress that looks like it belongs to a 1950s housewife, and a pair of flat red boots. Her hair is longer than I'd imagine would be practical; it's parted in the middle and hangs in brown waves almost to her waist. She peers around the room impassively. She doesn't look terrified. She doesn't look insanely overconfident, like Adrian that time in year seven when he performed a song as his book report for *The Outsiders*. Mike and I mark that event as ground zero for the downward social spiral of our group.

The girl looks neither scared nor full of herself. On the social scorecard, this is a plus one.

Mr. Nicholas smiles at her. "So, it seems we have a new addition to our Bowen Lakes family. I trust we'll make… Camilla…welcome. Tell us about yourself, Ms. Carter."

Camilla. Unusual name not filled with superfluous vowels. Plus one.

The girl shrugs, like addressing twenty-eight possibly hostile strangers is no big deal. "Well, we've just moved here. My dad and I. We're from here, originally, but we've been living all over the place for a while now."

11

She has a British accent. Plus two.

She is, objectively, attractive. Plus three. Although she is dressed pretty weirdly. I have no idea what girls find acceptable, but I suspect her clothes might be a minus.

She has a tattoo. An honest-to-god tattoo, a curly thing with blue flowers on her shoulder. I do not know a single other year-eleven student with a tattoo. There are a few murmurs around the room now. Plus five.

"Dad's a writer. A journalist. We lived in London for ages, but he was working in New York for the last year, and, well, we were bumming around the States for a while before that." She shrugs again with a half smile. "Guess he was missing home."

She's from New York. With a British accent. Plus twenty.

Something weird happens to Mr. Nicholas's face. "Wait—is your dad *Henry* Carter?"

The faint whiff of celebrity is in the air. The energy in the room changes. My mental pencil hovers uncertainly over the scorecard.

"Ah, yeah. You're a fan?" she says.

"Are you *kidding*?" Mr. Nicholas stares at her like she's wandered into the classroom brandishing Shakespeare's head in a box. "Your dad—he wrote that piece on Grand Funk Railroad for *NME*, right?"

"Yup. Dad loves his old school stadium rock. Mark Farner's pretty cool, though."

She smiles. It isn't embarrassed or self-important. It's just a smile. Plus twelve.

Mr. Nicholas seems to realize that there are twenty-eight other people in his vicinity, because he closes his mouth and packs away the giant man-crush he clearly has for this girl's dad. He leans against his desk again. "What do you know. Class, Henry Carter has to be one of the best music journalists working today. He's interviewed everyone from Lou Reed to Bowie."

There are hushed whispers. Mostly from people who have no idea who he is talking about, but are vaguely aware that they are famous people and therefore worthy of hushed whispers.

Mr. Nicholas rolls his eyes. "He also interviewed Kenny Elfin for *Uncut* magazine."

Gasps and a flurry of hysterical murmurs rocket around the room. Kenny Elfin was runner-up on last year's *X Factor*.

New girl just nods, and gives him that half smile again. So her final score is plus fifteen billion. Another minion for the army of suck that is the A-group.

Mr. Nicholas shakes himself out of his stupor. He gestures to a seat in the second row next to Jackie Nguyen. New girl walks casually to the table. A roomful of eyes are on her, but she moves like she's in the room alone. Justin Zigoni almost falls out of his chair as he tries to get a look at her legs.

Mr. Nicholas turns his back on us and begins writing on the whiteboard. No one cares.

She sits. She pulls her long hair back into a lazy pony-tail. She slips a leather-bound notepad and a pair of cat-eye glasses out of her bag. She settles the glasses onto her face.

She pushes herself back from her desk and crosses her legs, balancing her notepad on her knee. Behind her, two girls discreetly do the same.

Victor Cho chokes on his own saliva and wakes up with a snort.

Beside me, Allison grimaces.

Mike removes the pencils from under his lip. He catches my eye. I know what he's thinking. *At least Justin and the Vessels should be preoccupied for the foreseeable future.*

I roll my eyes. He crosses his. I try not to laugh.

I return to my Fortress of Solitude.

3

Samuel Kinnison and the Extremely Gay Weekend

Mike told us he was gay a year ago, on the weekend my parents were away for a silent meditation retreat. Two days of sitting in a field and refusing to speak. Apart from the field, I couldn't really see how it varied from any other weekend in our house.

It was Friday night, and Mike, Adrian, and I were in my living room rifling through my DVD collection. I was trying to convince them to commit to a *Friday the 13th* marathon, rather than watching *Tron* for the eighteenth time, when Mike took a giant swig of his Coke and said:

"I think I might be gay."

I looked at Mike. Adrian looked at Mike. Adrian looked at me. Mike looked at his Coke. I finally managed to say something semi-useful, which I think was:

"Are you sure?"

Mike shrugged. "Probably."

Adrian's experience with sex extends as far as the various female-oids that plaster his bedroom walls. Since the likelihood was slim that either Princess Leia or a Number Six Cylon from *Battlestar Galactica* would be appearing in my vicinity, I was exploring the option of clinical asexuality.

So we did the only thing we could think of. We googled stuff.

After stumbling on some guy's Olivia Newton-John fan page, we downloaded *Xanadu*, possibly the worst cinematic abomination that my eyes have ever been subjected to. At Adrian's insistence we rented *Lesbian Vampire Killers*, which, quite frankly, was just confusing all around.

We watched *Dirty Dancing*. Mike fell asleep, but I had to admit I kind of liked it, which made me question my own sexuality, raising a whole heap of other questions I chose not to examine.

Adrian offered to take a bullet and kiss Mike. Mike suspected that Adrian hadn't brushed his teeth since grade four. We checked out a bunch of scared-straight websites, but, according to Mike, nothing on any of them could rival the horror he felt at the thought of kissing Adrian.

Eventually I raided Dad's vintage porn stash, and after poring over pages of girls with giant breasts bending over farm equipment, Mike sat back in Dad's La-Z-Boy and said: "Pretty sure I'm gay."

And that was that. We haven't really discussed it since.

Not that it's weird or anything. Mike is just Mike. Mike has been Mike ever since we met in that Building Self-Esteem Through Drama workshop both our mums signed us up for when we were eight.

I don't care that Mike is gay. I figure that since there's little chance of either of us ever touching anyone else's parts, our relative sexualities are somewhat pointless topics of conversation.

✳

The Extremely Gay Weekend is on my mind today for several reasons. Partly because I'm concerned about Mike. But mostly because of *Dirty Dancing*.

The chain of events that led to these thoughts is as follows:

3:20 P.M. The final bell rings, and I head toward the IT office to meet the others. Apart from the morning's arse-planting, I've coasted through this day under the radar. This is because the only thing on anyone's radar today is Camilla Carter. When I catch occasional glimpses of her, she's wallpapered by an adhesive layer of groupies.

There's been much googling of her dad in between classes. Adrian is even inspired to look him up on his iPhone, and Adrian is rarely inspired to use his iPhone for anything other than Angry Birds.

The net is full of Henry Carter's stuff: articles and reviews and photos of a dark-haired guy who looks way too young to be anyone's dad. There's one story about him and Camilla's mum—some English model who was almost big in the 90s, who was married to her dad for, like, five minutes. Two photos of Camilla are also making the rounds; in one, she is leaning over her dad at the launch of the new Wombats album. In the other she's hanging out with some of the cast of *Harry Potter*.

By this point I lose interest. I assume the vague proximity to celebrity will keep the Vessels occupied for at least a month. A potentially incident-free month, the likes of which have not been seen since we had that substitute teacher in year ten who looked like the Channel Seven weather girl. I can't guarantee that the reprieve will be anything other than passing. But I *can* guarantee a few things. There will be angst. There will be gossip. And unless new girl turns out to be a cyborg, she will be of no relevance to me.

What *is* relevant to me is the fact that Mike has dropped out of karate school.

Mike has been obsessed with karate since year seven, when he discovered that kicking people in the face was a legitimate sport. He trains almost religiously, and is actually fairly brilliant at it. He is definitely one of the best black belts at his school.

Today he has wandered into the IT office, dropped six cans of Coke onto Alessandro's pile of cables, and said in his monotone voice:

"I've decided to stop training. I'm hanging up my shin pads."

Even Alessandro, who only knows Mike from a distance, pauses.

Midway through last year, I was employed by the school as Alessandro's assistant. Our IT coordinator does not really need an assistant. He needs a shower, and possibly a dentist. Alessandro decided to finagle my services after stumbling on a lunchtime incident between me and Justin Zigoni. The incident involved a stick, a length of jump rope, and a geyser-like bloody nose that would have made even the most hardcore horror writers proud.

Alessandro looks like what I imagine Adrian might look like in ten years' time, except Alessandro is six-foot-four and knows the passwords to everyone's e-mail account.

No one messes with Alessandro. He's happy for us to hang out in his office whenever we like. When we are here we are, basically, free.

We are listening to Foals in the background, because we always listen to Foals in the background. There is order to Monday afternoons, and in a world of stupidity and looming hostility I have come to depend on it:

On a normal Monday, Mike and Allison will show up at three-thirty with Coke and Mars bars from the shop across the road. Allison will perch on top of the filing cabinet with whichever *Akira* novel is on rotation that day.

Adrian will engage Alessandro in approximately twelve minutes of argument about *Call of Duty*. I will have one computer playing *Battlestar Galactica*, which we don't really need to watch with the volume up since we pretty much know it all by heart. Adrian and Alessandro will conclude their argument with some variation of the phrase, *Why don't you stick to Space Invaders/Checkers/Pong.* And then Alessandro will storm out and not return until it's time for us to leave.

Today, Mike is spinning slowly in his chair, his eyes on the ceiling.

Allison has stopped tapping her shoes against the filing cabinet. She is chewing on her hair again.

Adrian is eating his second Mars bar because I am glaring at him so he doesn't say something stupid, and the only thing that ever stops Adrian from saying stupid things is having his mouth full.

Mike stops spinning. He looks sideways at me.

"Any reason why you're quitting?" I say eventually.

Mike shrugs.

"Is it because of a guy?" Adrian says, spitting a shower of chocolate over Mike's arm.

I up my glare from stun to kill.

Mike sighs. "No. It's not."

I feel like I should add something more. Something insightful. Something quote-worthy.

But then comes the segue to *Dirty Dancing*.

My top five all-time greatest movie lines is a constantly evolving list. The ratio of *Star Wars* to horror movie quotes varies depending on my mood—but there's one line I can't seem to shake from the list:

"Nobody puts Baby in a corner."

I agonized over its inclusion. For a start, it's a girl movie. And it's a dance movie. And it's forever associated with the Extremely Gay Weekend, which, as mentioned, we do not discuss. If I'm narrowing it down to five lines only, a *Dirty Dancing* quote should not even make the top-hundred long list. But, for pure cheese and applicability to multiple situations, I cannot *not* include this line.

I have very little hope that my own life will ever produce anything close to a single great line. I'm desperately running through my mental movie-quote list as I try to think of something passably encouraging to say to Mike.

Except Mike is looking over my shoulder. His eyes widen. Adrian stops chewing on his Mars bar. Allison stops chewing on her hair.

And then I hear a voice behind me. The voice says:

"Dude. Nice laptop wallpaper. Six in the slinky red dress? Did the blonde on a corvette have the night off?"

It may not be *Dirty Dancing*-worthy. But it turns my head anyway.

Camilla Carter is standing in my doorway.

"I'm looking for Sam," she says.

The few times I've spotted her during the day, the only thing I noticed—apart from being surrounded by suck— is that she keeps changing her hair. Sometimes it's up. Sometimes it's down. At the moment it is twisted into some sort of bun-thing on the top of her head. I'm not sure I understand the schizophrenic hair thing—I thought girls spent hours getting their hair right before they ventured into the world.

Adrian points at me. Mike points at me. Allison points at me. I realize—after staring at Six in the slinky red dress on my *Battlestar Galactica* laptop wallpaper for eight seconds—that I am, in fact, Sam.

"I'm Sam," I mumble.

"Hey," she says. "Camilla."

I do not detect any exclamation marks in her voice. I detest people who talk with exclamation marks. Plus one.

She raises an eyebrow at my computer. "You do know she's an evil bitch, though, right? Despite the spectacular boobs."

No one moves.

"Sooo...the office sent me down here. I can't get on the network. They told me you were the person to speak to?"

She is holding a MacBook Air in her hands. She sounds like Kate Beckinsale in *Underworld*.

"If it's a bad time I can come back later. Only I have some sort of welcome pack in my inbox, apparently. You know, map to the toilets and secret S&M dungeons and everything..."

No one moves for another six and a half seconds.

Adrian stands. "Mars bar?" He holds one out.

Camilla steps into the room and takes it.

The sequence of actions has the same effect as Neo finally figuring out how to control the Matrix. The room bursts into a flurry of misdirected activity.

Allison leaps down from her cabinet and Mike jumps out of his chair, and together they shove past Adrian and push a stool toward Camilla. She sits. She unwraps the Mars bar and takes a bite. She holds her MacBook out to me.

The only thoughts I am capable of thinking are that the sanctity of my safe house has been compromised, and the order of my Monday has been disturbed. I take the laptop from her without a word.

"Thanks," she says with a mouth full of chocolate. "Sorry, I don't think I've met you guys yet. It's been a blurry day."

Adrian sticks out his hand. "Adrian, Mike, Sam, Allison," he says quickly. "But you've already met Sam. I'm Adrian. *Adrian*."

Camilla shakes his hand. She smiles at Allison. "Guess that makes you not Mike?"

Allison grimaces. "No. I'm Allison. Uh...nice to meet you?"

"Likewise," Camilla says brightly.

I open up her laptop. Her wallpaper is a picture from a black and white movie that I think is called *Manhattan*.

I do not know what this means. But I figure the faster I work, the faster I can return the four of us to our status quo. I also know that no good can come from having someone like her in a confined space with Adrian.

I balance her laptop on my knees and start typing as quickly as I can. It is not quick enough.

Adrian pokes at her tattoo. He actually jabs his stupid fat index finger into her arm. I don't need to look at Mike to know that he is holding his breath.

I know basically nothing about girls. But I'm fairly certain they don't like it when you poke at them like they're a half-ripe avocado.

"Is that real?" Adrian asks.

Camilla looks down at her arm. "Yup."

Adrian frowns. "How'd you get it?"

She shrugs. "We've travelled a lot. There are plenty of places that don't ask for ID. And Dad's big on self-expression." She flicks her fingers over the ink like she's brushing off some imaginary dirt. I notice a row of tiny music notes twisted in between the blue flowers.

"Did it hurt?" Allison whispers. Several strands of hair are still caught in her mouth.

Camilla grins. "Like a bastard."

No one seems to know how to respond to that.

I click the Firefox icon on her MacBook and the school homepage pops up. I feel that I may be a few moments away from starting to sweat profusely.

"Done," I mumble. I hand the laptop back. She takes it, and she smiles at me. I notice that Alessandro has tacked a new *Barbarella* poster to his pin board. I notice that Adrian has a dribble of caramel stuck to his chin fuzz. I notice that her eyes are hazel.

"So what's your realm?" she says.

"Pardon?" I croak.

She points at my laptop, which has kicked over to my screensaver. It's an image of a night elf from World of Warcraft.

I can feel the eyes of my friends burning into my head. "Oh, ah...Alliance...Frostmourne."

"Hey, cool. I'm trying to level up a dwarf on Frostmourne." Camilla grabs a Post-it. She scribbles something and then hands the Post-it to me.

The Post-it says "AltheaZorg."

"I'm usually on around nine. It's more fun when you're not surrounded by bots." She slips her MacBook into her satchel. "Thanks, Sam. And thanks for the Mars bar, Adrian. Nice meeting you all. See ya." She waves, and smiles, and disappears from the office.

I stare at the Post-it.

Did she just ask me to play Warcraft? Is she a noob that I'm going to have to walk through a simple quest? Or have Justin and the Vessels of Wank put her up to something? Will there be a cast of the school's biggest arsehats hanging out over a computer this evening plotting some brainless, but no doubt still humiliating, practical joke?

I have no idea. But there is only one solution.

I am never playing Warcraft again.

4

How I never played Warcraft again,
and other useless resolutions

Monday's routine has effectively been ruined, so I'm feeling less than cheerful as Mike and I walk home. Not even the combination of *Battlestar* and Foals could drown out the droneage that resulted from new girl's visit. A school full of morons is supposed to be fawning over her; my friends are supposed to have more sense.

Besides, Alessandro's office is my Neutral Zone, one of the few places I can be free of the many nemeses put on this earth solely to cause me pain.

I'm explaining all of this to Mike as we walk, but I'm not sure Mike is listening.

Mike is busy threading the cord on his sweatshirt from left to right. He tugs the brown rope until it almost disappears inside his hood, and then he pulls it slowly the other way. He has been doing this for three blocks now.

I am an idiot. How did I not notice this sooner?

Mike Adams does not say much. His face is capable of displaying maybe three distinct expressions. But right now he might as well be holding a megaphone and yelling, "I! Am! Having! A! Problem!"

I forget about Camilla Carter. "So...karate?"

Mike squints at the road. "Yeah. Think I've had enough."

We walk another block in silence. Unless he's been replaced by a pod person, Mike would not just quit karate. His bedroom smells like Deep Heat and runners. Every available surface is covered with trophies. And last year he skipped the *Star Wars* six-film marathon at the Astor—one of the most important events on our calendar—because his dojo had a training weekend.

I clear my throat. "Just had enough?"

He shrugs. "Yup. Just had enough."

I know he's lying. I don't know why. So we don't talk about it.

We do stand on the street corner near the park for fourteen minutes, discussing Mr. Norrell's history assignment, the latest episode of *The Walking Dead*, and whether Adrian is going to make it through the month without someone punching him in the face. We conclude: pointless, awesome, and probably not. And then Mike waves, and I wave, and we go our own ways.

I add the karate situation to my list of problems.

I walk the four blocks from the park to my house,

past the topiary trees and people with baby buggies that seem to be multiplying daily, *Night of the Living Dead* zombie-style. I sometimes wonder what would happen if zombie hordes did invade. I doubt anyone would actually notice.

I know I should be able to find a story in anything. Good screenwriters can pull interesting films out of the asinine and mundane. But everything I've read about writing always begins with "write what you know." What I know is: quiet streets, topiaries, moronic high school arse-hats, and homework. Has anyone ever made a film about homework? Probably. I bet it was French.

I step between the fake Grecian columns and open my front door. Mum is hunched over the piano in the living room with one of her students hunched next to her, a skinny kid named Kendra or Kendal or something. Kendra/Kendal is butchering Rachmaninoff, one finger at a time. She slips on the notes and turns. Mum swings around as well.

"Hey, Sam! How was your day!"

How was your day! Not even an attempt at being anything other than vanilla. And yes, my mother is an exclamation-talker.

"Hey, Mum. Biology quiz. Think I did okay."

"Well, that's great! Sam, you remember Kelly?"

"Hi, Sam," Kelly whispers. She kicks her shoes along the peach carpet, her cheeks turning scarlet.

I'm trying to think of something suitably insipid to say when I notice Mum is wearing her favorite necklace, the expensive one that she only wears when she's feeling particularly miserable. My eyes wander across the living room. They land on a pile of DVDs that Mum has set aside near the TV. I see *Beaches* on top.

This is not a good sign. This is a sign that my mother will shortly be descending into a blubbery mess as she sits in the dark watching movies where women die of various diseases while looking vulnerable and attractive.

Mum steers Kelly back to her lesson. I wander into the living room and covertly hide *Beaches* behind *The Thing* in the bookshelves. I scan through my DVD collection until I find my box set of *28 Days Later* and *28 Weeks Later*.

"Mum? Zombie movie marathon later?"

Mum turns around. The relief on her face makes me itchy. "Classic?"

"Nah. Danny Boyle?"

Mum smiles. "Sounds great, Sam."

Mum and Kelly are now both looking at me with watery eyes, so I back out of the room quickly.

Dad sticks his head out of the kitchen just as I attempt to sneak past. His face is set in that expression he always seems to wear lately: a little bit vague and a whole lot baffled.

"Dad," I mumble.

Dad clears his throat. "Sam," he mumbles back.

We stare at each other for five more seconds. If my dad's skin suddenly slipped off his body to reveal that he was in fact a lost, man-sized alien cockroach like that one from *Men in Black*, I'm not sure I would really be surprised.

I don't mean to be completely rude about my father. Being mediocre is probably not a crime. But I do believe in reducing things to their component elements. And Dad is, unfortunately, really easy to reduce:

My father likes Harvey Norman, the Discovery Channel, and, for some reason, lizards. He last smiled sometime in 2008, which is one of the few things we have in common. I think that was also about the time of his last proper conversation with Mum.

My dad also looks like me—i.e. sort of like a storm trooper. And not the cool *Star Wars* kind. We're both tall and blond and our facial hair is so useless it might as well not even bother to make an appearance.

I take the stairs two at a time and then close my door, exhaling the breath that's been stuck in my throat all day. I clear a space on my desk and turn on my laptop, and I run a search for Yu Kan-do It Karate. Their latest newsletter has just been posted; there's a training weekend coming up, and someone is selling raffle tickets. They have a new instructor from Queensland, and the DVDs of their last tournament are on sale. I can't see anything that could shed light on the Mike situation. Apparently, I also suck at detective work.

I turn off my computer with a sigh. I should probably start on some homework. Instead, I open my desk drawer. I reach underneath my *Empire* and *Total Film* magazines, and Dad's vintage porn that for some reason is still wedged between my stuff, and dig out my latest red notebook.

Killer Cats from the Third Moon of Jupiter is a screenplay idea I had while Mum was cat-sitting Aunt Jenny's psychotic tabby. It's supposed to be a combination of a classic invasion movie, with a bit of werewolf mythology, and a nod to Sam Raimi's *Evil Dead* films. It's still a working title—I did want to just call it *Cats*, but Mike pointed out that someone might have used that already. Anyway, the *KCftTMoJ* project is in serious danger of ending up in the same place as the rest of my notebooks—buried in the back of my closet.

Thing is, I know what it's *supposed* to be—a sleek sci-fi/horror with Tarantino-worthy dialogue and a kick-arse opening sequence. But right now, basically all I have is an unwieldy title, and a sketch of a giant cat.

I fight back a growing sense of doom as I stare at the page. Nothing in my closet is good enough for my college portfolio. And everything depends on The Plan. I will move to Sydney to study film, and Mike will move there to study law, and we'll share a sketchy flat in a cool neighborhood and it'll be fine because high school will be nothing but a tedious, vague memory and I'll never have to see Justin Zigoni or anyone from Bowen Lakes Secondary ever again.

I *will* write my cult classic. It will be full of quote-worthy lines. But until then, I will endure the status quo, and I will suffer the Domestic Routine.

I kill an hour on my screenplay and then face dinner with my parents—Dad's orange chicken, which tastes like marmalade slathered on KFC. No one says anything remotely memorable.

Dad disappears into his study like he does most nights. For all I know, he's attempting to invent an alternative fuel source down there. I don't bother checking in with him.

I watch two zombie movies with Mum, who makes popcorn and doesn't cry once, which is as successful a night as I can hope for.

It's partway through the second movie—about the time the pretty doctor chick shows up—that a thought starts prickling the back of my brain. I try to concentrate on the flesh-eating hordes on the screen, shoving the irritating thought aside.

It shoves back.

The second movie finishes and Mum goes to bed. Dad is still confined to his study. Perhaps my father is secretly Batman. Bruce Wayne is a bit of an arse as well. It would explain a lot of things.

I shower and throw on my track pants and the old Superman T-shirt that passes for pajamas. I stick a random *Supernatural* DVD on.

The school diary is still sitting on top of my book pile.

I open it, planning only to sort through the worksheets and other junk that has become lodged in there.

A yellow Post-it flashes at me. *AltheaZorg*.

What does it mean?

It means nothing. It belongs to a minion, an A-group hell spawn, which cannot, in any universe, be a good thing.

But if the knob-jockeys *were* plotting some new evil, surely they would have given up and gone home by now?

I turn on my computer.

I go downstairs to make a sandwich.

I return to my room.

I drink a can of Red Bull from the stash under my bed.

I stare at my *Halloween* and *Evil Dead* and *Star Wars* posters for three minutes.

I log on to Warcraft.

I haven't played in a while. I only get caught in the game when my brain feels drained of movie ideas. And my friends aren't really into it; Adrian has the attention span of a concussed fish, and Mike has training eight times a week so won't engage in anything else that requires commitment. Or he did until recently, anyway. Allison occasionally plays, with a level-twelve gnome named "Mizuno," but she is slow and hesitant and always seems to be facing the wrong way in Battlegrounds.

I connect to the server where my level-eighty night elf has been waiting since the last time I played. And then I do nothing. This is stupid. Besides, the whole point of

Warcraft, like the best movies, is to sink into another world with zero reminder of my own pathetic one. There is no logic to this course of action.

I stare at my night elf. I open a chat window. I type "AltheaZorg." I click enter.

A line of text appears on my screen. "Hey there, level 80. Cool name. DexGrifnor?"

I have a minor freak-out and consider logging off. My hands are frozen onto my desk.

"Sam?"

My fingers somehow manage to find the keyboard. "Hey—you knew it was me?"

"Well, I don't know anyone else on here. Been playing on US servers till last week."

"Oh."

I actually type "Oh." So now, apparently, I am both verbally challenged and borderline illiterate.

AltheaZorg writes back anyway. "Sam, wanna help with a quest? I could use a hand."

I check out the map. She's not that far from me.

I picture the A-group gathered around her MacBook, Justin laughing his supervillain laugh. I think about *KCftTMoJ*. I really should be working on my screenplay.

I consider logging off. And then I look at the map again.

"K. Can help. On my way."

"Cool," Camilla types. "Was about to give up. I'm wiped. First days are killers."

It's going to take me at least a couple of minutes to find her. I think for a moment as I watch my night elf fly. "You've had more than one?"

"First days? Ha, yup. Lost count."

Well, at least she didn't type "lol." I crack open another can of Red Bull.

"How does Bowen Lakes compare?" It seems like a reasonable thing to ask.

"First glance? Same as every other school in this dimension. School is school. Unless it's secretly training X-Men. I live in hope."

I snort and some Red Bull comes out of my nose. I don't know what to say. I type a smiley face. And then I feel like an idiot. I am not a user of emoticons.

She types a winking face back.

I remove my hands from the keyboard in case I'm tempted to type something else asinine. The chat window blinks at me. It's just a couple of lines of flashing text. It's not a real conversation. Is it?

I find her white-haired girl dwarf in a tavern. I jog alongside it, and Camilla makes it perform a few seconds of a dwarf dance, its fat legs bouncing in an uncoordinated jig. It looks ridiculous. I feel my face tug into a smile. I type the dance command for my night elf, but then backspace over it. I can't bring myself to make even a virtual me dance.

"Hi," I type instead.

"Hi," she types back. "Thanks for the assist."

I take a deep breath. "What do you need?"

"Trying to complete this stupid quest. I need to steal a sword. But I can't get close enough without dying. Help?"

"K. You lead, I'll follow."

"Cool. Maybe this time I won't end up in a graveyard. It's becoming embarrassing." Her dwarf trots out of the tavern. My night elf scrambles behind her.

I steer my character with one hand and crack open the window above my desk with the other. The warm night breeze circles around my room. I can't quite shake the image of Camilla surrounded by Justin and those guys, though I'm starting to accept that I might be somewhat, slightly, paranoid. Still, I can't form a picture at all of where she might be. Mike would be perched on his black bedspread with his laptop on his knees. Adrian would be stomach-down somewhere beneath his piles of clothes and moldy coffee cups, his computer on the floor in front of him. Allison would be stuck in front of the Mac in her parents' study, since they won't let her have a computer in her bedroom. Having a person I don't know on the other end of the chat window is disconcerting—like speaking to someone who's floating in a vacuum.

And then we reach the caverns and we don't have much time for typing, which is probably a good thing since I've already used up the four sentences of polite conversation that I know.

Camilla is fast, and skilled with her weapons. Occasionally she will throw a question at me, and I will respond with a suggestion or comment, but mostly our characters fight side by side in silence.

We reach the heart of the lair. We shoot our way through the mobs, and Camilla grabs the sword. Her dwarf performs another dance. I make my night elf bow.

"Nice work, Dex," she types. "I'm impressed by your crossbow action."

I don't know what to say. I type another smiley face. I feel like a moron.

She types a smiley face back. "Time for bed. Thanks again. See you later!"

AltheaZorg logs off.

See you later? What does that mean?

I glance at my phone. It is almost 1 A.M. I sweep the empty Red Bulls from the desk into my trash can. Somehow, I have consumed five cans.

I think I may be experiencing a caffeine-induced heart arrhythmia.

In total, I manage approximately eight minutes of sleep.

5

The unforeseen consequences of eggplant casserole

'm standing near my locker waiting for Mike and, even though I've checked my timetable three times now, I can't seem to remember which class we have this morning. I'm feeling fuzzy from lack of sleep and twitchy from the remnants of the energy drinks still circling through my blood. I also have a headache that is working its way from my brain through to my eyeballs.

After some deliberation, I have decided that five cans of Red Bull at midnight is not a great idea.

Mike appears next to me. He frowns at the English textbook in my hands. "We have math."

"Math. Right. Thanks."

"Might want to hurry," he says.

I follow his eyes down the corridor.

Justin Zigoni and Sharni Vane are walking toward us, like royalty surveying their subjects. Steve Stanton is behind them with his arm around Michelle Argus, as if he's worried she'll do a runner if he doesn't keep her attached to his hip. They're surrounded by a bunch of girls who I've gone to school with for years but whose names I keep mixing up.

It's normally about this point that I would make a run for it, but before I can slam my locker closed, something catches my eye. Right in the center of their group is Camilla. She's wearing red jeans, a faded Mickey Mouse T-shirt and a yellow cardigan that reaches her knees. She should look ridiculous. She doesn't.

Sharni is whispering something in Camilla's ear. My stomach knots but I can't get my feet to move. I brace myself to end up—literally or otherwise—on my arse again.

Camilla untangles herself from Sharni. She raises her hand and gives me a short, sharp salute.

"Dex."

The volume of conversation dims. I can just about hear the gears cranking inside Justin's thick head, but I can tell he hasn't made up his mind how to react yet. I think this might be a good thing.

So I ignore him. I nod back at her. And I say the only word my mouth is capable of forming.

"Zorg."

Camilla winks at me and continues down the corridor with the Vessels in tow.

There is a scene in the very first *Alien* movie, where the alien spawn bursts out of the guy's chest and runs off inside the spaceship. Everyone else just stands around, mouths hanging open, brains unable to process what has taken place in front of them.

I have a feeling that Camilla Carter has just created her very own alien-exploding-out-of-a-chest-cavity moment. I'm not entirely sure how I figure into this scenario. I've always imagined myself as that disposable member of the crew who gets killed first and who no one remembers anyway. Judging by the look Justin gives me as he walks away, I have just been upgraded to the guy who later has his entrails smeared all over the corridor walls.

Mike nudges my shoulder. "Explain?"

I swallow a couple of times. "She's a dwarf."

Mike considers this. "Okay then." He is looking closely at my face. That questioning look of Mike's is never a good thing.

I clear my throat. "So. Math?"

Mike nods at my hands. I am now holding my history textbook. I close my eyes for a moment. "Can it please be Friday already?"

Mike opens my locker and swaps my books. "If you could speed up time, would you really just skip one week?"

"You mean if I was gifted with a talisman like the Time-Turner from *Harry Potter*? Do I have the option of fast-forwarding to thirty?"

Mike grunts as he slams my locker closed. "Why thirty?"

"Well, I figure by then I'll be living in LA, in a cool house with views of the Hollywood sign, and my first two indie movies will be on their way to achieving cult status. Oh, and I'll have a dog."

Mike pauses in the classroom doorway. "So you'll have the sign and the dog—are you also planning on meeting any actresses?"

I think about this as we take our seats. I try to imagine myself surrounded by a bunch of blonde girls, but I can't exactly see it. I try again. Now they're in the picture, in bikinis and stuff like in all those dumb comedies Adrian makes us watch. They're standing around my swimming pool. They aren't doing anything much. I think I'm supposed to do something, only I have no idea what that might be. The blonde girls all seem to be staring at me now. One of them points and laughs.

I focus on Mrs. Chow's varicose veins. "I dunno," I whisper. "Do you think I can find some that look like Princess Leia?"

Mike shrugs. "It's Hollywood," he whispers back. "And you'll be in the movies. Probably."

I think about Princess Leia sitting on a lounge chair by the side of my pool. She doesn't look at all happy about this situation.

"Maybe I should just skip to forty?"

✳

I am not a complete moron. I know that movies, especially the movies I love, do not reflect the real world. Those films that try—the Eastern European ones about life on the farm or gulag or whatever—tend to be as depressing as my own life, which I think kind of defeats the purpose of film. However, everything useful I do know about real life I know from movies.

Through an intense study of the characters who live and those that die gruesomely in final scenes, I have narrowed down three basic approaches to dealing with the world:

1. Keep your head down and your face out of anyone's line of fire.

2. Charge headfirst into the fray and hope the enemy is too confused to aim straight.

3. Cry and hide in the toilets.

From as far back as I can remember, Mike, Allison, and I knew the first option was the rational one. Adrian, for as long as I have known him, has attempted the second option. Unfortunately, Adrian's weaponry consists of the equivalent of a backfiring pistol and plastic Viking helmet. The enemy is usually in no way confused. Often, the third option is hastily implemented as a fallback plan.

Camilla Carter, clearly, selects option number two. In her first week she joins the volleyball team and the chess club. She also joins the Spring Dance Committee, which I guess was inevitable. Details about her filter through the grapevine: her mum runs a modeling agency in Singapore. Camilla has a boyfriend named Dave who still lives in New York. There is much speculation over the identity of Dave the Boyfriend but, as yet, no one is sure who he might be.

She smiles whenever she sees me, and occasionally chirps "Dex" as she passes by. I have no idea what her angle is, so I have defaulted to a standard response of a furtive half wave before fleeing in the opposite direction. She is in my history and English classes, but is always knee-deep in Vessels-of-Wank suckage. She seems to slot right in, like the missing piece of a really lame puzzle.

I do not play Warcraft again all week. This is not entirely my choice.

On Tuesday, Mike and Adrian show up after school. We try to work on my screenplay, but since Adrian's idea of a good movie is to have girls in PVC jumpsuits appear at random moments, I give up and put on *Wolf Creek* instead. Despite Adrian's sledgehammer questioning, Mike refuses to discuss karate.

On Wednesday, I come home to find Mum sniffling over *The Notebook*. Apparently Dad decided he "needed a night off" and has gone to a movie, alone. I'm not sure what pisses me off more: the fact that he's ditching Mum, again, or the fact that he's doing it in a movie theater. It's like, he might as well just walk into my place of worship and pee all over the pews. Mum and I make tacos and watch *The Texas Chainsaw Massacre*. We discuss the development of the slasher genre since the 70s; I know Mum is just exercising the former English teacher in her, but I don't mind. It's almost midnight when I fall into bed. I try to rewrite the opening scene of my movie. It still sucks arse.

On Thursday, Alessandro corners me in the IT office at lunchtime with a request to help test some new software after school. I end up stuck for hours while he scours IMDb for news of the latest *Superman* movie. When I get home, Dad is locked in his study and Mum is in bed. Not even the prospect of an *Evil Dead* marathon can entice her out. I make toasted cheese sandwiches for Mum and me, and watch *The Evil Dead* in my bedroom, vaguely contemplating the various ways in which a face-eating curse might be unleashed upon my father. I am not in the mood for Warcraft.

Except that I do log on, briefly. My night elf is alone.

By Friday I am tired. I am tired of school, and home, and *Killer Cats from the Third Moon of Jupiter*, and hiding out in Alessandro's office, which—since the five of us have been crammed in there every lunch hour and free period this week—is starting to smell like the inside of a body bag.

"I think we should have lunch in the dining hall," I say as I walk into the IT office. I didn't even know the words were planning to work their way out of my mouth until I said them. Everyone stares at me.

We do not eat lunch in the dining hall. Not since last year, when Justin Zigoni and his minions and four strawberry milkshakes made it clear that it was best if we ate elsewhere. I was more than happy to maintain the status quo until graduation. I have no idea why I'm feeling so twitchy now, but regardless—I can't spend another lunchtime stuck in this office talking about *Battlestar*.

"Look, it's just lunch," I say. "Besides, has anyone copped anything other than a couple of looks this week?"

Mike and Allison glance at each other. I'm starting to feel inexplicably annoyed.

Allison tugs her Doraemon T-shirt over her knees. "Well, no. But aren't we better off not tempting fate?"

"Tempting fate? What's the worst that could happen?"

Allison looks pained. "I think that might be the definition of tempting fate," she mumbles.

Adrian tosses his sandwich in the trash can. "Come on, guys. No fate but what we make." He grins at me. For once, his *Terminator* quotage might prove to be useful.

Mike stands and straightens his glasses. "Okay. I'm in," he says quietly.

Allison scrambles out of her chair. "If you want, Sam, I'll come as well. I think it's supposed to be apple crumble day."

Alessandro appears to be trying to clean his teeth with a USB key. "You guys need company?"

My friends are looking at me like I've become the

leader of a possibly doomed expedition. I swallow. "Thanks, but we don't need a bodyguard."

Alessandro shrugs. "Your funeral."

I grab my backpack and try my best to look casual. The ridiculousness of this situation is not lost on me; then again, neither is the memory of a strawberry milkshake shower. I march out of the office before my legs have the chance to change their mind.

The four of us scamper into the too-bright dining hall, blinking like hibernating gerbils on the first day of spring. I grab a tray and join the line near the steaming double boilers. Mike files in after me. Adrian is already in the middle of a conversation with the lunch lady about the Friday special—a graying eggplant casserole that looks like the chemical sludge from which comic-book supervillains are born. Allison huddles behind us, clutching her tray like a shield.

I pay for my lunch and make a beeline for an empty table near the door. A bunch of year sevens at the next table look up in alarm; I balk before I realize it's actually me that they're looking at.

"This isn't so bad," Adrian says cheerfully as he slides into the seat across from mine.

Mike pokes at his eggplant casserole and frowns. Allison sits down with a small bowl of dessert. She looks paler than usual.

"You okay, Allison?" I ask.

She smiles faintly. "I'm good. Thanks, Sam."

The noise of a hundred voices and chairs scraping on linoleum is verging on painful. I'm not exactly sure what part of this plan I thought was a good idea, or why. In my rush to break the tedium of my week, I'd forgotten I never actually liked eating in the dining hall, even pre-strawberry-milkshake incident.

I shovel in a forkful of casserole. If malevolence has a flavor, I now believe it might be eggplant. Just as I'm wishing I was four years old and could acceptably spit my food out, a shadow falls across my tray. I freeze, a half-chewed mouthful lodged in my cheek.

"I would say to avoid the special, but I fear I'm too late. I think whoever made it hates taste buds."

"Hey, Camilla," Adrian says, waving his fork in the air.

I spin around. Of course, I then proceed to choke.

Mike thumps me across the back a couple of times. Allison hastily pushes her bottle of water across the table. I take a few giant mouthfuls, my eyes watering.

Camilla's smile wavers. "Sorry, Sam. Didn't mean to lurk." She pulls out a chair and drops into it without even asking first. "You okay? Do we need a medic?"

"No—I'm—fine," I manage to gasp.

"Are you sure?"

I gulp another mouthful of water. My esophagus takes a few moments to decide whether it will swallow or projectile-vomit it across the table.

I swallow. "Uh-huh," I say with as much dignity as I can muster.

Camilla takes a bite of the apple in her hand. She is wearing a T-shirt that has the words "Cobra Kai" stenciled on the front. Her hair is shoved underneath an old-man hat. "I don't think I've seen you guys here at all this week? Though I'm impressed the school actually has a dining hall. It's like an homage to *The Breakfast Club*."

I glance around the room. I can see Sharni Vane and Michelle Argus staring in our direction. Justin Zigoni is looking at me with this smirk on his face. I fear that the plan to remain inconspicuous may have failed miserably.

Camilla nudges my arm like she's known me for longer than five minutes. I flinch. From the corner of my eye, I see Allison grimace.

"Hey, you haven't been on Warcraft this week. My dwarf had to fight all on her lonesome."

"Um, yeah. I've had stuff going on."

Her eyes widen. "And here I was thinking you and I might be soul mates. Unfortunately, I cannot be friends with anyone who prioritizes real life over WoW."

It takes me a moment to figure out that she's joking. I risk another glance at Justin. He's still looking in my direction, and he's laughing. He also has a banana in his hand. I am uncertain of the anatomical correctness of the gesture he is making with it, but it looks painful.

"Um, so, was there something you needed?" I say.

Even to my ears, it sounds a little testy.

Mike shoots me a look.

Camilla nods. "Actually, yeah. See, for some reason I thought it was a good idea to sign up for history, only I'm a little behind. Actually, I'm going to get my arse majorly kicked in history if I don't have help. And since we're in the same class, and I figure you guys probably crack open a book every now and again...?"

"You want to study with us?" Mike says. His eyes dart over to the Vessels' table. Allison's eyes dart over to the Vessels' table. I keep my eyes on Camilla. She looks back at me innocently.

"Why are you taking history then?" I manage to ask. I don't think it comes out rude, but Mike gives me that look again anyway.

Camilla shrugs. "I was pretty decent at it in my other schools. But I'm not exactly up on Australian history. I was six years old last time we lived here."

Adrian is busy shoveling lunch into his mouth. He doesn't look up from his plate. But with a mouthful of toxic-sludge eggplant casserole, Adrian says:

"Sure. We should catch up for a study group. How 'bout Fridays after class? We could go to Mike's place. Or Sam's. They live near here. Tonight?"

Camilla takes another bite of her apple. "Can't tonight. I'm going to Sydney with Dad. He has a thing. But next week? I mean, if that's okay with the rest of you?"

Allison glances at Mike. He shrugs. "I could do with extra study. But my house is out. Mum…has her book club over on Fridays."

Mike catches my eye. I know the real reason he wouldn't want a stranger at his house is because his parents have turned it into a shrine for their okayness about their gay son—complete with a giant rainbow flag hanging in the foyer. The only fight I've ever seen Mike have with his parents was when his dad wanted to hang a rainbow flag off the antenna of their car. Mike thinks his parents are just happy to have something interesting to tell their friends.

Either way, we are not going to Mike's.

Adrian nods. "Sam's it is then."

Everyone looks at me. I make a noise that apparently passes for assent.

Camilla grins. "Awesome. Maybe I won't be looking at a total embarrassment of a history score after all. Cheers, guys." She pushes her chair back and stands. And then she actually tips her hat a bit and smiles. "Well, guess I'll see you in class then. Bye!"

Adrian waves. "Bye, Camilla!"

Apparently we now have a history study group. Is that even a thing people do?

I keep my eyes off the A-group's table. I don't know if Camilla made it back there, or if she's pointing and laughing at us, or if Justin is making his way over with a milky beverage of some kind in hand.

I do not eat the eggplant casserole.

The four of us make a run for history before the bell rings.

History on a Friday is supposed to be my best class. The four of us are together, it's light on suck-factor, and Mr. Norrell is massively lazy so often just shoves a DVD on and leaves us alone. We have our normal seats: Mike and me side by side, third row, and Allison and Adrian in the two seats behind us. There is order to our Friday afternoons.

Today, Camilla skips into the classroom and takes the seat next to mine. The hat is gone and in its place are head-phones that look like two giant speakers mounted on either side of her head. I've seen her walking around with those in the corridors a few times before, her face in this kind of faraway haze. She slides them off and shakes out her hair with a "hey" in my direction.

Camilla perches her glasses on her nose. Then she leans backward over Allison's table and starts talking about the psychology class they're both taking until Mr. Norrell walks in with a DVD of *Gallipoli* in hand.

Allison actually responds with more than monosyllabic whispers, which is weird in itself.

People are looking at us. Camilla doesn't seem to notice.

We should have just eaten lunch in the IT office.

6

Why Princess Leia hair is always a bad idea

The "thing" Camilla's dad had in Sydney? It turned out to be a party for the new Starfig Soles record. I find this out when I receive a hysterical call from Adrian on Sunday morning; apparently Camilla is in the paper. I look it up online; sure enough, at the bottom of the entertainment section, there are photos of the launch. Camilla is smiling at someone off camera with the arm of the bass guitarist around her shoulder. Her hair is poker straight. Her lips are cherry red.

I've never liked Starfig Soles. I turn off my computer and go back to bed.

My weekend is pathetically uneventful.

At eight twenty-four on Sunday night, Camilla logs on to Warcraft.

The chat window flashes at me. "Hallo, Dex," she types. "What's happening?"

The original *Halloween* is blaring from the mini DVD player on my desk. I have my *Anatomy of Story* book open on the bed in front of me. I wasn't really concentrating on Warcraft. I shove my book to the other side of my bed and grab the laptop from my pillow. After some consideration, and a few deleted sentences, I type:

"Hey. How was Sydney?"

"Meh. One of Dad's work things. Lots of being hit on by drunk old guys. Heaps o' fun. How was your weekend?"

I've spent my weekend alternating between homework and my movie. *KCftTMoJ* has reached this point where my three guys are trapped in the basement of a burning building, and one of the guys has been bitten and is freaking out about turning into a Killer Cat person. I'm not really sure what comes next. I'm also worried that the special effects needed may render my script unfilmable. And I think I may have written my characters into a corner.

I tried to catch up with Mike, but he's been busy doing unspecified things all weekend. Ever since we were kids, I've been able to decipher Mike's grunts and half sentences, like one of those British war guys who could read German codes. It's strange, because I'm not exactly the most intuitive person in the world. Apart from his coming out, which was kind of a surprise, Mike has always been an open book to me. But now I'm drawing blanks. He's starting to freak me out. I don't know what, if anything, to do about it.

"Not much happening," I type. "Planning on bed soon."

I hit enter before it strikes me what a dumb-arse thing that was to say. It is now eight twenty-seven. Why the hell did I say I was going to bed?

Camilla types a smiley face. "Whoa. Big night last night?"

Right. Saturday night. I spent my Saturday night analyzing the opening scenes of every Hammer horror movie in my collection, and trying to drown out Mum and Dad's theatrically whispered fighting, which they assume I can't hear because it's whispered.

"Something like that," I type.

"You up for a quest before you crash? I'm a little wired." Her dwarf jogs into view. It jumps around hysterically before bowing at me.

I shrug, and then realize that I am an idiot. "Sure. Lead the way."

I check out the map, and then our characters jog toward the path that will take them where they need to go.

I drum my fingers over the keyboard. "So…you seem to have settled in quickly?"

There is a pause on the other end of the window as her dwarf chats to a weapons seller. "Yeah. Kinda mandatory when you move around a lot."

I think about this for a moment. I wonder what it

would be like to be able to start somewhere new, some-where with no Vessels or minions or miserable dining halls with strawberry milkshake histories.

"Must be cool," I type.

"What's that?"

"Fresh starts," I type back, before I realize that it might be a lame thing to say.

Her dwarf spins around to face my night elf. The cursor blinks for eight seconds. I panic and consider log-ging off. It was, objectively, a lame thing to say.

"Wherever you go, there you are," she says.

What does that mean?

"What does that mean?" I type.

"I think it's Buddhist. You'd prefer something about being stuck in your own bell jar? We had to read Plath at my last school. It means fresh starts are fresh for all of twenty-five seconds. Unless you can factor in a brain or personality transplant—there's no such thing as a fresh start. You drag yourself with you wherever you go."

I push my laptop away a bit. She makes her dwarf do that stupid dance in front of my night elf. I place my hands back on the keyboard.

"So the person you drag with you—she manages to fit in no matter where she goes?"

"Well—she didn't always. But she's leveled up a lot since she started out. She just upgrades her equipment and hopes that there aren't any evil guilds waiting to shoot her in the back. And anyway, it's not always about fitting in, Dex."

"It's not?"

"Nope. Sometimes it's about reading your environment real quick, and then finding the bits of it that fit you."

I can see my face reflected in the laptop screen. It appears to be smiling. "Does your dwarf have a philosophy degree, AltheaZorg?"

"Ha. Not exactly. She does however have a PhD in new-girl-ness."

"And her thesis was on what?"

"Well, Dex, it was called: You can rock the boat, but you better make sure you have a very safe seat first."

Jamie Lee Curtis screams on my DVD player. I jump, and my laptop almost slides off my bed. I grab it with both hands. My fingers have been flying over the keyboard seemingly without being connected to my brain. I read over what she has written. I can't help but laugh a little bit.

"Anyway, Sam—school is school. I've never been to Mongolia or Afghanistan, but I'd bet money that school is the same in those places as well. Maybe the school dances involve more horsehair in Mongolia. But you get the idea."

"Yeah, I'm not really into dancing. Or horsehair. Or glitter."

"Ha, the dance committee did go kinda heavy on the sparkle. But it's Hollywood themed. Thought you'd be excited?"

"How did you know that?" I type quickly.

"Well, you're hiding a copy of *The Screenwriter's Handbook* underneath your *Macbeth*. And, you get very animated when you talk to Mike about old *Halloween* versus new. I'm in your English class as well, remember?"

Jesus. How the hell did she notice that?

"Crap. Sorry, Sam. Something's come up. Play another time?"

"Sure," I manage to type. My fingers feel a little numb. "Another time."

She types a smiley face and logs off.

I stare at the chat window. I swap the old *Halloween* for the new version in my DVD player. I think about fitting, and making things fit. I wait for an hour and seventeen minutes, but her dwarf doesn't reappear.

I'm not sure, but I think I'm a tiny bit disappointed.

✳

Monday morning, it's not Mike waiting by my locker, but Allison. She's holding her Japanese textbook tightly against her chest. A couple of girl minions are sticking a new Spring Dance poster to the opposite wall, and I can hear their conversation as I walk closer; they're talking about Camilla, and the bass guitarist who is, apparently, hot. There is a plethora of exclamation marks in their speech. Allison is wearing a purple dress that almost matches their poster. From a distance, she looks like she might have wandered in from a primary school.

"Allison?"

"Hey, Sam," she says, jumping a little. "How's it going?"

"Okay. Monday excitement. I see that an asteroid didn't crush the school into a crater over the weekend. How are you?"

She smiles. "Great? I went with Nate and Bill to see that anime double feature at the Kino on Saturday. It was cool. You should have come?"

Nathan and Bill are Allison's brothers. Bill is doing a Masters in English, and Nathan is studying Art History, and most of their conversations are peppered with references to Foucault and existentialism and stuff. The Kino is one of my top five favorite cinemas, but I tend to get a brain ache after more than three minutes around Allison's brothers.

"Maybe next time," I say.

Allison smiles. "Cool."

"So...what's up? Everything okay?"

"Yeah. Except, I wanted to talk to you alone. Have you noticed anything weird with Mike lately?"

I slam my locker closed. "Why? Has he said something?"

"Well, no. But the karate thing is weird, isn't it? And I know he's always quiet, but this quiet seems more *meaningfully* quiet, don't you think?"

"I think…something's up with him. I have no idea what, though."

"But do you think it's a guy thing? I mean, a *gay* thing," she whispers.

I glance at the poster girls again. Mike may not broadcast himself to the entire school, but I know he's not ashamed of who he is. And Mike knows he can tell me anything. But he also knows that if he really is having a problem with his love life, the drinks machine in the teacher's lounge might be of more use to him than me.

"I don't know, Allison. We'll keep an eye on him, okay? If it seems like it's something serious, then—I dunno. I'll think of something."

Allison looks thoughtfully down the corridor. She threads a strand of hair through her lips.

I don't exactly consider Allison attractive—not in a real-girl way or anything—but she does, objectively, have nice eyes. They're blue-green and mega-expressive. And right now they're peering at the girl minions. They're looking troubled, and a little wistful. They remind me that I have decided to conduct a small social experiment of my own this morning.

"Hey, Allison? Meet you in English? I have something I need to do."

She grimaces. "Um, sure. Okay?"

I sneak behind the minions as silently as I can, and duck around the corner near the art rooms where the second set of year-eleven lockers are. And I see her straightaway. Camilla is standing against her locker with Michelle Argus and another chick who I think might be Susan, or Sophie. Or maybe Sandra. Camilla is saying something to them, her hands gesturing wildly.

I take a deep breath and, with a brief, stealthy survey of my surroundings, I walk up to them. "Um, hi, Camilla."

"Oh, hiya, Sam," she says brightly.

I ignore Michelle and Susan/Sophie/Sandra. "So… was everything okay last night?"

Michelle and Susan/Sophie/Sandra look at each other, then at Camilla, then at me. Michelle's eyebrows shoot skyward. Score one for the surprise factor.

I watch Camilla's face. She doesn't shoot them any loaded looks. She just sighs. "Yeah. I forgot I was supposed to Skype with my mum. She gets a bit angsty if I mess with her schedule."

"Oh. Okay. I just thought…you disappeared pretty quickly. Just wanted to make sure everything was okay?"

She smiles. "Thanks, Sam. Everything's fine. Trying to keep two parents in different countries happy is sometimes a bit traumatic, though." Camilla swings her satchel onto her shoulder. "Heading to English? I'll come."

Michelle glares at me before turning back to Camilla.

"I guess we'll see you at break, CC?"

"Yeah, great. Bye, guys!"

Camilla trots off down the corridor. I stand where I am for four more seconds, until Susan/Sophie/Sandra points in the opposite direction and says, "Dude, are you lost? I think the hobbit village is that way."

I consider telling her that if I was looking for the hobbit village it would be because I'd just completed a quest that has saved the known world, and, also, that she has lipstick on her teeth, but then I think about my testicles and how I am somewhat attached to them, so I scramble after Camilla without saying anything.

"CC?"

Camilla wrinkles her nose. "Yeah. Apparently I have a nickname."

"That's…not a nickname. That's a corn chip."

She snorts. "Well, it's better than Coco. Or Cammie. Or Millie. Jesus, I hated Millie."

"Who called you that?"

She thinks for a moment. "Three schools ago. Chicago. I don't even know how that one stuck. Lucky we were only there a couple of months."

"Right. *Millie.*"

"Yeah. Great name for a cat. Or a weird aunt who lives in a trailer."

She looks up at me and grins. She must have a really

expensive dentist, because she pretty much has perfect teeth. As yet I am uncertain of the results of my social experiment. I focus down the corridor where our English classroom is looming. Justin Zigoni is hovering in the doorway. My intestines knot.

Random people smile at Camilla, and nod, and wave. She doesn't seem embarrassed to be seen walking next to me. Surely she knows by now that the four of us are the social equivalent of weed killer? Maybe all that stuff about reading the environment quickly was a bunch of crap.

We reach our classroom. Justin's face breaks into a slow, maniacal smile. He looks at me, then Camilla, and his eyes narrow. I have a sudden urge to shield my groin, on the offhand chance that one of Justin's arbitrary nut-slaps is forthcoming. He opens his mouth.

"Hey, Justin," Camilla says cheerfully. "Good weekend?"

Justin looks momentarily bewildered. "Uh, yeah, good. Football practice. We kicked arse. Uh...how was yours?"

"Same old. Hung out with Dad. Skyped with my boyfriend." She shrugs. "So, football? Steve said your first away game is in Brighton—that's near the beach, right? I haven't been to the beach in ages. Winter in New York and all."

Justin tries to frown and smile and look at her and me

all at the same time. He ends up looking like he's been stuck with a cattle prod. "Yeah, it is," he says. "Near the beach, I mean. Hey, we should have a beach party. I'll sort it out with the guys?"

"Sounds cool," Camilla says with a smile.

I glance into the classroom. Mike and Allison are in their seats, eyeballing me through the doorway. Justin's eyes remain on Camilla. I'm not willing to turn my back on him, but I've braced myself, and I'm waiting for it. That thing he's stored up, the thing that will humiliate me, and possibly Mike and Allison as well. The thing that will make Camilla look around her and think, *Oh, right, so* that's *who those guys are. The quarantined end of the social spectrum. Duh. That was a close call.*

Justin seems to recover, because the mask of smarm is suddenly back in place. He pushes past me as if I'm part of the classroom furniture. "So, sit with us, CC. I wanna hear about Sydney. I love Starfig Soles."

Camilla brandishes her glasses in the air. "I need to sit close to the board," she says mildly. "I have little-old-lady eyesight. I'll see you at lunch, though!"

She waves at a couple of people in the back of the room, and waves at Mike and Allison, and then she takes the desk in the second row, right in front of mine.

Mike looks at me as I slide into my seat. I raise my shoulders in a vague shrug. Justin bypasses my table without so much as a glance in my direction. Camilla digs out her books and doodles in her notebook for the entire double period.

I don't get her at all.

✳

As social experiments go, the Camilla test is, at best, inconclusive. I am not sure I'm equipped for involving myself in any further *Saw*-like death trap situations. So I figure the only logical course of action is to restore the four of us to our status quo as quickly as possible.

We eat lunch in Alessandro's office. We avoid the Vessels and minions, but the Vessels and minions seem to have forgotten that we exist.

I stick my head up long enough to notice that weird things are happening in year eleven. Stupid headphones the size of small cars suddenly become commonplace. Mismatched vintage clothes creep into the standard Vessel uniform. The day Sharni Vane showed up in leopard-print pants and a Nirvana T-shirt, Mike almost wet himself trying not to laugh. I can't decide why it works for Camilla, when everyone else looks like they've tripped and fallen headfirst into a Salvation Army bin.

On Friday, I think I figure it out. Adrian and I are hovering near Mike's chem class. The bell for morning break rang five minutes ago, but Mr. Francavelli appears to be

65

having one of his psychotic episodes, and his muffled yelling filters through the walls. Eventually the class dribbles out. Most looked drained of the will to live.

"What inspired today's meltdown?" I ask as Mike pushes his way through the crowd.

Mike sighs. "The usual. Only half the class did their homework. Chris DeCruise set fire to his sleeve, again."

"Again? Dude, learn to use a Bunsen burner!" Adrian calls out as Chris and his blackened sleeve shoot past us.

"Apparently the concept of fire escapes some people," Mike says. "And now we have double homework as punishment for the slack percentile of the class."

"Ouch. So are we still on for Minotaur tomorrow?" I ask.

Mike shrugs. "Dunno. Maybe."

Adrian glances at me. This is not good.

There is a casual indifference that Mike has mastered, which I know is typically cover for various levels of interest and/or excitement. Mike is usually happy to spend hours poring over the comic-book bins and bookshelves at Minotaur. But I don't think this is just casual indifference. Mike looks distracted and vague. He looks like he genuinely does not care about Minotaur. Unfortunately, my Mike train of thought lasts all of four seconds.

Adrian waves at someone over my shoulder, and I turn around to see Camilla bounding up the corridor in a long-sleeved yellow dress that looks like something my grandma might have worn in the 70s. And she's done something weird to her hair. It's split in the middle and scooped up in intricate twists on both sides of her head, just behind her—

Jesus. She has her hair in goddamned Princess Leia buns.

"Hey guys," she says breathlessly. "Have you bought your tickets yet?"

"Tickets?" I manage to stutter.

"For the Spring Dance? I don't know why we're selling them so early, only I think the committee needs more money for glitter or something." She winks at me. I have not processed a single word that she has said. "So they're only twenty each, because the school is subsidizing the cost. Anyway—six?"

"Six?" Mike mumbles.

"*Riiight*," Camilla says slowly. "For the three of you and your dates? I assume you're doing the chivalrous thing and paying for your dates?"

I pause for a moment to backtrack over the last thirty seconds, and am suddenly aware of how far this conversation has gone off track. I want to laugh, as the phrase, *You're kidding, right?* floats to mind.

But before I can say anything, Adrian—with his stupid Willy Wonka hair, and his monkey-like chin fuzz, and his faded *Lord of the Rings* T-shirt—Adrian, who has never spoken to a girl other than Allison and his sisters in his entire life and who is destined to die a virgin surrounded by nothing but *Doctor Who* DVDs, says:

"Sure. Six tickets. Can we buy them now?"

Camilla rifles through her things. "Yup. If you have cash that's great. If not, you can give me an IOU. I know where you live."

Adrian looks at me. "I don't have my wallet. Sam?"

I have seventy-five dollars in my wallet that was earmarked for a Dario Argento box set from Minotaur. My mouth is trying to say this, as well as a lot of other stuff, but Camilla is looking at me with her Princess Leia hair and that cheerful smile, and my consciousness detaches from my body and floats somewhere onto the ceiling. I see myself from a great distance away as my hand opens up my wallet and hands over the money. Mike looks at me and tugs out his own wallet. Ceiling-me sees him hand over the rest of the bills. The expression on his face does not change. I know, however, that he is horrified.

Camilla tears off a bunch of pink slips from the stack in her hand. "Cool. It'll be fun. Start working on those dates. And we're still on for study group tonight, right? I brought chips." She smiles and skips on her way without waiting for a response.

I stare at the glittery cards in my hand. My consciousness crash-lands back into my body.

What just happened?

Seriously, what just happened?

We are now three people with six tickets to a dance not one of us is planning to attend. I am supposed to be a nerd. But I cannot work out the math behind this equation.

Adrian grabs two tickets from me. "I have dibs on Allison," he says quickly.

Mike takes another two. "I'm meant to bring a date? This is going to be problematic."

Am I going to the Spring Dance? I am not going to the Spring Dance.

I really wanted to buy those DVDs.

I am blaming the hair.

7

The X-Men had an invisible chick, but still…

Adrian and I met in preschool when we were four. At least, that's what Mum tells me. It's not like I can remember the actual day he walked into my life. I don't remember a montage of conversations in the sandpit that would change our lives forever or anything like that. I just can't remember a time when Adrian wasn't around.

If Mike is the brother I never had, then Adrian Radley is the possibly inbred cousin who came for a visit and never left. I guess some people enter your orbit and get stuck, and there's nothing either of you can do about it.

"Yo," he says as he walks up to me at the school gates, his orange hoodie weaving through the crowds like a hazard beacon. Friday's final bell rang approximately eight minutes ago, but as yet no one else has shown up. Normally I'd be feeling the stomach-deep relief that comes from knowing I'm one week closer to getting out of this place. Today, all I feel is an inexplicable sense of panic.

Adrian heaves himself onto the wall beside me. "So I think we should visit Mike's karate school."

"What? Why?"

"Cos Mike doesn't want to go to *Minotaur!* Dude, something is seriously amiss. What if Mike's gone all manic-depressive over some guy? What if—"

"Man, first Allison and now you? Did you ever think that maybe Mike is sick of being kicked in the face eighteen times a week? Maybe he's just bored?"

But even as I'm saying it, I know it's not true. I know that my best friend is hiding something. Something serious enough to make him give up his favorite thing in the world, and something he feels he can't tell me about. And I'm thinking it's my job, whether he likes it or not, to find out what the problem is. I'm also thinking that leftover lasagna for lunch was not a good idea, because my stomach is churning.

Allison and Mike push their way through a bunch of year sevens who are scrambling to catch the bus.

"Heya," Allison says. "Where's Camilla?"

This is really stupid. Who even has study groups, outside of American high school musicals? And what made me think she would remember we—

"There she is," Adrian says, leaping down from the wall.

She's tapping at her mobile as she races out of school, her forehead creased in a frown. It's weird; I don't think I've actually seen Camilla frown before.

"Hey, guys," she says, shoving the phone into her satchel. She smiles, the frown disappearing as if it were never part of her face. "Sorry I'm late. I think Mr. Nicholas might have a great big man-crush on my dad. Kinda hard to make a polite exit."

I peer aimlessly at her for five seconds.

"So. I assume you know the way home?" she says lightly.

Jesus. What am I doing? "Um, yeah. If you're ready?"

"Ready as I'll ever be for 'Pastoral Expansion in the Port Phillip District'. I'm already nodding off."

"Tell me about it," Adrian says. "Nothing even a bit interesting has happened in this country in the last two hundred years. It's like, we found gold, woo hoo! And then some guys went to war."

Camilla nods sagely. "Right. We need a revolution. Or a plague."

Adrian grins. Mike nudges Allison and the two of them start walking down the road. Adrian and Camilla follow. And somehow, my feet make their way after them.

Walking at a normal human pace, it is approximately twenty-two minutes from the school to my door. This evening, the walk seems to take something like eighty-four hours. Camilla seems to be keeping up with Adrian's stream-of-consciousness conversation: American history, which leads to cowboys and Indians, which leads to the Village People, which almost leads to the Extremely Gay Weekend, at which point Allison casually asks Camilla about New York, and then, thankfully, we're at my house.

Mike shoves open the door and walks in without waiting for me. I weave through everyone else and bolt after him.

"Hi, Julie," Mike says, shooting a half wave at my mum, who is hovering in the living room in her slippers.

"Hello, Mike! Sam!" Mum's eyes are rimmed red, but Mike is already in the middle of a conversation with her about the new lilacs in the front yard. I say a silent prayer of thanks for my best friend; Mike has become the guru when it comes to dealing with my mum and her weepiness. I am not so useful.

"Hey, Mrs. K," Adrian says, bypassing Mum and heading for the kitchen.

"Adrian—Allison, hello! It's been a while."

"Hey, Julie," Allison says quietly. "D'you mind if I use your bathroom?"

"Of course not, hon, you know where it is. I was just—"

And then Mum stops talking. Camilla walks through my front door, straightening her yellow dress and peering around her curiously. A slow, broad smile spreads across Mum's face as I begin to feel like I'm having an out-of-body experience. Before I can say anything, Camilla holds out her hand.

"Hi, Mrs. Kinnison. I'm Camilla. It's nice to meet you."

Mum shakes her hand. "Please, it's just Julie."

If Camilla notices Mum's puffy eyes, she doesn't react. "Julie. Your place is lovely."

Mum smooths down her hair. "Oh, you have such a pretty accent. Where are you from?"

I've heard Camilla recite this speech to various hangers-on, but she doesn't seem to mind. "Well, I was born here, but I grew up in England. We've been living in the States for the last couple of years. My dad and I are a bit nomadic."

She smiles at Mum. Mum smiles at her. Mum smiles at me. Then she smiles at Camilla again. I smile at no one. I'm finding this love-fest somewhat disconcerting.

Mike clears his throat. "We brought food. I'm going to help Adrian." He disappears into the kitchen.

Camilla is still looking around the foyer. Something catches her eye through the living room door, and a really strange thing happens to her face. "Whoa. You...have a baby grand?"

I glance into the living room as well. "Mum teaches piano. Do you play?"

"Um, a little. We haven't had a proper piano since London, though. They're a bit hard to schlep in a suitcase. Do *you* play?"

"Sam used to be wonderful," Mum says. "But he's probably a bit rusty now, aren't you, hon?"

I grunt noncommittally.

Mum hurries into the living room and brushes some imaginary dust from the piano keys. "Would you like to play, Camilla?"

Camilla walks over to the piano. She runs her fingers lightly over the keys and plays a few choppy, random notes. She glances back over her shoulder, really briefly, and another odd thing flickers across her face. For a split second, that self-assured mask wavers. I would swear, for just a second, she looks almost shy.

"No, that's okay. Wow. This is a beautiful instrument, though." She plays a few more notes with one hand, a light tune that I don't recognize. "You're lucky, Sam. I can't believe you can play her whenever you like and you don't."

Mum looks like someone has told her that Santa will shortly be arriving with that guy from *Pride and Prejudice* in tow. "I know! He really was wonderful when he was little. I have the cutest video of him practicing when he was six—"

"Mum! Jesus, I think we need to study now."

"Oh, okay, of course. I'll help with the snacks and then I'll be out of your hair."

Mum skips into the foyer. From the corner of my eye I can see that she's trying to get my attention. I keep my eyes determinedly on the bookshelves of DVDs in the hope that she will give up and go away. Unfortunately, my concentration wavers. I glance at Mum. And my mother actually points at Camilla, and then gives me a thumbs-up. Two-handed. Both thumbs.

Despite the fact that the smile on her face is the first proper one I have seen in ages, I sort of wish my mother was, at this moment, on a mountaintop in Brazil. She closes the door behind her.

"Your mum's nice," Camilla says. She turns away from the piano and drops onto the floor near the coffee table like she's been here a hundred times before.

I'm not sure what to do, so I sit on the floor on the opposite side of her. I unpack my bag and stack my books in order of size. Then I shuffle the books around again. I suddenly find that the polished surface of the coffee table is one of the most interesting features of my house, and I can't believe I haven't actually noticed this before. I see my reflection. I look like an idiot. I clear my throat.

Camilla drops her books onto the table with a thump. "Are these all yours?" she says, waving at the shelves.

"Mostly. Yeah."

"Wow." She stands up and runs her fingers along the DVDs. "And they're alphabetized? How OCD of you." She tilts her head and peers at the spines. "Horror, horror, sci-fi, horror, zombie—I'm noticing a theme here."

"I like movies," I say weakly.

She laughs. "Yeah, I'm getting that."

I scramble up beside her. "No, I mean…I study them. It's sort of what I want to do."

She tugs out a random German horror film. "Screen-writing?"

"Um, yeah. Maybe. I guess."

"And so, have you written anything?"

"Sam's written loads," says Adrian as he shoves open the living room door with his knee. He's carrying one of Mum's good trays piled with fruit and chips. Mike and Allison follow behind with glasses and a giant bottle of Coke.

Camilla slides the DVD back into the shelf. "Really? Like what? Can I read something?"

"No!" I feel my face start to burn. "I mean, I've only been playing around with ideas. Nothing I have is good enough."

"That's crap," Adrian says. "Sam's stuff is awesome. The new one's going to be ace—it's about these three guys, and an asteroid that crashes—"

"Adrian, Jesus, Camilla doesn't want to hear about it!" I'm not sure how red my cheeks are, but I'm thinking beet probably doesn't cover it. I look at the piano and hope that when I turn around again, the four people behind me have miraculously turned into house plants. I agonize over showing even Mike and Adrian my movie ideas—Allison has never seen anything. The thought of Camilla Carter seeing my stuff makes me want to vanish into the peach carpet.

I turn around. Camilla looks at my face for four long,

painful seconds. I have no idea what is ticking behind her eyes.

"That's okay," she says mildly. Then she flops onto the floor again.

The other three settle themselves around the coffee table. I wait for a moment till I think my face has returned to its normal color, and then I join them.

Mike opens his textbook with a frown. "So. Should we start with a practice quiz?"

Camilla straightens her shoulders. "Consider me some weird little alien who has crash-landed on planet Australia. I need the local customs explained to me. Maybe with diagrams."

"We have faith," Allison says shyly.

"Diagrams can be provided on request," I add, just because I feel like I should say something. Camilla gives me a mischievous grin.

"Anyway," says Adrian, "you're probably more like Spock in *The Voyage Home*. You know, when they go back in time to 1980s Earth and—"

"Sorry, Camilla," Mike says. You're gonna have to learn to filter the *Star Trek* references from Adrian's conversation."

Camilla narrows her eyes. "That's the one with the whales? I know it's not the best *Trek* movie, but I still liked it." She giggles, probably at the various looks of incomprehension on our faces. "Okay. Study time, then."

And so, we study. Well, sort of. Mostly we eat, and answer Camilla's questions that are half about history and half about us. We work for an hour and thirteen minutes and then give up on the pretense of studying altogether.

"So how did you end up at Bowen Lakes?" Adrian asks, cramming the last of the grapes into his mouth. "It's a pretty crap school. Isn't your dad loaded?"

I've given up trying to keep him in line. So far Camilla hasn't seemed either offended or weirded out by him. A definite, if curious, plus one.

Camilla leans back against the floral couch and stretches out her legs. "Well, believe it or not, journalists don't get paid a fortune. Dad grew up around here, and BLS was the closest public school that'd take a late enrollment. We were supposed to come back before Christmas, but then Dad ended up going on tour with this band and—anyway. I had to go to school somewhere."

I drain my glass of Coke. "So is your dad planning on sticking around?"

She shrugs. "Who knows? He's kind of unpredictable. He gets antsy if he's stuck in one place for too long."

"Must be hard," Allison says. "Leaving your friends behind all the time?"

Camilla looks at her Moleskine notebook. She's doing some sort of music-note doodle thing in the margins. "Sometimes. We haven't really been anywhere long enough. I've got lots of Facebook friends, but they're mostly some nice people who've already forgotten about me."

I store away the inflection in her voice for later analysis.

"And your boyfriend? Leaving him behind must have sucked," Allison says quietly.

I glance at Camilla's phone, which is resting on the coffee table. Her wallpaper is a picture of a floppy-haired guy, presumably floppy-haired Dave the Boyfriend. He looks sufficiently dark and brooding: one of those I-play-guitar-and-write-crap-poetry guys that girls seem to be into.

Camilla nods. "Yeah. That was weird."

Weird. Interesting choice of adjective.

Adrian's phone beeps. "Sorry, guys, gotta go. My sister's picking me up. It's pizza night," he says. "Need a ride, Al?"

Allison gathers her books. "Yeah. Should probably go. I'm working breakfast tomorrow."

"Where do you work?" Camilla asks.

"Um, just at this café. I waitress. It's a bit sketchy."

Allison has worked at Schwartzman's for almost a year now. Schwartzman's is a local diner, famous for its wonky formica tables, its clientele of grumpy old men, and its coffee, which is possibly the worst in Melbourne. It's close, though, and the sort of place no one from school would be caught dead in. It has proven to be a viable after-school alternative to Alessandro's office.

Mike closes his history folder. "I'm gonna go too."

"Why? It's not like you're training tonight," I say.

He shrugs. "No, but I have stuff to do."

"Stuff?"

He looks at me with his blank face, but I can tell it's close to becoming his blank-annoyed face. "Yeah. Stuff."

"Okay. Cool," I say. It is definitely not cool.

Normally Mike and Adrian's exit would be marked by nothing more than a half wave as the door slammed behind them. This evening there is a flurry of goodbyes, and Mum reappears and flutters around everyone like they're going on safari, and Camilla and Allison are both juggling their phones, exchanging numbers because apparently they now have plans to "do something" together.

Then suddenly everyone is gone, and Mum disappears to answer the house phone which is ringing with what feels like frenetic speed, and I am standing in my living room, alone, with Camilla.

"I should go too," she says. "Need to jump on the bus before it gets dark. I still keep getting lost. Are the streets around here supposed to look the same?"

"Yeah...they may have been designed with the uprising of the robot clones in mind."

"And the topiaries? What did trees ever do to these people?"

"Well, I think it has something to do with wrestling nature into submission. It's like, hello, natural world, you think you're so great, but can you grow a tree that looks like a moose?"

She laughs. "I shouldn't complain, though. It does beat living in an apartment building with a couple hundred grumpy New Yorkers. And we have a yard for the first time in ages, which is nice. No topiaries in sight," she adds quickly.

I can't imagine how someone could move from New York to Bowen Lakes and still look as cheerful as she does. "Do you miss it?" I ask.

"New York? Well, we were only there a year. Sometimes I miss the energy, but this place has an energy all of its own. And everything is useful."

"Useful?"

Camilla starts to gather up her books. "I just meant that every place has its own…energy," she says lightly.

I perch on the edge of one of the couch armrests. A billion questions are circulating through my head. I select the most innocuous one. "So, then, have you always lived with your dad?"

She shoves her books into her satchel. "Yep. Pretty much since I was a baby. Mum is—well, she's really into shoes. She's not really into kids."

I'm running out of context for this conversation. I wrack my brains over the movies that I know, but I'm struggling to find a non-zombie or -vampire reference for a mum who's "not really into" kids.

Camilla swings her bag over her shoulder. "So. Point me toward the bus?"

"Sure. I'll walk you." It seems like the polite thing to do.

She smiles. "Thanks, Sam."

And then neither of us moves. Camilla glances at my DVDs again. "So, do you have a favorite? I suppose it's impossible for a true buff to pick just one favorite movie?"

"It is impossible," I answer.

"But if you *had* to narrow it down? Say someone had a gun to your head and your only hope of survival was to pick your—"

"My top five all-time favorite movies?" I grin. I don't know why, but for a second she looks a little surprised. I hurry over to my shelves. "Well—and keep in mind that if I had to have just five I would probably be some kind of psycho mess, and, really, these should be broken down into the top five by subgenre—"

"Subgenre?"

"Yeah. You know, slasher, stalker, virus, monster, alien —"

"I didn't realize there was such subtle detail."

"You have no idea. It's almost painful to pick a universal top five, but—here."

I pull out my copy of *The Evil Dead.* "Best low-budget possession movie ever made. And it was written by Sam Raimi, who is cool beyond cool."

She takes the DVD from me. "You'll probably think I'm completely unworthy, but I'm not really into gore."

"But, see, that's just it—it's not just about gore! At least, not in the old ones, and the really good ones. I mean, watch the opening scenes of the original *Halloween*—there's barely any blood, but it's seriously some of the creepiest stuff ever filmed. You can splatter as much blood as you want, but unless you can give your audience a nemesis that's truly worthy—then you're basically just covering a screen with corn syrup and food dye. It's not just about the killing. It's what happens *before* and *around* the killing that makes a really great horror movie."

She laughs and hands the DVD back to me. "I'll take your word for it, Sam. Next?"

"Well—okay, the original *Alien*. The first one was, like, the first real sci-fi/horror hybrid. And, you know, the alien-exploding-out-of-the-chest-cavity thing is unquestionably awesome, even though, okay, I guess it's a bit gross. And then, if I'm picking the most influential horror movies, I have to include *Halloween*, cos it was written by John Carpenter. It really was the first great modern slasher film and everything that came afterward was in some way a rip-off, I mean, after *The Texas Chainsaw Massacre*, which—"

Camilla laughs again. "Wow, there are a lot of movies I haven't seen. I guess I've never understood the appeal of sitting in the dark and having the bejesus scared out of me. Clearly I need to reconsider. What else?"

I pick another DVD off the shelf. "Well, you know...

Star Wars. The original one. It doesn't have much blood. But it's still…cool." I rein in my *Star Wars* worship. I think it might make me sound like a bit of a loser.

She takes the DVD from my hand. "Now *this* is one I can get on board with."

I blink. "Are you telling me you like *Star Wars*?"

"Are you *kidding*? I saw it for the first time when I was a kid. We'd just moved to London, and I was really, pathetically miserable. Dad took me to a revival at this theater in Paddington. I saw it, like, fifteen times afterward. I had the biggest crush on Luke Skywalker."

"I think we might have liked it for different reasons. But yeah, I saw it when I was a kid too. It is…awesome."

"Agreed," she says with a serious nod. "It would definitely make my desert-island-slash-radioactive-fallout-shelter-slash-death-row list."

I stare at the cover of *Star Wars*. My brain feels like it's experiencing a processing malfunction.

Mum appears in the doorway. She is smiling, but it's twisted on the edges in a way that signifies she's one step away from tears again.

"Mum?"

"Heya, kids," she says. "That was your father, Sam. He's going out with your Uncle Richard tonight. So it'll just be the two of us for dinner again."

"Oh," I say. I'm unsure if the overwhelming urge to punch your father in the face is ever justifiable.

Mum smiles at Camilla. I wonder if Camilla has any frame of reference for my mother's strange, sad smile. "So, Camilla, do you have big plans tonight?"

"I did. I mean, not big plans. Dad and I were supposed to be going out for dinner. Dad's working tonight, though. He has a gig. Or something."

Mum seems momentarily distracted. "Oh? Well you should stay and have dinner with us."

Camilla glances at me. "I don't want to impose. Dad leaves money for pizza. I'm fine."

Mum frowns. "You've been working hard. Eat with us and I'll drive you home later."

Camilla looks at me again. I shrug. I'm not exactly sure what else to do. "You should stay. If you want," I say eventually.

"Well, okay. If you're sure...?"

Am I sure? Of what exactly?

Routine is a weird thing. I don't know how one is formed, or how one manages to stick. All I know is, Camilla wanders into the kitchen chatting to my mother about London, and suddenly my routine has morphed, seemingly without me having any say in it, to include Camilla Carter having dinner at my house on Fridays after study group.

Of course, on this Friday, I have no idea that my routine has been irrevocably altered. On this Friday, all I am aware of is that a Vessel-adjacent girl with Princess Leia hair is helping my mum make a goat's cheese salad in my kitchen.

I am finding this just a little bit unprocessable. So I help her chop tomatoes. It seems like a reasonable thing to do.

Camilla nudges my shoulder. "Then I get to see your room. I want to be able to say I knew the next Hal Hartley way back when."

"Who?"

She looks at me in mock horror. "Sam, seriously. You need to expand your horizons."

"Um, I think my horizons are plenty expanded, thanks."

She grins. "We'll see. Remind me to lend you a DVD sometime."

"Okay, fine. If you'll give *The Evil Dead* a shot."

"'Kay, deal. Let me borrow it. But be prepared for a grouchy talking-to on Monday if I have nightmares."

I drop the tomatoes into the salad bowl. "Okay. Deal."

She smiles at me. I smile back. It feels strange on my face.

Routine is a weird thing.

Camilla Carter is having dinner at my house.

And our group, apparently, has expanded from four to five.

8

Proof that math and meat cleavers
will only ever be metaphorically useful

We are now going to the Spring Dance. I am still not entirely sure how this happened. After some intense discussion of the kind I was hoping to make it through high school avoiding, we have concluded that Mike is taking his cousin Gemma, and Adrian is taking his sister Roxanne, who has only promised to come if Adrian washes her car for the rest of the year, and also if he agrees to shave the fuzz.

For some reason, Allison found it offensive that Adrian called dibs on her. It therefore seemed logical for her to go with me. Apparently, I was still expected to ask. I don't understand the purpose of this ritual since the six of us are going together anyway, but, after some prompting from Mike and Camilla, I cornered Allison at her locker after school one Thursday. I did not rehearse the conversation. But when I mumbled something that had the words "Spring" and "Dance" in it, Allison's face lit up in a way that made me feel all twitchy and nervous.

Allison seems to have taken a small break from reality since then, because her conversation shifts from Robin Hobb books and Japanese movies to what dress she should wear and if we should hire a limo. She flashes magazine pictures in my direction and asks my opinion on colors and cleavage-appropriateness. Apparently, I am now supposed to have an opinion on cleavage-appropriateness. I grunt at random intervals and hope it passes for intelligent comment. Allison doesn't seem to notice.

Camilla is now a key member of the Spring Dance decorating committee, which I learn is one of many subcommittees within the main one. It means she will be working on the day of the dance and so will be meeting us there. She coos over dresses with Allison, and ribs me about having to wear a suit, and creates a countdown calendar for Adrian's diary with a picture of Johnny Depp from *Sweeney Todd* stuck to the date of his scheduled shave. She makes us watch *Sweeney Todd* one afternoon after school, which is a musical about a serial killer barber that actually proves to be somewhat cool, despite all the singing.

In math, we learn about outliers—statistical anomalies that lie outside the main data set. The outliers don't fit the pattern the rest of the figures are trying to make. They tend to throw all the other figures off balance.

I realize that Camilla is our very own statistical anomaly, an outlier that no one seems to know where to place.

Sometimes she hangs out with the scary girls from the

volleyball team, and she's friends with Victor Cho and those guys from the chess club, although she has admitted to me that she kind of sucks at chess. She seems to be part of the A-group, but she doesn't spend a whole lot of her time around them.

The group that she seems to spend the most time around is us. I don't know what planet she is from, but she is simply immune to crap. And because she has decided that she is our friend, we somehow find that we are immune too.

She makes us eat lunch in the dining hall. We now have our own table, not too close to the Vessels, but not in the middle of the shivering year sevens either. We sometimes take advantage of the last warm days and eat outside in the quad. Surprisingly, no one tries to kill us. I feel a bit bad for Alessandro, so we still spend a couple of lunches a week in the IT office. Camilla occasionally shows up to play poker. She might suck at chess, but I think she is some sort of poker genius. I cannot read her face at all when she is playing. I find this a bit intriguing.

Justin Zigoni looks somewhere behind my head whenever he sees me, but he hasn't breathed a comment to us in weeks. Susan/Sophie/Sandra, whose name it turns out is actually Veronica Singh, sits next to me in biology one afternoon, complaining about Miss Geramondi's latest test and asking me questions about our homework like she hasn't spent the last four years ignoring me.

I do not know what is happening to my life. My theory is that Camilla is some sort of reverse demon-spawn, like the Candarian resurrected from *The Evil Dead*, only instead of inspiring homicide and face-eating, she's spreading—well, whatever the opposite of demonic face-eating is.

I mention this theory to her one Friday after everyone else has left my house.

The Friday routine has quickly settled into a pattern: study, food, and a conversation about something pointless that everyone will have a resolute opinion on. Then Mike will leave, and somehow everyone else will leave with him. Mike does not eat at my house on Fridays, despite me asking more than once. I'm getting more and more worried about him, but I'm also starting to get pissed off with the whole secretive thing. I haven't decided how to deal with it yet.

Camilla stays for dinner since her dad is always out on Friday nights. I know she likes music, but she doesn't seem keen on tagging along with her dad to gigs; when I asked her about it, all she would say was that they have different tastes. I got the feeling she didn't want to talk about it.

Sometimes she brings her laptop and we spend a couple of hours playing Warcraft. Sometimes she disappears home without explanation—presumably for marathon Skype sessions with guitar-playing, poetry-writing, probably motorcycle-riding Dave the Boyfriend. Sometimes, she just hangs out and watches movies with me.

If Camilla notices the weirdness between my parents, she chooses not to comment. Anyway, she's always so chatty that the weirdness is hardly noticeable when she's around. Even Dad finds her interesting enough to ask her stuff about her life, which is more than me and Mum ever get from him. If I really stop to think about it, the only time my house fills with proper conversation anymore is when Camilla is around.

This Friday, Camilla is sitting on my bed, flicking lazily through my latest *Total Film*.

"So, I have developed a theory that you are some sort of reverse demon-spawn," I say. I'm at my desk burning *Drag Me to Hell* onto DVD for her. She's working her way through Sam Raimi's movies, though I think I have yet to convince her of his genius.

She tosses the magazine aside. "Is that so? Explain."

The first time she walked into my bedroom, admittedly, I had a minor freak-out. She sat on my bed, and the only thing I could think was, *Jesus, there's a girl on my bed*, which I understood only as the catalyst scene in a whole subgenre of horror movies. Then Adrian suggested I just consider her a non-gay girl Mike, which, surprisingly, did help. But as with lots of things in my weird new universe, Camilla Carter perching herself on my blue bedspread after dinner has become just—routine.

The DVD is going to take a while to copy. I spin around in my chair. "Well, basically, in any possession movie you've got an evil spirit released from a cursed book or wacky piece of gypsy jewelry—whatever. And said evil spirit's sole purpose is to cause carnage and destruction, right?"

"Okay. This relates to me how?"

"Well, put it this way—a couple of months ago, Justin and those guys would have caused us actual, physical harm if we dared stray into their territory. But now, it's like someone has waved fairy dust over their eyes or something. Reverse evil. I think that might be you."

She swings her legs off my bed. "Sam, seriously. You don't think that *maybe* you're overestimating my superpowers?"

"I never said superpowers. I said reverse evil."

"Look, I know you're not the biggest fan of Justin and those guys, but, you know, none of them are all that bad. D'you think you might be just a bit biased?"

I snort and snigger and make a bunch of sounds that I hope transmits my skepticism. "I'm not biased. They are, objectively, knobs. No reason, no conscience, not even the most rudimentary sense of life or death, good or evil—"

"Wait, I know this one. *Halloween*?"

"Aha. Very good."

She rolls her eyes. "All your speeches have a *Halloween* quote in them. Justin isn't exactly a knife-wielding psychopath."

"That remains to be seen. Anyway, I still haven't figured out why you would want to be friends with them."

"*Sammy*," she barks.

"*Millie*," I respond.

She knows I hate Sammy. I know she hates Millie. We seem to have fallen into this pattern.

Camilla rubs her hands over her eyes. "Look, the thing you have to realize…I've been to *so* many schools, Sam. And there are Justin Zigonis at every single one of them." She smooths her hair back with a sigh. She is wearing it loose today, which means that I will be finding errant strands of it around my bedroom for days after she leaves. "You know what Michelle Argus asked me yesterday? Could I get her the phone number for any of the guys from *Twilight*. Not one specific guy—just anyone would do. I mean, seriously. Do I think she would give a toss about me if my dad didn't get photographed with celebrities? I'm not that dumb, Sam. But for as long as I'm here, I can't do anything about the people I'm stuck with, so stressing about it is useless."

She stands up and perches herself on the edge of my desk with another sigh. I find that I'm staring at the faded knees of her jeans.

"I'm not that naive, Sam. I know why people are nice to me. But as soon as I stopped being so hung up on it— well, everything just became *soooo* much easier."

Camilla isn't big on speechifying. And she rarely says anything without a mischievous gleam in her eye. I'm concerned that I've genuinely pissed her off. Or worse, that I've upset her. But then she looks at me, and she smiles.

"Sam, you guys are so great. You have no idea how nice it is to be around people who aren't obsessed with which D-grade celebs I might have bumped shoulders with once. But you, it's like…well, like you're the scared blonde chick at the start of every horror film. She spends most of the movie freaking out, but then she picks up a meat cleaver and goes after the monster. She runs face-first into him, because the movie doesn't work if she spends the entire ninety minutes hiding in a cupboard, does it?"

"I'm…not sure who my monster would be in this scenario, Camilla."

"Yeah. I'm not sure either, Sam."

"But I am, just, extremely impressed that you worked a horror movie metaphor into that speech. Even if I did have to be the scared blonde chick."

Camilla stands and bows with a flourish. The smile is back on her face. "Thanks. I thought that was not bad at all for a speech on the fly."

"I should have taken notes. I could have borrowed some of it for my movie."

She laughs. "Which reminds me—am I ever going to see these screenplays?"

I glance at the desk drawer containing my red notebooks and movie mags and vintage porn that I should really throw out at some point. "They're not ready," I mumble. I may be okay with her sitting on my bed, but I am so not ready to show her my movies.

"Sam..." She peers at her feet. Her feet shuffle for a moment. "It's just that..." She looks up and shakes her head. "Never mind. I should go."

"You don't want to wait for the disc?"

She yawns. "Nah. Tired. I can't watch it tonight anyway. Have a hot date on Skype with some friends in the States. Give it to me tomorrow."

I'm momentarily distracted by an inexplicable flash of shirtless Dave the Boyfriend reclining, Adonis-like, in front of a webcam, but when I open my mouth the only thing that comes out is this:

"Tomorrow?"

"Right. Beach party? Post BLS arse-kicking of Shaleford High? It's going to be warm, and I've been promised that there will be beverages of some kind."

I laugh. I can't help it. "Really? Justin Zigoni's beach party? As much faith as I have in your powers, *Millie*, I am not willing to test them out in any scenario that involves Justin Zigoni and a large body of water."

She narrows her eyes. "Sammy! Scared little blonde, remember?"

Sometimes I forget that Camilla Carter is relatively new to my universe. "Camilla, I can't. I mean, I'm pretty sure I'm not even invited."

She frowns and gives me that wide-eyed innocent look

of hers. I've learned, surprisingly quickly, that this look is in no way innocent. "But *I'm* inviting you."

You'd think I'd know better by now. I focus on my desk, where the Freddy Krueger doll that Allison bought for my last birthday sits. Its little finger-knives gleam in the light from my computer screen.

"Camilla, the thing is, maybe I do need to pick up the meat cleaver—metaphorically—but I don't need to run into an abandoned cabin in the middle of the woods that's decked out with wind chimes made of human ears. That'd just be stupid."

She shrugs. "Fine. Guess it's just me and Adrian then."

"What? *Adrian* is going to this thing?"

Camilla picks up her bag from the floor. "Uh-huh. He was completely up for it when I asked. Said he was going home to dig out his boardies."

I close my eyes. "Camilla, those guys...you have no idea the sort of torture they'll have stored up for him."

She doesn't answer, but she starts humming something. It takes me a moment to figure out that it's a song from *Sweeney Todd*. I think it goes something like: *Nothing's gonna harm you. Not while I'm around.*

Admittedly, I have never felt all that tough. However—having a girl hum a song from a musical at you that implies she will be watching out for you at a party you are too scared to attend is a new level of feebleness, even for me. I am pretty sure my manhood does not approve.

When I open my eyes, she's giving me that reckless grin again. "Jesus. Okay, fine. I'll come."

"Great! You should ask Mike. He said no, but I told him you'd be calling."

Camilla disappears from my room. I hear her rapid conversation with Mum from the place where I am temporarily frozen to my bedroom floor.

"I'll be here at ten-thirty," she yells up the stairs. "Call Mike! Pack sunscreen! Bye, Sam!"

Apparently, I am going to a beach party.

I really need to learn how Camilla does that.

9

When the theme music from Jaws
is completely inadequate

wake up feeling like a very small person has been punching me in the chest from inside, repeatedly, for most of the night. The sun is streaming through the gaps in my curtains. I can already tell that it'll be way too hot today.

I extract my feet from my tangled sheets and grab my phone from the nightstand. It is 9:07 A.M., which means I have one hour and twenty-three minutes to develop a hospital-worthy disease, or for my parents to decide that we need to move, immediately, to Peru. I fear that neither of these options is going to be viable.

I drag myself out of bed and face the wardrobe situation with a sense of doom. I do not own anything remotely beach-appropriate. I mean, I'm not exactly scrawny, and I'm tall, which I think sort of balances out the lack of bulk, but the idea of being in any kind of flesh-baring scenario with Justin and those guys makes the few muscles I do have wither.

I take off my T-shirt and face the mirror inside my closet door. If my muscles could talk, I think they would be shrugging and saying something along the lines of, *Seriously. Dude. Whaddaya expect us to do?*

I shower, and after twenty-seven minutes of deliberation, settle for a pair of jeans, a faded gray *Transformers* T-shirt, and a dark blue hoodie. If Justin doesn't kill me, I am probably going to die of heat exhaustion. I will accept that as a viable outcome to this day.

Mike sticks his head in just as I'm double-knotting my Converses. "Hey. Maybe we're gonna have a big earthquake. They say things get really weird just before," he says, deadpan.

"Really? You think a *Nightmare on Elm Street* quote is going to help my mental situation?"

Mike throws himself onto my bed. It actually takes me a moment to remember the last time he was in my bedroom. "Probably not," he says. He's wearing army-style cargo pants and a brown hoodie zipped to the neck. He looks me up and down blankly. "So. No Speedos?"

"I left them in my other bag with my muscle shirts and tanning spray. You?"

He shrugs. "Figure the extra padding might come in handy."

I slump into my desk chair. "Mike, what the hell are we doing? I know things have been bizzaro lately, but still."

"Yeah. It's probably not gonna end well. But this was your call. I'm only coming for moral support. Or whatever. You know, you could always back out."

I glance at my phone. "Camilla will be here soon."

Mike looks at me impassively. "Uh-huh. So…what'd you two do last night?"

"Me? Nothing. I mean, she hung around for a while and then I worked on some dialogue bits in my screenplay—which still sucks by the way. What did you do?"

He shrugs. "TV. Stared at that math homework for, like, twelve hours. Feels like I'm trying to understand Swahili."

"You want mine?"

"You finished?"

"Well, yeah."

Mike shrugs. "Nah. I'll work it out on my own."

I slip my mobile into my pocket. "Guess it must be cool to have your Friday nights back. I never got the whole two-hour arse-kicking thing you guys did on Fridays."

"It was a fighting class," he says quietly. "For seniors. And yeah. Friday nights are mine again. So I can watch TV on the couch with a bag of chips if I want, right?"

"Sure. I'm just saying…I thought you'd be dying to to kick someone. But I guess you're not missing it at all. Friday night in front of the TV must be awesome."

"It is. Awesome."

Mike stares at me. I stare back. Mike and I used to get stuck in silent stares all the time when we were kids. This time, Mike looks away. Now he can't even hold my eye? This is not good.

Mike stands with a sigh. "Allison's waiting downstairs. Adrian's probably gonna be late." He reaches into my closet and pulls out a backpack. "You bringing a towel?"

I shelve the karate conversation, again. "Wasn't planning on getting wet."

"Right. They do serve other purposes, though. Sitting on. Soaking up blood. Bring a towel."

I groan, but retrieve one anyway. The only two beach towels we own have pictures of Ninja Turtles on them. After eight minutes of reflection I settle for a plain green thing that looks innocuous enough, cursing whatever creature of malevolence has plagued my life with the need to agonize over towel selection.

The doorbell rings. My stomach flip-flops. Jesus. I cannot be this nervous about going to the beach.

I bound down the stairs just as Allison emerges from the living room and opens my front door. She smiles at me as I skid into the foyer. "Hey, Sam. It's such a nice day. This should be good?"

"Yeah," I mumble. "Good."

Camilla swings in through the doorway with one arm braced on the frame. She gives me a brief salute.

She has her hair in two loose braids, and she's wearing

tiny shorts and a see-through top thing that looks a bit ineffectual as a piece of clothing. I can see the tattoo on her arm through the thin fabric. I can also see that she's wearing a bikini underneath. It seems to have flowers on it. Maybe daisies. Though I'm fairly certain that Smurf-blue daisies don't exist in the real world. But I am not a florist. Maybe they do exist. They look a bit like the flowers on her tattoo, but it's hard to tell through the material.

I probably should not be staring at the blue flowers on her bikini.

My face suddenly feels like someone has waved a space heater in front of it. But Camilla is looking me up and down and hasn't seemed to notice. "Sam, sure you don't want to add your ski suit over the top of that?"

I focus on her braids. "I...don't own a ski suit."

"Do you own shorts?"

"No."

She looks at me appraisingly. "Do you have Wolfman fur? Are you hiding a superhero costume under there?"

"I don't wear shorts." I didn't think this was a difficult concept to grasp.

She rolls her eyes. "Fine, Sammy. Be that way. You ready to go? I should say hi to your mum."

My mum, at this moment, is sitting on the deck in the backyard, one of her emergency cigarettes in hand. Mum quit smoking years ago. Last time I checked, her emergency cigarette pack was looking pretty low.

Dad disappeared this morning with barely a glance in either of our directions. Apparently he had "stuff" going on.

I do not know what to do about this situation anymore. I feel like I'm watching my parents succumb to the slow infestation by a zombie virus, and I'm the loser from any one of a dozen movies, staring at them with his mouth open as they start to bleed from the eyeballs. I always hated that character. It's like, dude, run, get help, grab an axe—do something! Don't just stand around looking blank and waiting for your face to be eaten off.

All I know is every time I look at my mother recently, I feel like someone is strangling me. And aside from figuring out how to clone a non-arsehead version of my father for her, there's nothing at all I can do about it.

"S'okay," I say. "Think she's in the shower. Mike's here, but we need to wait for Adrian."

"Speaking of…," says Allison.

"Hey guys!" Adrian is bounding up the driveway. His sister Emma beeps her horn and tears off down the street.

Adrian is squeezed into board shorts and a *Fraggle Rock* T-shirt that looks two sizes too small for him. He also seems to be carrying half the contents of his house, and possibly someone else's, in his arms. He grins and waves, and a container of orange slices falls out of one of his grocery bags and spills over the driveway.

Yep. We are very probably going to die today. I wonder if it's too late to convince my friends that sitting in the dark with the director's cut of *The Driller Killer* is a healthier option.

Adrian hauls himself and his luggage and his stumpy, hairy legs into the foyer. Camilla grabs a couple of bags from him, giggling. "Nice work, Adrian. Neither us nor the population of Brighton Beach will go hungry today."

Adrian's face falls. "Do you think it's too much?"

Mike makes his way down the stairs with my backpack in hand. He takes one look at Adrian and his stuff, and he gets this pinched look around his eyes.

Camilla shakes her head. "Not at all. Oh, hey, Mike! Okay, let's just sort all of this. I have room in my bag. We should move, cos I'm dying to get my toes in the sand. Last beach I went to was in England. Lots of gray water and rocks. I'm excited!"

And with that, any thought of skipping out on this day disappears.

✳

I've never been out to Brighton. When the train pulls into the station, we pile onto the platform in a confusion of bags and towels, looking pretty much like every group of brain-dead college backpackers who've ever decided that exploring a derelict cannibal's house in arsecrack nowhere Texas is a good idea.

I fear we may shortly fulfill that horror-movie trope known as "too stupid to live."

Adrian skips ahead. Camilla threads an arm through Allison's, and Allison smiles at her gratefully. The two of them follow Adrian.

Mike drapes his towel around his neck. "Dude, are you gonna pass out? Cos I'm not sure unconsciousness will be your best defense."

"Mike—assuming we're not killed on sight—are we actually expected to talk to these people?"

In all my mental scenarios about this day, I hadn't taken the actual *party* into consideration until this moment. What possible conversation am I going to be able to manufacture with the Vessels? And how did I not think of this before?

"What do normal guys talk about?"

Mike shrugs. "Dunno. Football. Boobs. Think I'm gonna be screwed as well."

One of Camilla's words seems most appropriate at this juncture. "Bollocks."

Mike grins at me. "Pretty much."

I look behind me as the train pulls out of the platform. I allow myself one moment of imagining being on it, heading back to my bedroom and my movies and my screenplay. And then I face forward, and I make my legs march ahead in front of Adrian. I am not sure if this is the equivalent of picking up that metaphorical meat cleaver. But when I glance over my shoulder, Camilla is grinning at me.

＊

We find Justin's guys tossing a ball around near the water's edge. The girls are gathered on the sand in a loose arrangement of towels and picnic blankets.

I'm not sure what the protocol is for staring at the skin of girls you see at school every day. And then I have a moment of panic, because I don't know whether looking or not looking would be considered ruder. I focus on the city skyline, and try desperately to think thoughts that aren't bikini-related. It suddenly feels like that space heater is being waved in front of my face again. I note, with almost clinical detachment, that this is an interesting biological feat, as my blood supply is rushing somewhat south of my face.

There are lots of squeals and air kisses as "CC" drops next to the girls. I huddle down quickly on the other side of her. I'm guessing that now we probably look like we've wandered from a slasher film into one of those Elvis movies that Mum likes, but if people are surprised to see us, no one reacts. The girls actually give us a couple of lazy "hey"s, though Veronica Singh does glare at Adrian, whose eyes are glued somewhere in the vicinity of her bikini top. I nudge his arm. He looks down at the sand with a manic giggle.

I spread out my towel, and check the contents of my

backpack; Mike has shoved a spare T-shirt and bottle of SPF 30+ from our bathroom into it. "Thanks, Mum," I mutter.

He whips the towel from around his neck and shakes it out on the other side of mine. "I'm not the one who cried last time he got sunburned."

"I was nine."

"Dude, you still cried."

Adrian is busy opening his Tupperware and describing the contents in frenzied Adrian-detail. The girls actually make happy noises at him. Camilla stretches out next to me and looks at the water with a satisfied sigh.

I don't exactly relax. But I do kick off my shoes, and I dig my toes cautiously into the sand. Under the surface, it's remarkably cool. And I have not, as yet, been beaten to death. So far, so bizarre.

Camilla glances around. "Hey, where's Sharni?"

Veronica looks at Becky someone-or-another. Becky's face falls into a sad mask that looks suspiciously like a face full of glee is trying to work its way out. "You didn't hear?" she says forlornly. "Justin and Sharni broke up. The poor thing can't stop crying. They've been together *forever*!"

"Poor Sharni," Camilla murmurs. She looks out at the water where Justin and the guys are laughing. I follow her eyes. I see lots of tans and no shirts. Alistair McIlroy looks like he spends his spare time chopping wood or wrestling crocodiles. I resist the urge to tug my hood over my head.

"Justin seems to be coping?" Camilla says.

Veronica snorts. "Yeah. It's been thirteen hours. I think his mourning period is over."

I smile without really thinking about it. Veronica grins back at me.

A bunch of seagulls squawk around us. They scatter as Justin Zigoni and a couple of Vessels land in front of us in a flurry of sand and muscle. My colon decides that my stomach is a good place for it to set up shop. I can all but feel Mike's danger-status shoot up from yellow to red alert.

"Hey," Justin says vaguely in our direction. He grins at Camilla and kisses her cheek. He does not have anything else to say to us.

Reverse evil. There is no other explanation.

Justin flops into the sand. "You made it, CC. Did you hear? We kicked arse!"

There is much cheering from the other guys. Camilla smiles. Justin runs his eyes over her. They settle somewhere on the front of her top-thing.

I'm not sure whether he's trying to identify her mysterious blue flowers. I do notice that he has exceptionally bad skin on his forehead, which I've never observed before. Probably because my eyes have never had extended contact with Justin's face. I feel my spine straighten.

"So, CC, you gonna come for a swim? The water is awesome." Justin's eyes roam over her top again. I clear my throat. Justin ignores me.

"Maybe later," Camilla says lightly. "I pretty much have English skin. Gonna burn in two seconds if I take this off."

He smirks. "Shame to hide your gorgeous self under all of that."

I shake myself out of my stupor long enough to notice that the girls are watching this exchange, their expressions ranging from amusement to bated-breath eagerness.

Camilla shrugs. "Not really. Here. Have a celebratory cupcake."

Justin takes one of Adrian's mum's cupcakes from her with a wide smile. "I know it's gay, but I love cupcakes. My grandma makes them all the time."

He takes a bite. My mouth switches itself to autopilot. "Guessing those aren't your mum's cupcakes. Unless she uses shellac and bits of brick to make hers."

"Hey, don't pick on my mum's cooking," Adrian says loudly.

"I wasn't picking on her cooking. Just her baking."

Camilla laughs. Behind me, Mike groans quietly.

Justin gives me a tight-lipped smile, even as the muscles right across his neck tense. I plaster my most inoffensive expression on my face. I have no idea what I am doing. But whatever I'm doing—it feels kind of good.

Justin turns his back pointedly on me. "I'm really glad you made it, CC. I wanted to hear the rest of your story about the Brit Awards."

She shrugs. "Those things tend to all blend together. Jeez, that's sounds really stuck-up, doesn't it? I just mean, they're really not as exciting as you'd think."

"Aw, I reckon you have heaps of stories. I'd love to hear them sometime. We should hang out. Maybe at Mindy's after school one day?"

Time seems to stop. The girls on the picnic blanket freeze, like they're afraid to disturb even the molecules of salty air in case they miss a moment of this event. It takes me six additional seconds to figure out what is happening.

Justin Zigoni is inviting Camilla to the sad-arsed, 1950s-themed café next to the soulless multiplex cinema in the mall. Justin Zigoni is asking Camilla out. This is not possible. The mustache-twirling supervillain with the IQ of a lobotomized crustacean cannot be asking Camilla on a date. Even Adrian pauses his frantic unpacking and stares.

Camilla's phone beeps. A dozen people watch as she slips off her sunglasses and shades her hand over her screen. She smiles, but something weird is going on around her eyes. I can't place it at all. "It's Dave," she says lightly. "Jeez, it's pretty late in New York as well."

Becky someone-or-another *awws*. Justin's face falls.

Right. Dave the Boyfriend. The guitar-playing, poetry-writing, no doubt chest-hair-possessing Dave the Boyfriend who's obviously so cool that a few thousand kilometers is no obstacle.

Justin's face slips back into its mask of smarm. "Well, anyway, we should hang out. With the guys. And stuff. You know." And then he leaps up, and the guys seem to take it as a cue to grab their football and bolt back out to the water.

Camilla smiles sheepishly at me. "How you doing there, sweater-boy?"

"Just awesome. And stuff. You know."

She flops onto her back with a chuckle. I glance at Mike.

"Smooth," he says under his breath. "I was giving it at least another month before Zigoni took a shot."

"What? You knew he had a thing for her?" I whisper.

Mike shakes his head. "Dude. Sometimes, you are seriously…blind."

Clearly. Justin and Camilla. There is no way. Camilla Carter is off-limits. She has a boyfriend. And even if she didn't, Camilla would not be interested in Justin Zigoni. Would she?

I have a flash of a possible beach scene in my screenplay where the Killer Cat people morph spectacularly in the midday sun and proceed to relieve the supervillain of his limbs, slowly, one body part at a time, while a crowd of people stand around cheering. The thought makes me feel only slightly less annoyed.

Mike sighs. "It's frakking hot. Gonna go in the water. You staying put?"

"Someone has to keep an eye on Radley. You go. Watch out for sharks. Don't talk to strangers."

Mike glances at a group of non-BLS shirtless guys. "Not even the cute ones?" he whispers.

I snort. It's not the sort of conversation that Mike and I ever have. I suppose drooling over half-naked bodies is what normal guys are supposed to do at a beach party, but I'm not sure I can add another first to this already too-weird day. Even if Michelle Argus is now lying on her stomach, and her back does look incredibly smooth, although I'm pretty sure she should be wearing some sort of Cancer Council-approved shirt since she is so pale and, now that I look at her properly, bears more than a passing resemblance to that page-six cowgirl from Dad's vintage—

Mike clears his throat. I snap my eyes away. They land on Camilla. Beneath her giant glasses, her eyes are closed.

Mike glances at Adrian, who is attempting to teach Annie Curtis how to play poker. Annie actually seems semi-interested in this endeavor. Apparently satisfied that Adrian is safe, Mike unzips his hoodie, tosses it and his glasses onto his towel, and jogs toward the water.

I'd almost forgotten about Allison. She's still sitting on the edge of the girls, listening to them with that pensive, calculating look of hers. Veronica and Brie Dailey are poring over magazines and discussing Spring Dance hairstyles. I try to catch Allison's eye, but her brain appears to be otherwise engaged, cos she opens her mouth and utters what I can only guess is the password to some secret girl-dimension.

"I hate my hair."

Veronica and Brie look up.

"I never know what to do with it. I want to change it, but I don't know how."

Veronica and Brie scamper over and Allison disappears beneath their hands. For a second I panic, thinking that they're trying to bury her, but it turns out they're simply tugging her hair in different directions. Allison re-emerges, briefly. She looks pleased.

Everyone is okay. No one has died or looks in danger of imminent death. I lie down cautiously on my towel.

"Told you it would be fine," Camilla murmurs. "You worry too much, Sammy."

"Ugh. Do I really deserve a Sammy?"

"Yes," she says decisively. "For being a huge wuss."

"I never claimed to be anything other than a huge wuss. And you know my theory. I think your presence here might be unbalancing the natural order of the universe."

"Well, guess it's lucky I'm not going anywhere." She's looking sideways at me with a giant grin.

"Well...glad to hear it."

I bury my feet in the sand again. I don't know if it's the clear sky, or the crashing water, or the fact that I have my very own evil-repelling force field lying right next to me—but I am actually not having an awful time. The idea that I could be not having an awful time in any BLS-related context is somewhat mind-boggling.

I close my eyes. I'm half thinking about a new movie idea that's a hybrid between *Jaws* and *Resident Evil*, when I hear a sharp gasp from someone. I sit up. Camilla sits up beside me. Even she looks a little surprised.

I can see the guys passing the football along the sand. Jonah Warrington kicks the ball in Mike's direction. Mike has clearly succumbed to the heat and taken his T-shirt off. It's dangling from the back pocket of his pants like a flag.

Oh. I see.

My best friend might live in a uniform of thick hoodies, but he has also spent the majority of the last four years doing push-ups and sit-ups and whatever other stuff they get yelled at to do in karate classes. Maybe I look like a prepubescent girl with my shirt off. But Mike—well, Mike looks exactly like he has spent the last four years at the gym.

"Where has that been hiding?" I hear Becky say. There is much muttering from the other girls.

"Um. Mike's probably not going to appreciate all the girl-attention," I murmur.

Camilla laughs quietly. "Well, he should probably keep his shirt on then." She lies back on her towel and looks up at me through shaded eyes.

The eyes of the other girls are still firmly locked on Mike. I'm starting to feel somewhat hot and stupid, so I tug off my hoodie. No one throws anything at me. I will accept this as a good sign.

Camilla gives me a short, sharp clap. "See? Painless."

I lie down with my sweatshirt squashed under my head. "Compared to a killer bee invasion or zombie apocalypse—guess not. But I'm not the one being blinded by my pallid spaghetti arms."

Camilla looks sideways at me again. "As an impartial observer, Sam, I can safely say that your spaghetti arms are significantly less painful than a zombie apocalypse. And probably less spaghetti-ish than you think as well."

"Um…thanks?"

Camilla nods. "You're welcome." She waves her hands lazily above her head. "Although, the beach is probably the last place you'd want to be caught in a zombie apocalypse. Can zombies swim?"

I squint into the sun. "I'm not sure it's been scientifically tested. But yeah, a beach wouldn't feature in any sensible zombie survival plan. For one, it's impossible to run quickly on sand."

"True," she says with a yawn. "Might slow the zombies down, though?"

"Well, true. But unless you happen to have your Uzi, you're also going to be out of luck with weapons. And weapons are mandatory for zombie apocalypse survival."

Camilla is silent for a moment. "You couldn't just beat them to death with Tupperware? That stuff's tough."

I grin. "Maybe if it's filled with Adrian's mum's cupcakes. I think those are a valuable addition to any arsenal."

She rolls onto her stomach, laughing. "Right. I need to update my zombie survival plan. I am *so* going to be the first bimbo devoured by the hordes."

"Nah. You'd survive at least the first act of any movie. The pretty brunettes rarely get bumped off first." I realize what I've said the second the words leave my mouth. I'm wondering if her sunglasses also block the crimson that I know is creeping up my face.

"Aw. You think I'm *purr-ty*," she says in a singsong voice.

"Well, you know, objectively…" I clear my throat.

Camilla kicks some sand over my towel. "I shall take that as a compliment," she says, giggling.

There is a bloodcurdling scream from somewhere near the water. I sit up again, half expecting to see zombie hordes marching across the beach. Steve Stanton has gathered Michelle Argus in a fireman's hold and is ambling toward the sea. Michelle squeals and smacks her hands ineffectually against his arms as Steve tosses her into the surf. I can hear her yell combined with a laugh, even from here.

Camilla sits up quickly. "Listen, Sam—I cannot, under any circumstances, be thrown into the water."

"Why?"

"Because I can't swim!" she hisses.

I stare at her. "Are you serious?"

She shoves my shoulder. "Don't look at me like that! It's not considered a vital skill everywhere in the world."

Justin is walking languidly toward us. He is smiling and I think it's supposed to look teasing, but really he looks like he might have a dripping axe or severed human head hidden behind his back.

"*Camillllllaaaaaa*," he calls in a low voice.

I leap up. Camilla leaps up beside me. I shuffle in front of her. She shuffles behind me. I may have fantasized about some heroic moment where I stand up to Justin and perform a perfect roundhouse kick to his stupid square jaw, but I am not sure this is that moment. I am uncertain of the physics of performing a roundhouse kick on sand, for one.

"Bugger," Camilla whispers.

"Yeah, okay, we're going for ice cream," I say loudly.

Justin looks momentarily disappointed, but turns his attention to Becky, who squeals hysterically before bolting directly toward the water. Clearly, Becky is the movie chick who will never make it past the opening credits.

Camilla grabs my arm and pulls me along the sand. Her hand relaxes only when we are out of earshot of the group. She looks at me sheepishly. "Sorry, Sam. Didn't mean to imply that I needed a bodyguard."

"Noted. Anyway, you're in serious trouble if you're expecting a bodyguard service from me. I'm still waiting for my radioactive spider bite."

She grins. "Lucky I can fight my own battles. Most of the time. Lemme know when that spider makes an appearance."

"Sure. I promise you'll be the first person I take for a spin on my web."

She laughs. "That sounds slightly gross. But okay, I'll hold you to that."

We walk lazily in the direction of the confetti-colored beach huts. The sand is burning my feet, but I can't seem to make my legs move faster. Camilla turns her face to the sun and sighs. "I can't believe it's autumn and still so beautiful. How is it you guys don't take advantage of living in this place?"

"Melanoma, for one," I say. But I'm looking around at the people laughing and hanging out, and I'm kind of asking myself the same question.

Camilla kicks her feet along the sand distractedly. "Hey, Sam? Can I ask you something?"

"Um, okay?"

"Well...why screenwriting? I mean, I thought all movie nerds dream about directing their own stuff. All those guys you like are directors."

"Not all of them. All the great horror directors have written stuff for other people—and did you just call me a movie nerd?"

She nudges my hip with hers. "You know you are. But I'm serious. Why screenwriting?"

"I think, because…well, I like the idea of coming up with a story that never existed before, but I don't really want to be in charge. I don't want to be famous. I guess I like the idea of sitting in the dark and knowing that I created the thing on screen, that it's *my* story, but, like, no one else has to know it was me. Does that make sense?"

I'm not even sure if it makes sense to me. The thought of being the guy with the megaphone—the one who everyone is looking at to tell them what to do—just makes me want to crawl under my bed and hide. I want to do something with the stories in my head. But I'm happy to hand them over and let someone else make them real.

Camilla is silent for a long time. Actually, she is silent for approximately eighteen seconds, which is the time it takes us to walk across the sand and onto the path that leads to the ice cream vans.

"You're going to tell me I'm a huge wuss, aren't you?" I mumble.

Camilla turns around to face me. The sun is behind her so I can't see her face at all.

And then she does the weirdest thing.

She takes a step toward me, and she kisses me on the cheek. It's not even for half a second; it's so quick that I think maybe I imagined it. Then she skips off in the direction of the Esplanade.

"I don't think you're a wuss, Sam!" she yells over her shoulder. People turn and stare. My feet are starting to burn again. I think my face is burning too. "I don't think you're a wuss at all!"

10

When punching people in the face is a great idea

Maybe I have fallen through a wormhole into another universe. Maybe I have acquired a talisman and now have protection against evil. Whatever the reason, I make it through the beach party without being humiliated or drowned. Actually, we all do.

Adrian's poker knowledge has come in handy. Allison's hair has come in handy. Even Mike's abs have come in handy. The girls seem genuinely disappointed that we are leaving early, though I think the disappointment was mostly because Mike put his shirt back on. Justin Zigoni ignores me. Camilla waves at Justin and skips away before he can kiss her goodbye, leaving his lips hovering in midair.

It is not the greatest day of my life. But it is, by no means, the suckiest.

Now, Camilla's bare feet are propped up next to me on the train seat. She's humming something under her breath, her head resting against the opposite window. The sun is dipping as we chug slowly back home. I'm feeling oddly serene, despite having sand lodged in places where sand does not belong. I glance at Camilla's small feet, which are nestled in the space between the window and my thigh. Her toes are still dusted with brown and gold grains. I brush the sand off them absently.

Allison yawns. "How am I supposed to work now? I'm *soooo* tired."

"Shame," Camilla says with a matching yawn. "We could have done something. No one else has plans?"

Adrian leans over the aisle with a box of cookies in hand. "Roxy has friends over, so I'll probably be banished to my room."

"Anyone want to come back to mine?" Camilla says. "We can order pizza?"

Adrian brightens. "That sounds awesome, I—"

Mike clears his throat. "We can't. We have that legal assignment we're supposed to be working on."

"Yeah, but it's not due for another—"

"Dude, do you not remember anything? It's my nana's birthday next weekend. This is the only time I have. And we're already behind. I told you we're gonna work on it tonight."

"I...guess. I must have forgotten."

"You must have," Mike says mildly.

Camilla nudges me with her foot. "What about you? Big plans tonight?"

My immediate plans are a de-sandifying shower, but I have to admit, I'm more than a bit curious to see Camilla's house. "No. I guess I'm free."

Mike is staring vacantly out of the window on the other side of the aisle. I toss a potato chip at his head. "Hey, Mike, guys, you should come. It's only legal—the assignment won't take that long."

Mike turns around and glares at me. He actually glares. Mike never glares. Mike has never actually been pissed off with me—not since that one time when we were eleven and I accidentally dropped his Optimus Prime toothbrush in the toilet.

"We need to work on it. Tonight. It's important."

"Really? It's vital to the universe that your legal assignment is done tonight?"

Behind his glasses, Mike's eyes narrow. "Maybe it is. Maybe the universe doesn't know how vital it is. Is that okay with you?"

That doesn't even make sense. I don't know why I'm snapping at him, or why he's being so goddamned frosty with me. "Sure. Whatever."

Allison's and Adrian's eyes are ping-ponging between us. When I glance at Camilla, she is frowning at me. Then Allison starts talking about the new haircut she has settled on, and the weird moment passes. At least, I think it does.

When we reach Camilla's stop and the two of us jump off the train, Mike gives me a sort of wave. I kind of wave back. My hand feels weird and mechanical.

Camilla lives on the edge of my neighborhood, where the old suburbs end and Bowen Lakes begins. It's like there's an invisible line dividing this place with knotted trees and ancient houses from my neighborhood, which looks like it was beamed in from the suburb-making equivalent of an Ikea.

Her house is all high ceilings and creaking everything—a total serial-killer house, which is cool beyond cool. Camilla tosses her bag onto the floor and wanders through an archway into what I guess is their living room. It's just a guess, because the only things that indicate living-room-ness are a couple of leather couches and a flat screen sitting on a coffee table. Every other part of the room is covered with boxes, most of which are spilling records and CDs. It looks like a record store walked in and exploded.

"Sorry 'bout the mess," Camilla says. "Dad hasn't unpacked."

"How many months have you been here?"

She grimaces. "Yeah. I know." She squints into the darkness. "Dad! Hey, we have company!"

My eyes adjust to the dimness. At the far end of the room, in a leather armchair that looks somewhat throne-like, sits the guy whose face I've seen all over the net. He's leaning back with his eyes half closed, his head connected by headphones to a stereo the size and complexity of a smallish space shuttle.

If I lived to be seven hundred years old, and spent most of those seven hundred years searching for the elixir of coolness, I might possibly attain one-eighth of the coolness of Henry Carter. He's wearing jeans and a frayed black T-shirt, and his dark hair is longish, but not in that sad way that makes old guys look like they're from a *Doctor Who* convention or something. He has wriggly tribal tattoos underneath leather bands on both wrists. He does not look like anyone's dad that I know.

"Hey, baby," he says, tugging the headphones off his head. Then he glances at me, and I think, for all of three seconds, his face registers surprise. "Who's the boy?"

"A friend," Camilla says. "Henry, Sam, Sam, Henry."

Henry Carter doesn't look like he's in any rush to stand up. I'm not sure of the protocol of crossing the obstacle course of their living room to shake his hand. In the end I settle for a half-arsed wave and a mumbled "nice to meet you." But I have a feeling he's already lost interest in me.

"Check this out," he says, brandishing the headphones at Camilla.

She leaps over the couch and lands with a thump next to his armchair. Camilla presses an earpiece to her ear. "This is the new Sinking Wormholes?"

"Yup," he says with a kind of smug look on his face. "Demo came today. Whaddaya think?"

She closes her eyes. "Well…ooh, I like the violin arrangement. It's different from their first album, though—"

"Yeah, it's crap. It's like they've taken the glimmer of originality their first record had and mashed it into the ground with this pop garbage masquerading as indie. Completely ripped off early Pulp as well, don't you think?"

Camilla frowns. "Sounds like they're experimenting. Adding a couple more instruments—"

Her dad takes the headphones from her hand. "It's so completely derivative, I almost wanna contact Pulp's management and tell them to get their copyright lawyers onto it. I mean, listen to the bridge on that track!"

Camilla shakes her head. "Guess I'm going to have to give it a closer listen later."

"Don't bother. My ears are about to bleed." He tosses the headphones aside and reaches for the laptop on the armrest next to him.

Camilla turns around and smiles ruefully at me. I know basically nothing about music, and I'm guessing the couple of bits of Foals trivia I do know are not going to impress Henry Carter. I pretend to be extremely interested in the Turkish rug on the floor until Camilla picks her way through the detritus toward me again.

"Dad, Sam and I are gonna be upstairs. You home long?"

Her dad is focused on whatever he's typing. He doesn't even look up. "Nah, I'm out. You need dinner?"

Camilla shakes her head. "I'll sort something."

"Cool. Have fun."

"'Kay. You too, Dad."

She smiles at me again. I can't be certain, but I think it might be a different smile from her usual one. I don't think I'm a huge fan of Camilla's dad.

I follow her up the groaning stairs. I am not sure if going to a real girl's bedroom for the first time should be considered a momentous occasion or not. I know it's only Camilla, but still, I can't help feeling just a little bit weirdly nervous.

Camilla takes the dark doorway that leads from the first landing. I follow her cautiously, hovering near the door as my eyes adjust. She bounds over to the window and yanks across her heavy curtains.

"Whoa—this is your room?"

"Yeah. It's a bit of a sty, I know."

Camilla's room looks like—well, like no other place I've ever seen, not even in any of the movies I know. For a start, it's huge. Her ceiling is twice the height of mine, and the entire wall behind her futon is covered from floor to ceiling with music posters, most of which look like gig ads for the kind of obscure bands that Allison's brothers listen to. The opposite side around her door and dresser is plastered with photographs and pictures torn from magazines; only a few squares of purple paint peek out between them.

Her window reaches all the way to the floor and opens onto a balcony. And in front of the window, lined along the edge of the room, is an array of instruments. There are a few guitars, a keyboard and a violin, and a bunch of other things that I'm sure must have proper names but just look like those foreign instruments I sometimes see on the World Movies channel. Everything is jumbled in a mass of wires and headphones and endless piles of paper.

Camilla darts around and gathers up the chaos of papers. "Make yourself at home," she calls as she shoves them into her dresser drawer.

I drop my backpack near her door. My feet squeak on the dark floorboards as I spin in a circle trying to look at everything at once.

CDs and books are piled in thick stacks on the floor on one side of her mattress, her MacBook balanced precariously on one tall pile. A bar fridge doubles as her nightstand on the other side. The fridge is topped with a heap of junk: snow globes, and a ceramic London phone booth, and a giant yellow lamp that has three brass dachshunds for a base. She doesn't have a desk, so I'm guessing she's a homework-and-Warcraft-on-bed kind of person. Her room is messy and cool and makes my bedroom look as personality-full as a toaster factory.

"Camilla, I think I want to move in here."

She giggles. "I think I might snore, Sam."

She scoops up her crumpled volleyball uniform from the keyboard and shoves it into a drawer. She doesn't seem to see the yellow bra dangling from a handle on her dresser. My face starts to feel a bit warm, although, really, I'm not sure what I expected a girl's bedroom to hold, if not a heap of bras and stuff. Not that I've spent much time thinking about it. Girls' bedrooms. And bras. Have I?

I tear my eyes away from the yellow bra and hurry over to her picture wall. Different faces stare back at me from the scattered photographs. I see one picture of a group of people standing in front of a pretzel cart. They look American, in that shiny-teeth-and-perfect-hair way. Dave the Boyfriend's gloomy face peers out at me.

Camilla takes one last look at the floor, now clear of debris. She trots over to my side and follows the direction of my eyes.

"Dave seems cool," I say lamely. "So…how long have you guys been…going out?"

Camilla grimaces. "Actually, Sam, I have a confession to make. And I think it'll probably make me sound like a huge idiot. At the very least, it's gonna make me sound really weird." She drops onto her futon and looks up at me guiltily.

"What sort of confession?"

"Well, the thing is…Dave and I broke up. Before I moved here. We weren't even going out that long. It's just that the new school thing is…it's kinda hard being…" She shrugs. "Well, fresh meat. When Justin and those guys were buzzing around on day one, Dave just kinda slipped out. And I ran with it because, well, fending off random guys wasn't really part of my new-school plan."

"Oh. Well, yeah. Random guys. I guess that would be…annoying?"

She sighs. "I always try to make the best of wherever we end up, but the guy thing, it's just complicated."

"So then Dave is like your beard?"

She laughs. "Jesus, that's spectacularly pathetic, isn't it?"

"Well, I wouldn't know. I've never had to invent an imaginary girlfriend to keep swarming masses of girls at bay."

Camilla plucks absently at her bedspread. "He wasn't imaginary. Just exaggerated."

"Okay, but then who kept texting you today? You didn't look thrilled with whoever it was."

She looks up at me. "You noticed? That would be my mother. Gabriella is…tricky."

I glance at her wall again. Dave the suddenly-ex-Boyfriend stares out at me. This new information makes me feel a bit like I'm trying to decipher the plot of a David Lynch movie. For some reason I feel a little…untethered. I store it away for later analysis. "This must have taken you ages to do," I say, waving at her walls.

Camilla accepts the subject change with her customary shrug. "It did. But I'm considering it insurance. I'm hoping the thought of pulling all this stuff down is gonna be enough excuse for Dad to stay put, at least for a bit. Henry would have us living out of his car if he had his way."

I wander over to the instruments while she's talking. "Do you actually play these?"

"Um, with varying degrees of suckiness. Yeah."

"*All* of them?"

Camilla stands and skips over to my side again. "Well, I mean—bass guitar isn't that difficult. I pretty much taught myself. And acoustic isn't hard to pick up with a few lessons. And I learned piano when I was a kid. And the others I just...mess around with."

She blushes. I am not sure I have ever seen Camilla blush before. It is sort of...endearing.

"Would you play something? I haven't even heard you play the piano at my house."

She picks up her yellow cardigan from the floor. "Maybe later. Besides, it's still nice out." She grabs a couple of cans of Coke from her bar fridge and shimmies through the balcony door. I squeeze between the instruments and follow her.

Bright leather beanbags are scattered on the balcony. Camilla settles into a green one and tugs on the cardigan. I take the opposite beanbag, feeling sand grinding against my thighs, and I think maybe in a few other places. I almost don't care. The sun is setting over the city, and the sky is a hazy mash of purple and navy. Camilla stretches and looks out over the view. When I straighten my legs, they bump against hers. I move them quickly. She nudges my foot with her toes, her face set in that half smile. I nudge her foot back.

"So—do you approve?" she says.

"Of your place? It's awesome. I could set an entire slasher film here."

She laughs. "It's the nicest place we've lived in ages. The apartment in New York was the size of a dog kennel. And my last bedroom in London had an amazing view of my next-door neighbor's bathroom. She was eighty-three. And she didn't believe in curtains." She shudders.

I grin. "So much for your glamorous life?"

"Yup. It's been one party after another."

I hear a door slam downstairs. "Your dad?"

Camilla shrugs. "Guess I'll see him tomorrow."

I settle into the beanbag. "You must spend a lot of time on your own."

"Sort of. But I like having time to myself. Time to read and listen to music and…stuff. And Warcraft, of course."

"Of course."

"It's fine. It doesn't bother me." Camilla takes a slow sip of her Coke. "Anyway, it's good that Dad's keeping himself occupied. He gets restless when he's bored. And restless Henry rarely works out well for me."

I crack open my Coke. "You know, Camilla, you hardly ever talk about your mum."

She laughs dryly. "My parents. It's like being stuck between a tsunami and a tornado."

I'm fairly certain that I have nothing to contribute, parent-wise. But Camilla's eyes look like they're focusing somewhere not entirely here. I bump her toes again. She nudges my foot with a smile. "Anyway, I keep myself busy. Lucky I have some spectacularly nerdy friends who can fill entire days with movies and WoW. I'm kept sufficiently amusified."

"And I guess if the spectacularly nerdy friends ever fail, there's always Justin Zigoni. I'm sure you could fill entire days talking about his hair." I meant it to sound like a joke. I think it comes out sounding annoyed.

"Maybe I'll call that my Plan B," she says.

"Sure. I think Justin has your face lined up to replace Sharni's on those Spring Dance posters, though. You might need to practice your dead-eyed look." I have no idea why my mouth is still moving, only I can't seem to make it stop.

Camilla raises an eyebrow. "Jealous?" she says lightly.

I open my mouth. No words find their way out.

I am not jealous.

Of what?

Am I?

"I just think…Justin's an idiot," I mutter.

"So I keep hearing. D'you ever think that maybe he's jealous of *you*?"

I laugh, spluttering a mouthful of Coke over the balcony. Camilla's eyes narrow, but she's sort of smiling as well.

"I'm serious, Sam. Maybe someone like Justin, who is—let's face it—a straight-C average, might be intimidated by someone who aces everything while barely cracking a book?"

"I think you might be clutching at some serious straws. I doubt me and my IQ are giving Zigoni any sleepless nights. He's just a straight-up, run-of-the-mill knob."

Camilla groans. "Whatever. I'm sick of talking about Justin."

My head is whirling. I am more than ready to move on from this conversation. "Fine with me."

"Fine."

"Fine."

"So then, you wanna tell me what's going on with you and Mike?" she says casually.

I sigh without really meaning to. "You noticed?"

"That spat on the train was hard to miss. And my spider-sense is telling me something's been off for a while. I don't know Mike all that well, but he seems…sad?"

"Mike's been acting weird since the beginning of the year. I've asked him about it, but…Mike's never liked people prying into his stuff."

"So I've noticed. Mike's always kinda stoic. I mean, he's more stoic than you, which is saying something. It's hard to get a read on him. But you're his best friend—don't you have a prying exemption?"

I think about this. "Guess I've never needed one before."

Camilla twirls one of her braids around her hand. "Have you tried to find out?" she says eventually. "Maybe Mike doesn't realize he needs help."

"That's what Adrian thinks. He's been trying to get us to do recon for a while now."

"But?"

I take a deep breath. "But what if it's something I can't do anything about? What if it's something serious? I'm not an expert on all things…Mike-related."

What I can't really explain is how much I've come to rely on consistent, solid Mike. Solid Mike is possibly the only reason I haven't had a complete psychotic meltdown these last few years, what with school and my parents and everything. The current state of my life being what it is, un-solid Mike is not something I know how to deal with.

Camilla is silent for a moment. "Okay. What's your plan, then? I know you're worried about him, Sam. I can see it."

I stand up and lean out over the balcony railing. The sun is nothing but a blood smear in the sky now. "Do you have any suggestions?"

She hauls herself up and leans out beside me, her braids dangling midair. "Well, barring straight-out asking—if I were a psychological detective, I would suggest going back to the moment you noticed the weirdness. Maybe something happened at the beginning of the year?"

"Psychological detective?"

She grins. "Uh-huh. It's a thing. Look it up."

I can't help but smile back. "So I'm searching for the psychological equivalent of a bloodied ice pick in the library?"

"Correct. Follow the clues. And don't trust anyone with an eye patch. Or anyone who runs an antique store. They always turn out to be sketchy."

"Isn't it always the sweetest character who turns out to be the psychopath?"

"Oooh yeah, right. That's a basic movie cliché." She peers down at the flickering streetlights for a moment. "So does Allison own a chainsaw?"

I laugh. "Right, the baby-faced killer. That would definitely make my top five list of pathetic mystery movie clichés."

Camilla spins around to face me, bracing her elbows on the railing by my side. I'm not sure if it's my imagination, but she seems to have developed the faintest freckles across her nose since this morning.

"What about your top five list of truly clichéd death scenes, Sam?"

"Well, Camilla, that all depends on your genre…"

I seem to have forgotten what we were talking about.

✳

The Yu Kan-do It Karate dojo looks like a cross between a Japanese tea house and a medieval torture chamber. The last time we were here, Mike was doing his first dan black belt grading. The Japanese weaponry hanging on the walls was very cool; watching Mike get yelled at and kicked for six hours was not so cool. Allison spent most of it flinching every time someone so much as waved in Mike's direction. Adrian just yelled and cheered until Mike made him stand outside. Still, Mike's photograph—exhausted and grinning with his black belt in hand—is now hanging alongside the photos of the other black belts in the dojo foyer.

Adrian, Allison and I hover uncertainly in front of the photos. Harmonized shouts rattle through the walls from the main room. A bunch of kids with belts of varying colors wander past us and into the smaller side gym. A bucktoothed kid with a yellow belt shoots me a dirty look as he walks by. He comes up to my kneecaps. I am fairly confident I could take him. I glare back. He scampers away quickly.

"Any idea what we're looking for?" Allison whispers.

"Maybe we should just hang out for a bit and watch?" Adrian says.

I scowl. "Yeah. Let's hover near the changing rooms

while the little kids are training. That's not going to make us look suspicious at all."

"Well, should we split up? Maybe someone here has some idea—"

"Can I help you?"

The three of us spin around.

A guy in a crisp black uniform and black belt is standing behind us. His legs are braced apart, his hands crossed lightly over the knot on his belt. He looks no more than a couple of years older than us.

Allison stares at him with her mouth hanging open for approximately four seconds. Then she looks down at her toes, a mottled blush spreading down her neck.

I am not gay. I do not have gay tendencies, I don't think. But this guy towers over my six-foot frame; he has shoulders like a football player and black hair that flops across his forehead so perfectly it looks photoshopped. His goddamned chin even has one of those chin-arse things.

I am not gay. But even I can appreciate that, objectively, this guy makes the rest of us look like we're descendants of Leatherface, after some cosmetic work with his chainsaw.

Chin-arse guy holds out a hand to Allison. Allison looks at is as though it belongs to the Dalai Lama or someone. She shakes it with a nervous smile.

"I'm Travis Azumi. Can I help you?" His voice sounds like stones strained through silk. His blue eyes flick from

Allison to Adrian to me, before landing back on Allison. She grimaces and smooths down her static hair.

Adrian waves. "Hey, dude. How's it going? We're thinking about taking lessons."

Travis's expression does not change, but something in his eyes does. He looks at Adrian as if Adrian is a green thing that has dropped out of someone's nostril. Adrian doesn't seem to notice. Beet-red Allison doesn't seem to notice.

I notice.

I hold out my hand. "I'm Sam. Mind if we look around for a bit, Travis?"

Travis grips my hand. An X-ray might be required once he lets go, because I'm pretty sure he's fractured a few fingers. I shake my hand out furtively behind my back. A thought starts to worm its way into my head. "So...are you an instructor here?"

He crosses his arms over his barrel chest. "Senior instructor."

I cross my arms over my significantly less barrel-like chest. I try to sound casual, and try not to look like I'm about to pee my pants. "So...been teaching here long?"

"Since the beginning of the year. They wanted a new instructor. Some fresh talent. They brought me down from Queensland. This is the place to train, if you're serious."

His eyes flick over Adrian again. Adrian smiles cheerfully at him. I can practically see the moment the other shoe drops inside Adrian's head.

"Since...the beginning of the year?" Allison repeats.

Travis straightens his black uniform. "They have a couple of up-and-coming fighters. Future national, maybe even international champions. Someone needed to bring them up to speed."

A nervous-looking kid in a white belt is hovering near the front desk. Travis looks at him. The kid looks like he's about to cry.

"Um, thanks Travis," I say. "Maybe we'll come back and try out a class."

I grab Adrian by the sleeve and Allison by the wrist, and drag them backward toward the door. Allison's eyes are still locked on Travis. She waves with her free hand as the door spits us back onto the street.

"Wow," she says. "That was...a very nice-looking boy. Did you see those eyes?"

"Oh my god," Adrian says in an overly dramatic whisper. "*That's* why he quit! That guy! It makes perfect sense!"

"What perfect sense does it make?" I snap, even as I suspect the answer is obvious.

"Travis shows up and Mike does a runner? Mike practically lived in this place, but now he can't face coming here? Dude, it's so obvious! Mike is in love with Travis!"

Allison grimaces. "That's a big leap, Adrian. Just because Mike likes guys, and that guy is kind of a god—"

"But the fact that he quit just after this Travis guy appeared? You're telling me that's a coincidence, Al?"

Allison and Adrian look at me. "It seems like…the timing is about right," I manage to say.

As I suspected, I am in no way equipped to deal with this. I've stood on the sidelines for years with ice packs and first aid sprays; I know which strapping is best for weak ankles, and how many days between tournaments Mike needs to recover. I am not sure I know how to deal with any other sort of trauma.

Adrian sighs. "If Mike really is in love with this guy—"

"Which is kind of a major assumption," Allison says quickly.

"I said *if*. If Mike has a thing for this guy, or whatever, obviously he's not dealing with it. Should we talk to him?"

My friends look at me again. I am going to have to be the one who decides what to do. I suddenly wish we had brought Camilla with us; I'm not sure Camilla is ever stumped by anything.

"Look. It's not like Mike has ever dated anyone before. Or like he's even been interested in anyone before. Maybe he just needs time to get his head together?"

Adrian and Allison look at each other. "Maybe you're right," Allison says. "Maybe we just need to be there, and let him sort whatever this is out on his own?"

Adrian snorts. "Really? Do nothing? That's your plan?"

Allison catches my eye. Inwardly, I sigh. "Okay. We keep this to ourselves. Until we have more info, we do nothing."

Adrian looks displeased. Allison looks pensive.

I am so not qualified to make this call.

The beach party turned out to be one of the last decent warm days we had. Proper autumn kicked in soon after, rendering my neighborhood damp and barren and more like a zombie wasteland than ever.

The Justin-Sharni breakup was major news for the better part of a month. The dance committee was compelled to remove any trace of the ex-couple from the Spring Dance posters; Camilla used this opportunity to shrewdly maneuver them into modifying the entire event.

The Spring Dance is now also a costume party.

I was somewhat unhappy with this turn of events, until Camilla dragged me to a costume shop in Kensington that had honest-to-god *Star Wars* Stormtrooper outfits for hire, which suddenly rendered the Spring Dance passably endurable. Her exact words, as she paraded around the store wearing the arse end of a zebra, were:

"How many opportunities are you gonna have to dress up as a Stormtrooper?"

I couldn't really argue with that.

I normally find the approach of winter fairly depressing; this year, it sneaks up without me noticing. Camilla tries to convince me that winter depression is scientifically quantifiable, and that the only way to combat it is with Vitamin D and fake sunshine. She wears a lot of yellow and recruits me to help paint her purple room bright lemon. I don't know if I believe in the scientific reliability of any of this, but I do feel less depressed whenever I escape from my house to hang out at hers. Her dad even scores tickets for us to see Foals at the Forum for Mike's birthday, which I take as evidence that Henry doesn't think I'm a complete moron, despite the looks he regularly gives me.

Mike and I spend most of the Foals gig staring at the fake Roman statues in the theater, and trying to stop Adrian from hyperventilating with excitement. Camilla stares at the stage with that hazy look she gets whenever she listens to music. I haven't figured out what that's about yet.

The midyear break rolls around with the usual chaos of exams and filler activities that are supposed to pass as educational. Mr. Nicholas actually tries to make us play

Heads Up, Seven Up on our last day. There is much amusement at Victor Cho's expense.

Mike is spending the break with his cousins in Queensland. Adrian is taking a road trip with his sisters. Allison's parents have signed her up for an intensive math vacation program at Melbourne University. Camilla is being shipped off to stay with her mum in Singapore.

I am not going anywhere, because my parents decide to split up.

I always pictured the parental-separation thing as a scene that included both parents and some heartfelt speeches. In the last few months, I'd even begun to imagine the plinky, sad piano music that should accompany it. I thought I'd at least get a fancy breakfast. French toast. Anything.

Instead, I wander down the stairs on my first Saturday of freedom to find Mum leaning out the kitchen window with one of her emergency cigarettes in hand. The house is ominously quiet.

"Mum?"

She takes a final drag and throws the cigarette into the yard. When she turns around, her eyes are dry. "Hey, hon. Your father left this morning. I don't think he's going to be living here anymore."

"Oh," I say. I'm not sure what else to add. The thought-processing part of my brain appears to still be asleep.

"You don't *think*?" I say eventually.

Mum sighs. "He's moving in with your Uncle Richard for now. He'll look for a place once he gets himself sorted."

"Oh."

"Honey, we've been unhappy for a long time. We really wanted to wait till you finished school, but we just couldn't. This is for the best."

"Oh." I swallow a couple of times. My mouth remains stubbornly dry. "Did Dad say anything? Did he say…why…?"

Mum sighs again. "Sam, I'm not sure we can explain it like that. Things weren't always bad between us—you remember that, right? We used to be good…and then we weren't. I know that's not logical enough for you, but I don't have any other explanation." She smiles tiredly. "Believe me—I have been looking for one."

"Oh. So, then…are you all right?"

"Actually, I think so. For now, yes, I am."

I stare at the toaster. "What will you do?"

She shrugs. "I never thought I'd say it, but I actually miss teaching. Maybe I'll look for a job. Who knows?"

Who knows? Aren't you supposed to, Mum? If you don't know, who the hell does? But I don't say this, because she walks over and gives me a hug. I respond with an arm action that I think resembles a hug back.

"Dad's going to call you later. He thought he would give you a bit of time to digest."

"Oh. Okay."

She brushes my hair out of my eyes. "Are *you* all right?" she asks.

"Yep. Fine."

I stand where I am until I'm sure she's not going to dissolve into tears. Strangely, Mum's face looks more solid than I've seen it in ages. And then I walk back up to my bedroom. I should probably change out of my pajamas or shower or something. I hover in my room, my feet feeling weirdly distant from the rest of me. I try to talk them into moving, but they don't seem to want to do anything much. I pick up my phone instead. I don't really know why. It almost rings out before she answers.

"Jesus, the airport is freezing!"

"I just wanted to say bye."

"What's wrong?" Camilla says instantly.

"Nothing. Not really. My dad moved out. I think my parents are getting a divorce."

My knees do something strange when I say the words out loud. They seem to forget how to hold my body upright. I sit down on the edge of my bed. Dryness lodges in my throat again, achy and lump-like. There is silence on the other end of the line.

"Sam. Damn it, they finally decide to do this *now*? I mean, your poor mum, but—Mike's left already, hasn't he?"

"Yeah. It's okay. I just…I don't know…"

"Sam, I'm *so* sorry. This is horrible, and the worst possible timing. Not that there's ever a good time to hear that your folks are splitting, but—I'm not even going to ask if you're okay cos it's a stupid thing to ask—"

"It's fine, really. I think I just wanted to tell someone…"

"I'm glad you called me, but—bugger, damn it—Sam, I have to get on a plane!"

I hear the boarding announcement in the background, as if some faceless airport moron is also taking his shot at ruining my life. "You should go. Don't worry. I'm fine."

"Say anything!" she barks.

"What?"

"*Say Anything*. Late 80s movie, John Cusack—it's one of my go-to happy movies. Find it. Promise you'll watch it."

"It…doesn't sound like a guy movie, Camilla?"

"That doesn't matter. The point is, it's a feel-good movie. You don't need to be watching people having their brains splattered right now. And I don't need to be on a plane for eight hours worrying about you watching people having their brains splattered. What you need is an old school 80s rom-com."

"Are you sure?"

"Positive. You'll love it. I'll call you when I land."

"You don't have to—"

"Sam, shut up. I'll call you when I land. Just…be okay for a little while."

"Camilla, I'm fine." I think my hands are actually shaking.

"Sure. Sam, listen—your friends are all here for you, just not in your vicinity at this second. But we're here. I'll call when I land. Eight hours. *Say Anything*. I gotta go."

"Okay. Have a good flight."

"Eight hours. Bye, Sam." She hangs up.

I stare at my phone for what feels like an hour.

I open up my laptop and search for a torrent of her movie. I watch for a while as the file downloads, piece by piece, onto my computer.

I lie on my bed and stare at the ceiling for forty-three minutes. At some point Mum sticks her head in to tell me she's going to Aunt Jenny's. She asks if I am all right, and a bunch of other things that I nod and respond to without really processing. She walks into my room and kisses me on the forehead before she leaves.

I send Mike and Adrian a message. I'm not really sure what to write, so I text:

Dad moved out. Don't think he'll be moving back. Bout time, I guess.

Adrian calls straightaway. He is in the car, already halfway down the Great Ocean Road. I can hear Roxanne and Emma singing in the background. "Sam, man, that really sucks. What did your dad do?"

"Nothing specific. I don't think. Just being himself."

"That is just…arse. Big time." There is a pause. I'm pretty sure Adrian is eating something. "You gonna slash your wrists or anything?" he says eventually.

"Nah. Watching a movie. Camilla's recommendation."

"That's good. Don't stress. I mean, stress, but don't do anything dumb. Y'know."

"'Kay. I won't. Have fun."

"Will IM you if I find wifi. Catch ya."

Mike calls as soon as I hang up. He is silent for seven seconds. He sounds like he's in a car as well. "So. Are we concocting some elaborate scheme where we pretend to be twins to get your parents back together?"

"Am I supposed to know the reference?"

"Dude. *Parent Trap*?"

"Isn't that a Disney movie?"

"Yeah. So?"

"How gay are you, Mike?"

Mike snorts. "My cousin made me watch it last time I babysat. It was possibly the stupidest thing I've ever seen. Anyway, doubt we could pass for twins."

"Yeah. You can't pull off blond."

"You'd look even more emo with dark hair."

"Right. Besides, I think my parents might be better off in different houses. Actually, they'd be better off in different dimensions, but barring the discovery of a Stargate I guess this will have to do."

"Yeah. How's your mum?"

I shrug, then realize he can't see me. "I think she's okay. Right now, anyway."

Mike clears his throat. "And you?"

"Yeah."

We talk about nothing for another twelve minutes. Mike's family is on their way to Sea World. He promises to call back later. I hang up.

The rain starts to pelt on my window. I curl my body around my laptop and tug a blanket over my legs. I watch Camilla's movie with my face all but pressed up against the screen.

When the movie finishes I don't have the energy to do anything else. So I play it from the start again. I make a giant pile of toasted cheese sandwiches, and then fall asleep while I'm watching it the third time. When I'm playing the movie for the fourth time, I get a text message that reads:

Where are you? Turn on your computer!! Do it now!!!!

Camilla knows how I feel about exclamation marks. I jump out of bed, dump the laptop onto my desk and flick off the movie. I drop into my desk chair.

It takes a moment to sign in to Skype, and then Camilla's face appears on my screen. She is trying to yank her hair up and type at the same time. She smiles and waves, her messy ponytail bouncing over her shoulder. She's wearing a pale blue summer dress and her face looks flushed with heat. Outside, the rain beats down on my window and the wind rattles the roof tiles. It feels like she's on another planet.

"Okay, so you think your life is bad," Camilla says before I can speak. "Look at this." Her face disappears, and then the webcam bounces kind of erratically. She has picked up her laptop and is slowly circling around the room with it.

"Wow. That is…an awful lot of pink."

In fact, her room looks like an explosion inside a bubblegum machine. Her bedspread is pink, the cushions on her bed are pink, and the curtains are a different shade of pink. Her furniture is uniform, featureless white.

"I know, right?" I hear her disembodied voice say. "It's like living inside Barbie's campervan. And look at this."

She angles the camera upward. A giant black and white picture hangs above her bed. It features a woman stretched out on a leather couch. Her head is thrown back over the armrest. She is not wearing a single piece of clothing.

Camilla spins the laptop around and settles it onto her desk. Her face appears in the screen again. "That would be Simone, one of Mum's clients. Apparently this is an appropriate piece of artwork to hang in your kid's room."

"I'm…not sure I'm qualified to judge its appropriateness. Maybe I need to see it again?"

Camilla laughs. "Those boobs have been airbrushed beyond recognition. I saw the real thing at a photo shoot once. They're not so special."

I wonder if my blushing transmits over webcam?

Camilla glances sideways. "Hey, Sam, wait a sec…" She gestures wildly off camera. "Mum! Come here. There's someone I want you to meet."

I smooth down my T-shirt, suddenly wishing I had changed today. A woman appears over Camilla's shoulder. I sit up a little straighter. Her mum looks like an older, harsher version of Camilla, except her hair is inky black and iron-straight. She has the same full lips and the same long lashes, and her eyes are exactly the same shade of hazel. But Gabriella's face seems to be permanently frozen into an expression of disinterest. She peers at the computer screen.

"Mum, this is Sam. Sam is one of my best friends. Sam, meet my mum."

"Um, hello," I mumble at my computer.

"It's a pleasure," Camilla's mum says coolly, her clipped accent a couple of shades more English than Camilla's. "You have a great face, Sam. Have you thought about doing any modeling? The feminine look is in at the moment."

"Mum!" Camilla attempts to maneuver her mother out of the frame as I scramble to fix my bed hair. "Okay, enough with the intros. I'll be down for dinner in a sec."

Her mother rolls her eyes at the camera. "I think that is my cue to leave. Goodbye, Sam. Maybe think about shaping those eyebrows."

Camilla smiles sheepishly as the sound of a door closing echoes in the background. "And that, Samuel, was my mother. Questions? Comments?"

"You look exactly like her. Though she seems even scarier than you've let on."

"Oh, she is. We'll run out of things to talk about in approximately four minutes." Camilla settles her dress over her knees. "Anyway, Gabriella will keep. How are you?"

"I'm okay, I guess. I watched *Say Anything*."

Her face brightens. "And?"

"It was fairly girly. But it did have some awesome lines."

She grins. "I gave her my heart and she gave me a pen?"

I can't help but smile back. "How many times have you seen it?"

"This from the person who can recite *Halloween* backwards? No comment." She rests her chin in her palm. "But, really, Sam. How are you doing?"

I focus on my desk for a moment. How am I doing? Do I even know? "I'm okay. It's not like it was a surprise. Mum even seems relieved it's finally done with. I'm fine. Really."

"Sure. Wanna tell me why you're still in your jammies?"

I tug at my Superman T-shirt. It is starting to feel a bit gross. "Dunno. There's no one here. Didn't see the point of getting changed, I guess."

"Sam—"

"Hey, Camilla? I…don't really want to talk about it. I…can't. Okay?"

She looks at my face for a long moment. I focus my eyes determinedly on this one tendril of her hair that is curling around her neck. And then she leans in toward the webcam. "Okay, Sammy, this will not do. I am going to be summoned for dinner in a sec, but—I am setting you two tasks. Failure to carry out either of them will result in the automatic severing of our friendship. Or maybe I'll just give you a wedgie when I get back. Are you up for it?"

"Jesus, Camilla, what are you going to make me do?"

"Nothing traumatic. Promise. Are. You. Up. For. It?"

"Okay, whatever. What are these two tasks?"

"Task one—shower."

I roll my eyes. "I think I can manage that. Task two?"

She chews thoughtfully on the inside of her cheek. "You need to go to my house. Tomorrow. Nine A.M. No excuses."

"But—"

"Argh! No buts! No excuses! Be at my house at nine! Or I shall be forced to speak in exclamations for eternity!"

I laugh, even though I think it might sound more like a frightened sheep bleat. "Fine. Nine tomorrow. You won't even give me a clue what I'll be doing?"

She shakes her head. "Nope. And now I have to go. Mum's dragging me to some art show opening, which means I probably won't be back till four A.M. And she's scheduled a no doubt stimulating day of manicures and shopping for tomorrow. I'll try to buzz you, if I can. But in the meantime—your task has been set."

"Should I be scared?"

She gives me that evil smile of hers. "Depends on how big a wuss you are, Samuel Kinnison. I'll talk to you soon?"

"'Kay. Have fun. Bye, Camilla."

Her Skype window goes black. I stare at the empty screen for seven seconds, that ache-thing settling into my throat again.

My mobile beeps. Three times in a row.

Her first text reads:

9 A.M. tomorrow.

The second reads:

Or else…

And the third reads:

!!!!!!!!!!!!!!!!!!!!!!!!!

I am still laughing when I haul my depressed arse into the shower.

✳

It's two minutes to nine when I arrive on her doorstep. I don't know whether to ring the doorbell or look under the rocks for a secret message. I hover tentatively for thirty seconds. And then I ring the bell.

Henry Carter yanks open the door. He is wearing black jeans and no shirt. He looks like he's still half asleep, or maybe hasn't been to bed yet.

"Um, hi, Henry. Camilla told me to—"

"Yeah, hey, Sam. Hold on."

He disappears into the house. I shuffle from side to side in the doorway, my hands buried in my pockets. It's freezing and the sky is dark and low. Part of me wants to be back home in bed, but I am also kind of curious to know what Camilla is up to.

Her dad reappears, lugging a square black box that almost comes up to his chest. He thrusts it at me. "She ordered me to give this to you. Hope you know what she's handing over. This is a genuine Fender. It's not supposed to wear training wheels."

It takes me a second to realize that the box is a guitar case. "Um. Thanks?"

"Yeah. You'll need this too." He hands me a scrap of paper with an address scrawled across it. "See ya, Sam. When you speak to my kid, tell her to call her dad for more than just two minutes, if it isn't too much trouble." He lingers in the doorway like he's not entirely sure what to do with himself next. I resist the somewhat smug urge to remind him that she's been gone less than twenty-four hours.

"Sure. Bye, Henry."

I walk down her driveway with the heavy case in one

hand and the scrap of paper in the other. It's an address for some place in Fitzroy. I have only a vague idea where it is; I never head out that way. Under the address in a barely legible scribble is this:

Look for the blue door. Give the package in the case to Jasper.

Jesus. Maybe I should have just stayed in bed. Living in my pajamas for the next two weeks was shaping up to be an acceptable plan.

I swing the case over my shoulder and step onto the curb. The street is pooling with puddles and leaves, and everything looks washed out in hues of gray. I hover uncertainly on the side of the road.

I look over my shoulder at Camilla's house. From my place on the street I can see her bedroom window with its small balcony. Even from this distance, her room seems silent and empty.

I glance at the address on the paper again. And then I heave the guitar case over my other shoulder and head toward the station.

✳

A train and a tram ride later, and I'm standing on a drizzly street corner, squinting at the map on my phone and trying desperately to pinpoint where I am. I've triple-checked the address, but all I can see is a narrow bluestone alley across the road. The alley is guarded by graffiti of a rat with what I'm sure is unhealthily disproportionate genitalia. There is no street sign that I can see. I look at the map on my phone again. It is telling me that rodent-penis alley is where I need to be going.

I dodge the traffic and bolt across the road, the guitar case bouncing across my back.

The damp lane is wider than it appeared from across the street, although it still looks like the sort of place that should be adorned with flapping police tape. I hover for another twelve seconds. And then Camilla's voice echoes in my head.

How big a wuss are you, Samuel Kinnison?

"Guess there's only one way to find out," I murmur. I slip the phone into my pocket and step out into the alley.

✳

I see the blue door straight away, mostly because it is set in the biggest wall in the lane. White paint flakes off the bricks under balding red ivy. I can just about make out a faded sign on what is probably the third story. The sign reads: The Blue Delilah.

I realize I'm standing at the back end of an old pub. A moment later, the blue door is abruptly flung wide. A guy with pastel yellow hair is attempting to wheel a bike through the doorway. He glances at me and his eyes narrow suspiciously. "Yeah?"

"Um…I'm looking for Jasper?"

His face changes as if someone has flicked a lever under his skin. "Oh right. You're Henry's kid's friend. I'm Ethan. Go in. He's expecting you."

Yellow-haired Ethan squeezes the bike past me and pedals off with a wave. I stick my head in the doorway.

"Are you coming in? You're letting my heat out."

Inside is what I assume was once a bar, but is now a very large, very messy living room/dining room/refuge for a pool table and a heap of giant speakers and random music equipment. Half a dozen guys are lounging on orange velour armchairs that are scattered around the far end of the room. The air smells like coffee and old beer and stale cigarettes. I close the door behind me.

The people on the couches are staring vacantly at a TV that's balanced on some milk crates. They appear to be watching *Rage*. A couple of them peer at me; most look wholly uninterested. A twenty-something guy with a head full of chaotic curls stands.

"Lemme guess. Sam?" he says, stretching his arms languidly over his head. His T-shirt is ripped, revealing some sort of twisted tattoo across his stomach.

There is much shaggy facial hair and faded band T-shirts and flannel on the other guys in the room. I suddenly wish I had worn something other than my pale blue hoodie and Oscar the Grouch T-shirt. I have an inexplicable flashback to the first day of high school: loading my Ninja Turtles stationery into my locker as Justin Zigoni made out with Brooke Piper against the locker next to mine.

"Um, yeah. I'm Sam. Jasper?"

"One and the same." Jasper crosses the room and shakes my hand with a lopsided grin. He has a thick English accent that's nothing at all like Camilla's. Even though I'm looking down on him, I feel like he towers over me.

"So, I think you have something for me?"

"Ah, I think, yeah." I scramble to undo the clasps on the guitar case. Sitting on top of Camilla's acoustic guitar is a flat brown paper sleeve.

Jasper grabs at it eagerly. "Original press Burrito Brothers record." He gives me that half-smarmy grin again. "Thought I would have to pry this from her cold dead fingers."

The guys on the couch seem to have lost interest in us. They're talking about some gig they were at last night. I notice a couple of framed black and white posters propped up against the pool table. Jasper's face stares down the camera in front of a bunch of guys wearing expressions of pain and gloom. The swirling text beneath their faces reads *The Annabel Lees*.

Jasper clutches the record to his chest. "Righto. You ready? Let's go upstairs."

It seems pointless to argue. I follow him behind the old bar, which seems to have been converted into a combined storage space for food, shoes, and general junk. A wooden staircase leads upward. Jasper takes the stairs two at a time.

The level above branches into a wide corridor with chipped blue doors leading off it. I'm guessing it's the old hotel part of the building. I peek into bedrooms of various levels of disorder. If I wasn't having a minor freak-out about what I'm doing here, I might actually be able to contemplate what a cool place this would be to live, in spite of the filth.

Jasper leads me into a room at the far end. There is nothing in here but some mattresses propped up against the walls and a few cracked stools. He sits down heavily on one stool and gestures for me to take the one opposite. He places the record carefully on the floor beside him. "So. Camilla told me you're a virgin," he says.

"She did *what?*" I stammer. "She's not...why would she...it's not like she would know—"

Jasper laughs, loudly. "Relax, kid. I meant, she told me you've never played before. But thanks for sharing, yeah? Unfortunately, this is all I can help you with today."

He's still chuckling as he reaches behind him for a battered guitar that's resting against one of the mattresses. I must have missed it in all the mortal fear.

Apparently, I am having a guitar lesson. I sit down on shaky legs and wipe my palms on my thighs.

"Right, well, since this is your first time—I'll be gentle and all that." He laughs again. I am glad he's amusing someone. He starts to tune his guitar, his fingers plucking lightly at the strings.

I hoist Camilla's guitar awkwardly onto my lap. I'm not even sure I know how to hold the stupid thing. I feel like a massive knob.

"So…how do you know Camilla?" I mumble. It seems like a reasonable thing to ask at this point.

"London. Her dad was big on the scene when we lived there. I used to give little Cammie lessons, back in the day."

I make a mental note to rib her about the "Cammie" later. "You were her guitar teacher?"

He grimaces as he sets his guitar aside and takes mine from my hands. "Do I look like I'm wearing spectacles and a pocket protector? I'm not a *teacher*. I'm a musician. But yeah, I did a few lessons here and there. Select clientele, you understand?" He fiddles with the tuning things on Camilla's guitar. "I mean, I wouldn't be doing this for just anyone, right? But Cammie asked. I'm doing her a favor."

I get it, Jasper. It's an honor to be studying at your feet. "Well, thanks," I say.

He hands the guitar back to me. "Yeah. Tell her she owes me a visit, virgin-boy."

"Can we just stick with Sam?" I say. I hope it doesn't sound too pleading.

Jasper grins. "Whatever. Righto. Let's start with some basic chords."

*

"So? How was it?"

I made it back home just as the rain started again, and I've spent the last four hours alternating between staring at the drops on my window, staring at an empty page in my red notebook, and staring at my computer screen. When Camilla finally pings me on Skype, I have to turn the volume right up on my laptop just so I can hear her over the noise of the rain on my roof.

She's stretched out on her bed with her laptop perched on her pillow and a mug of what I'm guessing is that strong English tea she likes balanced beside her. Her hair is scooped up behind her neck. It looks wavier than normal today.

Her mum has dragged her out shopping for most of the day; I know Camilla can spend hours combing through vintage stores, but malls are some of her least favorite places. She hates the fluorescent lights, and the sameness makes her sad. Gabriella should know that. Camilla looks tired.

"It was actually okay. Jasper's a good teacher. I almost have three chords nailed. Sort of. Are my fingers supposed to feel like they're bleeding?"

She grins. "Yup. Keep practicing. You'll be surprised how quickly they'll toughen up. And three chords is ace, cos you can play a whole heap of stuff with three chords.

Hang on, I'll send you links for some good guitar tab sites."

"You think I'll be capable of playing actual songs?"

"By the time I get back, you'll be rivalling Jimmy Page."

I have no idea who that is. I move from the desk to my bed, settling the laptop onto my pillow. "Well, you'd know," I say casually. "Jasper tells me that the twelve-year-old you was some sort of musical genius."

Camilla's cheeks turn red. She takes a long, slow sip of her tea. "He would say that," she says eventually. "I think he might be talking up his own teaching skills."

I peer at her face. She's looking somewhere just left of the webcam, her fingers plucking at her bedspread. I've been busting to ask her a billion questions all day—number one being why I haven't ever heard her play anything if she's so good, and why she gets that weird expression whenever I mention it. But she looks awkward and embarrassed, and I'm suddenly not at all willing to make her any more uneasy. I shelve my interrogation, for now.

"Anyway, Jasper's place is very cool. I think there's about eighteen people living there."

"Yeah, I love it too. Though it does smell a bit too much like boy for me. I'll take you to see Jasper's band play one day. They might look like rejects from the 70s, but The Annabel Lees have a really great sound. I think you'll like them."

I sit up a little straighter. "Camilla, that record you gave him…was it worth a lot? I mean, I'll pay you back, but—"

"Don't worry about that. It's not important. But Sam…?" She leans closer to the camera. Even in the crappy laptop light, her eyes are twinkling.

I find myself leaning toward her as well. "Yes…?"

Her eyes narrow mischievously. "Are you ready for your next task?"

✳

She sends me to the National Gallery on a mission to photograph the top five weirdest nudes I can find. I text her the truly outstanding examples, and she texts back her rating while she's confined to her mum's office. The gallery has no windows, which makes me feel like I'm in a space-time warp, where my only connection to the outside world is Camilla on the other end of my phone. A bunch of scenes for my screenplay swirl through my head as I wander the gallery halls, but I don't bother writing any down. I'm not sure my story really works with my Killer Cat people trapped on opposite sides of a dimensional rift.

Camilla is so enthusiastic about the top five nudes project that she sends me into the city again to gather the top five examples of a whole heap of pointless things—the top five stupidest restaurant names, the top five street signs that could double as porn words, and the top five greatest mustaches on city waiters. The top five mustaches prove to be perilous to photograph with my phone, though I do manage to get a photo of me with a bartender at a Mexican restaurant who looks exactly like Lando Calrissian from *Star Wars*. I explain my mission to Mexican Lando, who is more than happy to pose with me, so long as we can both wear a sombrero. Camilla tells me that she loves the sombrero pic so much she has set it as her laptop wallpaper.

She makes me watch a movie called *Trust* by this guy called Hal Hartley. I watch it twice and then I download everything else that he has ever written. I can't sleep, but it almost doesn't matter that I'm blurry-eyed with exhaustion. The movies are awesome. I find myself filling half a red notebook with bits of dialogue while I wait by my laptop for her to Skype. Camilla gets stuck at some fashion launch thing with her mum and so ends up only texting, but I think she's a bit excited that I like him. She reminds me that I'd promised to watch one of his movies the very first time she came to my house. It seems like a lifetime ago now.

On Friday, Camilla makes me trek out to this vintage store on Smith Street, with the goal of finding the most ridiculous thing I can buy for under twenty dollars. It takes me about three hours to comb through the cavernous shop, but I eventually emerge with an electric blue velour top hat that has a giant peacock feather embedded in the side. When Camilla finally pings me on Skype, it is almost

2 A.M. and I'm staring blankly at the screen in my pajamas and the hat. She laughs so hard she actually has tears running down her cheeks. She tells me it is the best hat she has ever seen, and that she'll be borrowing it when she comes home. My stomach does this unnerving bouncing thing when she says that. I may have eaten too many tacos for dinner.

I know she's making this stuff up as she goes along. But I find that the only way I'm able to get out of bed every day is by doing exactly what she tells me to do. This is probably slightly pathetic. But everything feels out of sync and messed up and confused, and I'm so tired that I'm barely managing to function, and my house is way too quiet, and *KCftTMoJ* has hit a big fat dead end, and every time I try to write I just end up covering pages with half-arsed sketches and rows of tiny music notes.

Mum spends most of her time with Aunt Jenny. She updates her résumé and starts smoking full-time again. She is in tears at unpredictable moments, like whenever that ad for the Family Feast KFC box comes on TV. We circle around each other without talking about anything.

It rains for the entire second week of the break. Camilla and her mum go on a spa retreat in Malaysia for a few days, so we don't get to Skype for ages, but on her instruction I hang out at Schwartzman's on the evenings that Allison is working. I take my homework and notebooks and try to work on my screenplay, but it seems to have morphed into this weird experimental Sundance thing where my Killer Cat people do nothing but sit around licking themselves while yowling longingly at the moon.

I end up mostly just talking to Allison. I suspect she has spoken to Camilla and Mike, cos she doesn't ask me anything about my family, but she does give me sympathetic head tilts and doesn't make me pay for coffee. I learn that she is planning to apply for an Asian Studies course at college and that her dream job is working as a translator for the UN. I feel a bit bad that I've never asked her before what she wants to do with her life. She wears a blue uniform and a matching ribbon in her ponytail while she works. Without her hair clinging to her face, Allison looks older. She actually looks pretty. It is an odd revelation.

I have three more lessons with Jasper, who turns out to be really cool and not nearly as big a knob as I first thought. I spend a whole afternoon with him and his housemates, listening to music and playing pool. I become almost proficient at a sketchy three-chord *Ruby Tuesday*, the song that Henry once mentioned inspired Camilla's middle name. My fingertips start to feel tough and hard.

I have coffee with my dad like we're old friends or something. He still looks hopeless, like he's not entirely sure which planet he's beamed down onto. He has no explanation for what's happening with Mum, other than mumbling some stuff about "finding himself." I'm tempted to say that he should know where he is by now, but instead I just stop listening. The only silver lining of this whole situation is that I no longer need to deal with my father and his dumb-arsery.

I find myself writing a long e-mail to Camilla at three in the morning, which is mostly about the screenplay of *Amateur*, but also, in passing, about my dad. She e-mails back to say that I'm allowed to be mad with Dad, just not for forever. She doesn't say anything more.

When she manages to jump online in between her mum's frenzied scheduling, I help her Warcraft dwarf level-up another two times. Mostly, when she finds the time to Skype, we talk about movies, and *Battlestar Galactica*, and the places she has lived since she was a kid, and the stupid stories from Reddit, and how awesome Hal Hartley is, and how crap I am on guitar even though I'm loving it, and how we both might want to live in a converted pub one day. We talk about everything other than our parents, which suits me just fine.

And then, it is 7:16 on Thursday night, and I am in my living room watching *The Fog* with the volume way down low. Mum is out for dinner with Aunt Jenny; she's not due back for hours, but I jump every time the headlights of a car beam through my front window. Camilla is catching a cab home from the airport because Henry is working. She promised to stop by, but I can't imagine she'd want to do anything other than go home and unpack and—

Another set of headlights glow in the window. This time, the light lingers.

I stay where I am for seven seconds. At twelve seconds I attempt to stand, but end up hovering in this half-sitting pose, feeling a little dumb-arse. At fifteen seconds I hear the slamming of a car trunk, and I find myself at the front door with my fingers on the handle before my brain really registers that I have moved.

I hear footsteps thundering down the wet front path.

Camilla barrels through my door in a blur of suitcases and is already halfway through a conversation in the way she always seems to be when she breezes into my house. She untangles herself from her luggage and gloves and hat, dropping them one by one onto the floor, and then, all of a sudden, she is free. She gathers herself with a frantic breath. And she smiles at me.

I don't know if I move or if she does—it's almost as if someone skipped a scene in my movie and I missed a bit of the action—but the next thing I know, my arms are around her. Her heavy winter coat is damp from the rain, and it feels like the actual Camilla is somewhere miles beneath layers of wool—but it is still her. And she is home. I want to tell her that I'm happy she's back, but the first words that slip out of my mouth are bizarre, even by my standards:

"You were gone for too long."

She pulls loose from my arms a little and peers up at

me. Her face passes through a bunch of different things. For a rare second, it is serious. "I know."

She shrugs off her coat and shakes out her hair. Then she grabs my hand and tugs me into the living room, flopping onto the couch and pulling me down beside her. She shuffles closer, still holding my hand. I find that I'm not at all concerned about this invasion of my personal space. I find that my hand in hers is the best thing I have felt in weeks.

"Okay, Sam. So tell me."

And so I do.

I tell her about Mum and Dad, and the last couple of years of Mum's sadness, and of Dad's oblivious zombie-walking through everything, and how relieved they both seem now, and how pissed I have been with Dad for ages, and how sad I've been for Mum, and how I think I'm actually happy that it's going to be just me and Mum from now on. I keep talking and talking, feeling like a giant balloon that's slowly deflating. I talk until I have no more air left, till I feel empty and tired and still.

Camilla has been watching me closely the whole time I've been speaking. Maybe it's something to do with the cabin pressure in an airplane, but her eyes are flecked with colors I've never noticed before, tiny sparks of green and gold. Her eyes are way bigger and warmer than I remember.

"Everything just feels really…tilted," I mumble.

She squeezes my hand tightly between both of hers. "I'm sorry about your parents. I'm sorry I wasn't here when it happened. I'm sorry it's rained for ten days straight."

I don't know why, but that is all she needs to say. I look down at our hands. "Camilla, I wanted to say…thank you. I'm not sure what I would have done if…you know. If it wasn't for you." I swallow. Why do I suddenly sound like a four-year-old?

I glance at her face. Camilla's eyes seem to be focused on our hands as well. "I'm glad I'm back, Sam. Not sure if I could've coped with another day of Gabriella. At least I know what to expect from Henry. I'm almost excited about school. It'll be a relief to get back to some kind of… order."

I turn my hand over absently. My palm lies flat and warm against hers. "Status quo is good," I mumble.

She smiles at me, but for a second something almost hesitant flickers across her face. "Yeah. It really is," she says.

She lets go of my hand, and then she's buzzing around again, unpacking the thousand presents she's brought. I get knock-off DVDs and a miniature wind-up space robot from the Singapore Art Museum. She's also brought me a *Battlestar Galactica* Commander Adama figure with a suspiciously inauthentic face. She waves it in front of me.

"Does he look a bit…?"

"Asian?" she says with a giggle. "Yeah, thought you'd appreciate. Okay, so I do have one more thing for you." She rifles through her jacket pockets. "I found this at a vintage store, so you know it's not a Movie World souvenir…"

She holds her fist over mine and drops something small into my hand.

Nestled in my palm is a tiny movie clapperboard on a keychain. The front is a real chalkboard, the kind filmmakers used before they all went digital. If I had a tiny piece of chalk, I could even write the name of my movie on it.

"It's…awesome. Camilla, I don't know what to say. Thank you."

Her cheeks turn pink. "It's a keychain. Don't cry."

"Shut up. That's not what I meant. I just meant, thanks. Again. For everything."

She gives me a lopsided grin. "I'm really glad I'm home, Sam. For one thing, I haven't seen a horror movie in weeks. I never thought I'd say it, but I might be experiencing some withdrawal symptoms."

I flick through the DVD pile she has given me and pull out the new *Saw* movie. "Are you in a rush to go?"

She kicks off her boots. "I probably smell like airport. But I can stay for a bit."

She curls up on the side of the couch that she always defaults to. I put on the DVD and take the other side. The movie rolls on the screen. Neither of us really watches it.

Camilla has too many stories, and I'm finding that the movie chick getting sliced in half is not nearly as interesting as listening to her. Her voice fills my house, and I feel less and less like I'm swaying. I feel—-

What?

Relief, for sure. I mean, that's a rational response. Camilla is part of my everyday routine; a disturbance to that routine will produce a negative response, and a return to normality will produce a positive response. Objectively, it is perfectly reasonable that I would be happy she is home.

But it's something else, too.

It feels sort of like that moment in the cinema, those few seconds of quiet when the lights dim and the babble of the audience fades. It feels comfortable, and familiar, and somehow just...safe.

I think about the mess that is my life. I think about my Killer Cat people, lost and useless and pining for something that nothing in my screenplay could explain. I think about my dad, his confusion more destructive than any chainsaw-wielding psychopath. And then I think about how consistent, solid Camilla is the one thing left in my life that I understand.

So I don't let myself think about anything else. Because Camilla is home.

Mike and Adrian come home from their vacations too. Allison is released from math hell for our last few precious days of freedom. We sit at the park in the freezing cold, or at Schwartzman's in the almost-as-cold, or at the Astor, which is showing a 1940s comedy double feature on Saturday afternoon. The Astor is icy. The movies suck. It doesn't matter at all.

We take blankets. We huddle beneath them and whisper alternative Tarantino-inspired lines over the top of the rapid-fire 1940s dialogue. Allison proves to be surprisingly adept at Tarantino lines, as well as producing a whole vocab of swear words that makes Adrian blush and Mike choke on a mouthful of popcorn.

Camilla huddles sideways under a blanket with her cat-eye glasses perched on her nose and her knees touching mine. She pokes me in the side and giggles or groans whenever something particularly cheesy happens on screen, her eyes sparkling in the crackly movie light.

I feel like everything is exactly how it is supposed to be. Like nothing at all needs to change. And as soon as I think that thought, I freak.

I have seen enough movies to know how jinxes work.

I really should have known better.

12

The reason they call it a siren's song

I believe that in some parts of the world, events of actual significance are occurring. There are wars, and earthquakes, and people making scientific breakthroughs. But at Bowen Lakes Secondary, none of these things matter at all. Because the new semester is all about the Spring Dance.

The costume party idea has been enthusiastically adopted, but there is much controversy over what constitutes Old Hollywood. Apparently people are interested in my opinion on this. Camilla ropes me into a committee meeting, where, after a lengthy debate that I somehow find myself in charge of, it is decided that 1980 will be the official Old Hollywood cutoff. While this is objectively incorrect, I have no interest in arguing since it means that *Star Wars* just scrapes in.

Sharni Vane hooked up with Jonah Warrington over the break. Justin is now going out with some girl from a private school, but it doesn't stop him trying to weasel his way in with Camilla. He tends to touch her arm a lot when they talk, which sort of makes me wish I had a taser. He actually tries sucking up to me like he hasn't spent the last four years being a pus-filled tumor on the arse of my life. Justin and I have as much chance of becoming friends as Adrian has of captaining the Starship *Enterprise*. For Camilla's sake, I am passably polite. Even if Justin is still a massive knob.

Allison gets her long-awaited haircut. I think she may have been saving it for a new semester grand entrance. When she sidles up to me at my locker, I'm not sure who she is for four whole seconds.

"Well?" she says.

Her fine blonde hair is gone. What remains is a short pixie thing in a shade of bright coppery-red. The new hair makes her eyes look twice as big. She actually looks sixteen. She looks great.

"You look great," I say. I don't know why my opinion is important, but Allison beams. There is much fluttering around her from Veronica and Annie, as evidently Allison's hair is some sort of group achievement.

Mum starts a teaching job on the other side of the city. She initiates a Thursday dinner-and-movie routine with just the two of us, and invests in an industrial-sized box of nicotine patches. She also hugs me at random moments, and turns Dad's study into a yoga studio. I sort of wish she would wear less lycra around the house, but since she seems happy, I can let the lycra go.

My father moves into a flat near the city. I avoid going there for three and a half weeks, until Mike and Camilla drag me onto a tram to visit him. Dad has set up his second room for me. It has a single bed and a set of wobbly Ikea furniture. He has also stuck a *Friday the 13th* poster crookedly on the wall above the bed. I'm not sure what to feel about any of this, as I'm not planning on spending a lot of time here. I hover uselessly in the middle of the room until Camilla squeezes my arm and then tapes a photo above the night-stand. It is the slightly blurry shot of me and Mexican Lando, complete with giant sombreros.

"Just in case you change your mind," she says.

Camilla helps me buy a second-hand guitar so I can keep taking lessons with Jasper. In between Jasper sessions, she makes me practice some simple stuff and tries to look encouraging, but her face gets this pained look whenever I play and I feel a bit like I'm stabbing her in the eardrums with a fork. For some reason, Mike finds her zero patience with my musical incompetence hilarious.

Mike and I hang out less and less. I don't know how this happens. He goes to a normal gym and runs and lifts weights, but he has not set foot inside another karate class. We talk as much as we ever did at school, but it's always about stupid, trivial stuff. I've been on the verge of bringing up the Travis thing more than once, but the prospect of navigating that conversation with Mike makes me, predictably, wuss out. I keep thinking that whatever this is will fix itself—it's Mike, so it just has to—but the weirdness has crept in, and I don't know how to undo it.

As the cold gives way to longer days and bluer skies, Camilla's dad starts travelling more and more. When he's home he prowls around their house like the walls are closing in on him, throwing half sentences in our direction and generally being a morose pain in the arse.

Camilla picks up a waitressing job at Schwartzman's; she tells me that this is mostly so she has somewhere else to be other than hiding out at my house, but I suspect she's just digging her heels in, for "insurance" against her dad's antsiness.

I know she's worried about Henry taking her away again. It's not something I'm prepared to contemplate.

The girls save the same green booth in a corner for us whenever they're working. Adrian and I spend way too much time at Schwartzman's doing homework or playing poker; the old regulars call it the kiddie table, but no one really seems to mind.

Killer Cats from the Third Moon of Jupiter ends up in the back of my closet. I think it may possibly be one of the worst things ever written.

I find that I'm not hating this new routine at all. Unfortunately, this new routine is not to last.

✳

I read somewhere that significant events tend to happen on Thursdays. I don't know the logic behind this. All I know is one sunny Thursday, my life as I know it is nuked.

I'm in the lab at morning break, trying to fix a bug that has frozen all the printers. Camilla is perched on the desk, swinging her legs impatiently against my chair. She's wearing one of the presents I gave her for her birthday: a necklace with two enamel sausage-dog charms that clatter against each other when she moves. I don't know why she has a thing for dachshunds, but I'm grateful that all variations of weirdness are available on the net, if you look hard enough.

"Sam, come on! It's perfect outside and I need some sun. How much longer is this gonna take?"

I ignore the thumping of her feet against my chair. "I don't know. It's very complicated and important. You don't have to wait for me if you don't want."

"Well, I have volleyball practice lunchtime. You have your mum tonight. I have a dance committee meeting tomorrow lunch. Dad and I are in Adelaide this weekend. When else are we going to hang out?"

I lean back in my chair with a sigh. It does suck that she's away this weekend. The Astor is screening *The Shining*, which I know she hasn't seen before.

"Blame Alessandro," I say.

"Oh, I do. Seriously, how many times has he had food poisoning this year?"

I laugh as I scroll through the printer configuration settings. "I know. Dude needs to learn that six-day-old pizza is probably not the healthiest breakfast option."

"You'd think someone who lives on a diet of Coke and kebabs would have a slightly tougher constitution." She balances her boots on the edge of my seat and swivels my chair from side to side. "But Sammy, do you have to do this now? Can't it wait till Alessandro gets back?"

I plant my hands on the desk at either side of her, holding myself in place. Camilla's knee digs into my chest a little, but I resolutely refuse to let her move me again.

"Oooh, tough guy Sam," she says with a grin.

I roll my eyes. "You know I get paid to do this job, right? And besides—what if the committee has some poster-printing emergency? Fixing this might be all that stands between me and the wrath of Sharni Vane. Seriously—I'm not willing to put my man parts on the line for you."

She winks. "God forbid I do anything to put your man parts in danger, Sammy."

Her mobile beeps before I can respond. She pulls it out of the pocket of her blue dress and frowns at the screen.

"Everything okay?"

"Huh? Ah, yeah. I just…need to make a phone call.

I'll meet you back here in a min." She moves my arm out of her way and swings off the desk, hurrying from the room before I have a chance to say anything.

I wait in the lab till the bell rings, but she doesn't reappear. We have English next period, but I detour past her locker anyway. I can't find her anywhere, and no one seems to have seen her. I duck into the classroom but Camilla's chair is empty. Mike hasn't seen her. Allison hasn't seen her.

She bolts into Mr. Nicholas's classroom seven minutes late and drops into the closest seat to the door. I know straightaway that something is wrong. Her eyes are all wide and weird and her face is pale. I try to get her attention by staring at the side of her face, but she doesn't look at me once. Mr. Nicholas may have been speaking for some of the period, but all I hear is a vague rumble of sound in the background.

By lunchtime she's looking really sick. She dashes out of the classroom as soon as the bell rings, but I run behind her and corner her near her locker.

"Camilla?"

She jumps. "Oh. Hey, Sam."

"Hey...is everything all right?"

She fidgets with the dog charms on her necklace. "Yeah. Everything's fine." Her eyes are focused somewhere in the middle distance. The hand that holds the necklace is trembling.

"You sure?"

Camilla looks up at me for a moment. And then she grabs the sleeve of my hoodie and pulls me around the corner. She really does look awful. My palms start to sweat. I run through all the possible scenarios that could have reduced the unflappable Camilla Carter to the pale, wobbly thing in front of me. I'm thinking a family tragedy, a teenage pregnancy, or—

Jesus, she couldn't be—

She takes a deep breath. "Sam, I think I might have done something stupid. Well, not stupid, just hasty, and now I'm kind of stuck and—"

"Okay, tell me." For some reason, my voice is wobbling as well. I'm trying to remember that session with the Family Planning nurse who came in year nine, but I can only come up with a video of a screaming baby and some girl with braces talking about ruining her life. I have a feeling this won't help. What am I going to do? Mike has money. He could help her. Maybe I could get another job, or—

Camilla swallows. "I'm supposed to do this thing. I signed up for it ages ago, on a stupid whim, and now they've called me and I'm supposed to go tonight, but I don't think I can. I can't. I'm an idiot."

I try to decipher some meaning from her rambling. I fail. "Maybe try that again in English?"

Her cheeks become red. She looks up at me for three

long seconds. And then she closes her eyes. "Thing is, Sam, I sort of…write. Songs. Music. I'm not very good. I don't even want to perform, at all. Dad thinks I'm just messing around with instruments, which I am, but whenever he's gone…I work really hard at it. And I had this burst of something—recklessness or whatever—months ago, and I sent a demo disc out to this bar that does open-mic things. And they called me. They had someone drop out tonight. They asked me to fill in. *Tonight*."

The image of screaming babies is still circling in my head. I have to replay Camilla's words before any of them actually process. "You…sing?"

"No! Well, yes, but like I said, I'm not good. It's the writing I really like. And I've never sung in front of people. And it's a *bar*. People are going to pay actual, real money to hear me sing my own songs, and I'm supposed to be there on stage and—"

She groans and sways a little. I grab her arm. The relief that floods through my insides almost makes me sit down in the middle of the corridor. I burst out laughing.

"Don't laugh at me!"

"I'm not laughing *at* you. Jesus, I thought you were going to tell me you were having a baby or something—"

Her mouth drops open. "You thought I was *pregnant*? *That's* the first conclusion you jump to? How exactly did you assume that happened?"

I feel my face flush. "Well, I don't know…"

"Sam, jeez, did you fail sex ed?"

I fear we are heading off topic.

Camilla shakes off my hand. "It's so stupid! I recorded the stuff on my laptop in my bedroom! I know the music industry, Sam. It's brutal—my dad is *brutal*. Have you read his reviews? I don't know why I thought I could do this, and now I can't back out and I don't want Dad to know and—"

"Camilla, calm down—"

"I can't calm down! Sam, I'm supposed to *sing*. In front of *people*."

Some year twelves thunder past. They look curiously in our direction. I pull Camilla into the shadows of the lockers and lower my voice. "Okay, look. Obviously you've been thinking about this for a while, right? It's not like you've thrown a song together in one night, have you?"

She shakes her head. "No. I've been writing for ages. But I've never shown them to anyone. And I've never, ever sung in front of people before. It makes me want to vomit and pass out...I can get up in front of people and speak, but my music—I just can't, Sam, I can't, and—"

Her accent is almost painfully pronounced. The Britishness only ever comes out this strongly when she's excited—or, I guess, super stressed.

"Camilla. You...have stage fright?"

"Argh! Do you have to label it? It makes me sound like I have a psychological disorder and I really don't want to have to deal with that, since I already feel like I'm going to have a heart attack—"

"Okay, okay. How's this—you are somewhat, slightly concerned about getting up on stage?"

"Maybe," she whispers. Her face has gone from white to an awful shade of green.

"Right, okay. But…you like songwriting? It's something you want to do?"

"I don't know. Maybe. I mean, yes, I think so. I mean, I'd like to write songs for other people. I always have music and words floating around in my head, but I don't have dreams of winning a Grammy or anything. Yes, I want to write. But my dad—"

"Doesn't need to know anything," I say.

I try to slot this new development into my Camilla file. The idea of getting up in front of people and doing anything makes me want to vomit too. I have a vague flashback to the Building Self-Esteem Through Drama workshop where I met Mike. All I remember is jelly knees and a constant feeling of nakedness. But Camilla isn't me. Camilla can do anything. Except right now, she looks like she's about to faint.

"Camilla, forget about your dad. You're not doing this for him. If you really don't want to, you don't have to. It's your call. But…you sent the disc in. Didn't you?"

"I thought I could handle it," she says softly.

"And you can," I reply. I don't know what else to add.

She looks at me again. Her eyes are kind of shinier than normal. "Do you think so?"

I smile. I hope it looks encouraging. "It's just an open-mic night, right? It's not Rod Laver Arena. Aren't these things, like, a couple of drunk people in a dark bar? It's no big deal. You can handle it."

"You sound so confident. You've never even heard me sing before."

I shrug. "Doesn't matter. It's you."

She exhales slowly. She seems to have lost the power of speech, which does not bode well for her singing debut. But she catches my eye and nods, just once. "Sam…if I'm really going to do this…I could use a friendly face? I mean, I know you have plans with your mum, but—"

"I'll come. Of course I'll be there," I say, without really thinking about it.

"You and the guys? I think…I'd like that. As long as you're aware that I might majorly suck. Probably will majorly suck."

A bunch of things swim through my head—how the hell we're supposed to get into a bar being number one. But she's looking at me with those eyes, and all of a sudden the only image I have in my head is of Princess Leia asking Obi-Wan for help, which pretty much renders me incapable of any further logical thought. "Just us. I promise. I'll spread the word among the guys on the possible major suckage. But Millie?"

"Yeah?"

"You're going to be great. I'm sure of it."

She laughs, this shaky thing that sounds like it might dissolve into tears at any second. "Sammy, I think you might have seriously overestimated my abilities. If I make it on stage without puking, it's going to be a miracle."

I take a deep breath. For some reason, I suddenly feel a bit sick myself.

*

The taxi drops us off on a dimly lit street corner at the edge of the city. Our CIA-worthy cover story is that Mike is studying at my house and I am studying at his. Adrian has no curfew, but Allison had no hope of escaping without the third degree from her parents. I'm supposed to give Camilla a hug from her—that is, if we ever actually find Camilla.

I have no idea where we are, only that, if I were writing a horror movie scene, the three vague-looking guys wandering around a dark alley behind a row of dumpsters would probably be too obvious a setup.

Adrian frowns at the map on his iPhone. "This is supposed to be it."

The alley terminates at a dead end. My eyes take a moment to adjust to the dark. There is a guy sitting on a milk crate at the far end. There is no signage that I can see.

We shuffle toward the milk crate guy. In the dark I

can't exactly tell where his long hair ends and his giant beard begins. The effect is disconcerting, like the top and bottom halves of his head are swappable, Mr. Potato Head-style. Crate-man is standing guard by a featureless red door. He looks us up and down. "ID?"

Beside me I feel Mike adjust his glasses. I swallow involuntarily. "We're supposed to meet a friend. She's playing tonight. Camilla Carter?"

The guy leaps up from his crate. "Camilla? That's cool, no probs. Hey, you don't know if her dad's coming, do you?"

I glance back down the alley. I consider making a run for it. "I don't know. Maybe."

It seems like the right thing to say. Crate-man opens the red door and sweeps us inside. A narrow concrete staircase, lit by a single naked globe, leads downwards. Mike and I pause on the top step. Music drifts from somewhere below.

"It looks a bit sketchy," Mike offers.

Adrian snorts. He pushes past us and takes the stairs two at a time. "It's a *bar*," he calls behind him. "It's supposed to look sketchy. Don't you guys know anything?"

Mike shrugs. "He's right, I guess. C'mon."

Adrian is waiting at another red door, three flights down. A cloakroom window is set in the left wall. An irritated-looking chick with a chin piercing stares out at us.

"Five bucks," she says in a bored voice.

I hand over the money for all three of us, hoping the bills aren't dripping with clammy palm sweat. I have no idea why I'm so nervous. Mike pokes me in the side, and I realize that angry-girl is waving a stamp in my face. Then she pounds a black horseshoe onto my wrist. Adrian blows on his stamp like Mum when she's drying her nail polish. He ends up with a crescent of ink on his top lip. Somehow, this is not how I pictured my first bar experience.

The bar is slightly bigger than a classroom. Candles in red glasses light up the tables in front of the stage, which is smallish and framed by strings of lights. A row of red cracked vinyl booths line the back wall. Mike and I herd a gaping Adrian into an empty booth in the corner.

The place is just about half full. Camilla's audience looks like the college crowd that hangs around near the Nova cinema; there are lots of vintage shirts and thick glasses and bizarre hair. I am wearing my most inconspicuous clothes—a black T-shirt and dark jeans—but I still feel somewhat sore-thumb-like.

"How cool is this!" Adrian barks. Several people turn and stare. I sink into my seat.

Two young guys are strumming guitars on stage. Their song is about trees or ferns or something. The song fades out, and there is some light applause from the room, but mostly people seem to be concentrating on their drinks and animated conversations. An upright piano is set to one side of the stage. Even under the dim lights, it looks awfully exposed.

I stand up. "I'm going to see if I can find Camilla."

Adrian stands as well. A twenty dollar bill appears in Mike's hand, seemingly plucked out of the air. He waves it at Adrian. "You wanna get drinks?"

Adrian's eyes widen as he looks at the bar. "Awesome. Whisky? How 'bout tequila?"

Mike rolls his eyes. "How about three beers? This isn't *Sex and the City*. I'm not holding your hair back while you puke."

Adrian snatches the bill from Mike and practically skips over to the bar. Mike looks impassively at the guitar players on stage. "Say hey to her for me, yeah?"

There is a gap to the side of the stage with a metal sign pointing to the toilets. There's nowhere else to go, so I squeeze between the tables and head toward it.

A guy in a Radiohead T-shirt stumbles past me and shoves open a door with a picture of a cowboy on it. I'm probably not going to find Camilla in the guys' toilets. I turn around and smack straight into her.

"S*aaaaaaaam!*" she wails, grabbing my forearm with both hands. "You're here. I think I'm going to throw up."

She's wearing a green dress that reaches her ankles. Her hair is swept to one side and spills over her tattooed shoulder, and she's framed her eyes with some sort of dark stuff that makes them look even brighter than normal.

"You look great," I murmur. I have a feeling my cheeks have turned red. I'm sort of glad we're in semi-darkness.

I don't think she's listening to me anyway. Camilla's face is chalk white. She really does look like she's about to be sick. "Sam, I don't think I can do this," she whispers.

"Okay…you need to relax. Calm down."

She takes a deep breath but doesn't seem to let it go. She starts to pace the tiny corridor, her hands flapping like wayward birds. "I can't. *I can't, I can't, I can't, I can't, I can't —*"

She paces back toward me. I grab her hands, even though mine are still clammy. I don't think it matters, since hers are just as damp. I don't know what else to do.

"Camilla, look at me."

She stops flapping. She looks up at me. Her eyes are terrified.

I think about my top five all-time greatest movie inspirational speeches. Most of them take place just before expendable soldiers are sent off to battle aliens or killer cyborgs. There's that speech from *Army of Darkness* I know by heart. I'm not sure if an inspirational speech from *Army of Darkness* is going to be relevant in this situation. Camilla is still looking at me. I am still holding her hands.

"You can do this. You always know the right thing to say. I can't imagine it'll be any different when you sing."

I wouldn't want to send the troops off with that. But

it seems to do something useful for her. She takes a couple of slow, deep breaths. Camilla's hands are really soft, but her fingertips are rough with guitar-string calluses. My hands feel too big and clumsy around hers; I've never noticed that before. I have a sudden flash of the lonely piano on stage, and I'm struck with this overwhelming urge to grab her and haul her someplace safe. I grip her hands a little tighter instead.

"Okay, Sam…I think I can do this." She smiles weakly. "Hey. What's the worst that could happen?"

"You could die a horrible violent death if legions of the undead invade. But that probably won't happen. So relax."

She laughs a bit as she lets go of me and shakes out her hands. "Okay. It's four songs. It's no big deal. I can do this."

"You can. You will kick arse."

She grins. Then there is a smattering of applause from the front room, and I hear the guys on stage mumbling thanks into their microphones. Camilla's smile vanishes. Radiohead guy reappears behind her and pushes past with a slurred apology. She stumbles and lurches into me. I grab her by the shoulders, my hand curving around the blue flowers of her tattoo. I can all but feel her heart trying to beat its way out of her chest. She smells like vanilla and lilacs.

I have run out of inspirational material. I seem to have run out of words entirely.

And then someone on stage calls her name. There is more polite clapping, and a hysterical voice that sounds suspiciously Adrian-like cheering from the front room.

I look down at her. She looks up at me. She is trembling beneath my hands. "See you afterward?" she says quietly.

"Right. Afterward."

I turn around and walk away, realizing that I didn't even wish her good luck.

Mike glances up as I slide into the booth. He pushes a glass toward me, and turns silently back to the stage.

Adrian takes a big swig of his beer. "What are we going to do if she sucks?"

I can't answer him. I wrap my hands around my glass, not really caring that this is, officially, my first drink in a bar. I can still feel my palms sweating through the cold.

The noise in the room has increased since the guitar guys finished their set. A single weak spotlight lands on the piano, and the guy on the mic who called Camilla's name wanders back behind the bar.

She walks out on stage. On the table in front of us, two guys are talking, loudly, about the latest Michel Gondry movie. It's all I can do not to leap out of my seat and tell them to shut the hell up.

I can see Camilla's bottom lip trembling as she takes the piano stool and adjusts the microphone. She pauses for a moment, her eyes laser-fixed on the keys. She chews on the inside of her cheek a little bit, a thing I know she does when she's tossing up options inside her head. Then she slips off her shoes and rests her bare feet on the foot pedals. She squeezes her eyes shut.

She takes a deep breath. I'm holding mine. And then she places her hands on the keys and begins to play.

Her voice is breathy, and odd, and sweet. It isn't note-perfect, but it doesn't matter at all. It is almost exactly what I imagined Camilla would sound like. Her eyes are still squeezed shut, but her voice doesn't tremble. Her feet tap at the foot pedals. Her hands don't miss a note.

Mike nudges my foot. He grins at me.

"Hey...she's really good!" Adrian says brightly.

"*Shush*," Mike hisses.

Her lyrics are kind of weird, but not at all in a bad way. They're not about guys or broken hearts or anything else I assumed girls would write songs about. Her first song seems to be about a crazy lost dog. A few people chuckle, but it's in the right spots. The guys in front of us stop talking.

I rest my palms on the stained table and my chin on the back of my hands. Camilla's voice soars over the chorus, more powerful than breathy now. The hair that's tumbling over her shoulder brushes against the keys, but she moves it aside without skipping a beat.

She finishes her first song with a few notes at the top end of the piano, and the audience claps. A guy in front of us whistles. Adrian swings his hands above his head, cheering way too loudly. Camilla glances around, shading her eyes against the stage lights. I know there is no way she can see me without her glasses, but somehow, I think I catch her eye for a second. Then she turns back to the piano. She still looks shaky, but her eyes are open this time.

Her first three songs are light and funny, and they seem to hold the attention of even the cranky-looking guys behind the bar. The conversations around the room are definitely quieter than before. I even catch a glimpse of drunken Radiohead guy tapping his fingers against his table.

The applause is louder at the end of the third song. Camilla smiles shyly at the room. "Thanks, everyone," she says softly. "Well, um, this is my last song. I just want to say thanks to my friends for coming tonight. Especially my friend Sam. I might've passed out on my way to the stage if it wasn't for you." She waves in my direction. A few people turn and stare. I think my face becomes crimson. And my stomach does that uncontrollable bouncing thing again.

Camilla turns back to the piano and starts to play again. Her last song is different from the others. It's still strange, but it's also a bit darker and sadder than her first three. Her fingers fly super quickly over the keys; she really is an amazing piano player. The lyrics aren't exactly obvious, but I think, somehow, I know what this song is about.

It's about absent people, and uncertain things. I'm pretty sure it's a song about Henry. I don't think I like this song.

And then she finishes. The room explodes with applause. Adrian tries to climb onto the table, but Mike yanks him back into his seat. Camilla stands and bows. She looks sheepish and flushed. And then she disappears from the stage.

I sit up. I think I may have been holding my breath for the last seventeen minutes.

Mike takes a cautious sip of his beer. "Well. I'm kinda relieved that's over. Lucky she's good."

"*Good?*" Adrian says. "She was awesome! Don't you think so, Sam? I mean, it's not the sort of music I'd normally listen to, but she was so cool, and she's wicked on the piano. And she looked hot, too."

"Don't call Camilla hot," I say automatically.

"Why?"

"Cos it's *weird*, that's why. And girls don't like it when you say that stuff behind their back."

"What stuff?" she says from behind me.

I spin around. She's standing at the edge of our booth, looking at me with a raised eyebrow.

Adrian grins. "I was just saying that you looked hot up there. Sam was disagreeing."

"Adrian! That's not what I—"

Camilla sticks out her bottom lip. "You didn't think so?"

"I did *not* say that. I mean, I didn't—I wasn't—Adrian, you're an *idiot!*"

Camilla giggles. Mike climbs out of the booth. He shoots Adrian and me a look, and then he gives her a hug. "You were great," he says quietly. "Really, really good."

She collapses against him. "God, I thought I was going to die up there. I've never been so nervous in my entire life. My knees are still shaking."

Adrian flies out of the booth behind Mike. He grabs Camilla around the waist in a ferocious bear hug. "You were really awesome. Wow. Just very, very cool. I loved the one about the donkey."

Camilla laughs as she hugs them both back. "Thanks, guys. Jesus, I need a drink."

I scramble backward and she slides next to me with a shudder.

"Here." I push my untouched beer over to her. She grabs it with both hands and drinks half the glass in a few giant gulps. Then she looks sideways at me. Her eyes are uncertain and self-conscious and completely un-Camilla-like.

"So…?" she says quietly.

Suddenly I'm not exactly sure what to say. Somehow, *you were awesome* just doesn't seem enough. I try to think, objectively, about the sort of things that a songwriter might want to hear. Objectively, her songs were funny and cool, and her voice was unique and worked perfectly for the music. Objectively, it was a great set.

"You were awesome," I murmur.

She smiles. "Thanks, Sam. Really. You have no idea. Even though I thought I was going to cry up there, I think I almost feel good now. I'm really glad you didn't let me flee." She looks around the table. "Hey, where's Allie?"

"Al really wanted to be here, but she couldn't escape the Winfield fortress," Adrian says.

Mike peers at the empty stage. "She said to wish you luck. Sam's supposed to give you a hug from her."

Camilla looks at me. Her face is almost back to its normal color. "Well?" she says.

"Oh…right."

The booth we're in is too small, and the table in front of us is marked with half-moon stains and scratched graffiti, and the entire bar smells like old beer and foot odor, and Mike is suddenly engaged in an intense discussion with Adrian about why college students all have the same glasses. Camilla is still looking at me expectantly, so I drape the arm that's resting on the back of the booth around her, in a half-arsed thing that's more awkward-shoulder-squeeze than hug. And then Camilla wraps both her arms around my middle and looks up at me with a smile.

"Thanks, Sam. If it wasn't for your pep talk—I couldn't have done it without you. Sorry you had to see my pile-o-nervous-jelly side."

She feels really, unusually warm. It might just be the

stage lights, or it might be the fact that the last time I hugged her she was buried under a coat, but now her dress is pretty thin and I can feel the shape of her beneath it, which feels like nothing I actually have words for. All I can think is that the vanilla is her shampoo, and that my hands might be shaking. And then I move my other arm from its place on the table, and suddenly, both of mine are wrapped around her as well.

She rests her head against me. I can feel the warmth of her palms through my T-shirt. The fog of bar noise seems to fade. My brain is telling me to move my arms away now. My arms do not move anywhere.

From somewhere that seems miles away, I hear the scraping of chairs. Camilla quickly untangles herself from me and the room comes back into focus. My skin is prickly, too hot and too cold all at the same time.

Two guys have pulled chairs up at the edge of our booth. It takes me a few seconds to realize that they are the guitar players who were on before Camilla. They settle on the edge of our table, propping their beers in front of them.

"Hey!" she says. "Guys, this is James and Noah. We fumbled through our sound check together earlier." She sits up straighter and puts on her best game-show-host voice. "James is a budding singer-slash-songwriter who's studying industrial design and hopes to travel to Nashville. His brother Noah is in year twelve at City High, and enjoys…" She raises an eyebrow at him.

"Um, I guess, guitar, New Folk, photography, and, um…lamb pizza?" he says quietly. Noah has shaggy dark hair and a checkered shirt scattered with holes. He looks exactly like he belongs on stage in a dingy bar, not in a year-twelve classroom. He clears his throat and looks uncertainly around the table.

Camilla introduces everyone else. Adrian is already in the middle of a conversation with James. James seems either nice enough or drunk enough to deal with Adrian. Noah clears his throat again and glances at Mike.

"I liked your music," Mike murmurs.

"Yeah? We mangled the last one. Timing was all off."

"Oh? I didn't notice."

Camilla turns around to face me, ignoring the conversations around her. I stare at her for seven seconds.

"Why so quiet?" she says eventually.

"It's just…I can't believe I've never heard you sing. I can't believe you never told me you write. There's this whole *thing* you do that I didn't know about."

She runs her fingernails over the graffiti on the table. "It's not like I meant to hide it, Sam, but it's just so…*personal*, you know? And I have no—well, in your words, no objective measure for anything I write. I mean, Jesus, how many sad emos are out there calling themselves songwriters? As if bad hair and a rhyming dictionary is a qualification. I listen to myself in my bedroom and sometimes I think that maybe bits of my stuff are okay, but—"

"Camilla—objectively—your music was more than okay. You were really great. Hey, even if I am biased, you heard that applause."

"Well, that was just simple stuff. Since I wasn't sure if my hands or voice were going to crap out on me. But...I have other music too," she says shyly. "More instruments. More complex arrangements. Lyrics that aren't about animals."

I think about this. It suddenly hits me that Camilla has always been vague about her plans after high school. I always assumed it was because she didn't know where she would be or what she wanted to do, but now—

"What do you want to do after year twelve?"

She takes a slow sip of my beer. "I've thought about lots of different things. But maybe...music composition?" She glances at my face. "At a proper conservatory. Though I'd have to audition. I think I might be too freaked to even play 'Chopsticks' properly."

"I think, Camilla...I would really like to hear your other stuff. Have you really *never* been on stage before? With all the people you know, all your dad's contacts—"

"That, Sam, is part of the problem." She sighs, curling her legs underneath her and resting the side of her head against the booth. "I think that if I grew up like most normal people, maybe I'd feel differently. But I've been around music people my whole life. And they can be *soooo* judgmental. I mean, hello—you've met Henry. Do you have any idea what it's like listening to him rip shreds off everything? I can only imagine what Dad would have to say about my music."

"Okay, so I guess I understand the thing with your dad. But you've never cared what other people think."

"No. Not about stupid things. But my music is different. Putting something out in the world like that, it's like—stripping naked and asking people to comment. It's a different kind of judgment. It's just…harder."

"Well, okay. I get that."

She smiles at me, but for an instant that hesitant, non-Camilla look flickers across her face again. "I know," she says.

The guys behind the bar have moved the tables off to the side of the room. The music becomes louder and thumpier. A couple of girls sweep in front of the stage and start waving their hands around. It takes me several seconds to figure out that this is some form of dancing.

James disappears to the bar. I can't really hear anyone over the music, but Noah seems to be talking to Mike about a photography course at college. Mike's face is blank.

Camilla scuttles out of the booth and pulls at my hand. I remain firmly in my seat.

"I like this song," she calls over the music. "And I feel like celebrating. I did not die today, Sam! And I didn't vomit on stage! This is a good thing!"

"Sam doesn't dance," Adrian says.

At the same time, I say, "I don't dance."

Camilla rolls her eyes and lets go of my hand. "Whatever, Sammy. Adrian?"

Adrian climbs over Mike and is halfway to the dance floor before she has finished speaking. Camilla looks down at me. "You sure? Last chance...?"

I shuffle back into the booth. "Positive. You go."

She shrugs. She spins around and follows in Adrian's wake.

I sink back into the shadows and watch them through the crowd. Adrian dances like a hobbit who's just peed on an electrified fence. People seem to be giving him a wide clearance area as his hands and hair flail about in every direction in time to no discernible beat that I can make out.

Camilla dances the way Camilla does everything else. Her arms and legs and hips don't seem to be moving in any logical pattern, but she looks like she knows exactly what she's doing. She isn't watching other people, or noticing other people watching her. She isn't moving like anyone else. She's just dancing. Her green dress spins around her legs, and she laughs at Adrian but doesn't seem embarrassed to be dancing with him. She looks like she's actually having fun. She looks really...amazing.

At some point I glance at the clock on my phone.

Mike and Noah's conversation floats back into my consciousness.

James has, inexplicably, not returned.

I realize I have no idea what's been happening around me.

I realize I have been watching her dance for forty-seven minutes.

Uh-oh.

13

Awkward realizations
[that should have been fairly obvious]

I do not know what is happening to my life.

But I can't stop thinking about her.

I close my eyes, and her face floats in front of me.

I close my eyes, and I smell lilacs and vanilla.

I think about her writing a song because Henry made her sad, and my stomach wants to crawl out of my mouth.

I really want to touch her hair.

I do not know what is happening to my life.

So I do the only thing I can:

I unplug my computer.

I turn off my phone.

I dig out my DVDs of the entire five seasons of *Andromeda*.

I do not go to school for three days.

Also:

I kiss Allison Winfield.

I punch Adrian in the face.

There must be a logical sequence of events that led to the above. I'm still trying to figure out what it is.

14

The logical sequence of events that led to the above

I wake up Friday morning not really sure that I've slept at all. At some point I must have fallen asleep, because I'm unconscious when my alarm blares. But I don't remember sleeping. What I do remember is lying awake, staring at the shadows on my ceiling and thinking about Camilla. Actually, I spent most of the night lying awake and thinking about how many other nights I've spent thinking about Camilla, only clearly I have been too dumb-arsed—and terrified—to acknowledge what it meant. I want to punch myself in the face.

How could I have been so stupid?

More importantly, how did I not recognize this sooner?

I've also tried to rationally pinpoint the moments that may have led to this situation.

I met her…

This is the last rational moment I'm able to pinpoint.

Everything else that followed is just this confused, insane tangle, like a jumble of movie scenes that have somehow become mashed together with no particular order or logic, an out-of-focus montage of her smile and laugh and eyes and voice and—

What am I going to do?

At some point before dawn, I realize the answer is simple. I am going to do nothing. I am going to recognize this for what it is—a simple crush, like I've heard normal human beings occasionally get on other human beings. That's all. I've been spending too much time around her. If I reverse that situation, this *thing* will go away.

There's no other option. I have to get this under control.

Then my alarm screams, and I wake up thinking about seeing her at school today. My stomach leaps into my throat. I think I might be panicking. I think I also want to run out of the house in my pajamas, just so I can see her sooner.

This is, objectively, not getting anything under control. I roll over and bury my face under my pillow.

Camilla. I cannot possibly be feeling what I am feeling for Camilla. For one, it's her. For two, she is my friend— one of my best friends. For three, it's *her*. Camilla knows exactly what she is doing. She's had a *boyfriend* before. If

Camilla thought of me as anything other than her friend, she would have done something about it by now. There is no way, in this universe or any other, that Camilla would feel anything for me. The thought makes me feel like a creature of some kind is shredding its way through my intestines.

There is a logical solution. It is Friday today. If I skip school, that gives me three days to get my head back into a reasonable state. I can avoid Camilla for three days. Three days of not seeing her, or speaking to her, or saying her name. Like detox. Like putting myself into quarantine until this horrible alien virus is flushed out of my system.

Hell, Luke Skywalker had a crush on his sister. If he managed to get over that, I can manage this.

I send Mike a text that says, *Sick. Staying home.* And then I turn my phone off. I haul myself out of bed and turn off my laptop. I climb back into bed. And then I climb out again, and I bury my laptop underneath the old clothes on the top shelf of my closet. I close my closet door. I prop a chair in front of the door.

I dig out Dad's stupid goddamned farm-girl vintage porn from its hiding place in my drawer and chuck it in the trash can. I am not taking any chances.

Since I'm hardly ever sick, Mum doesn't protest when I tell her I'm not going to school. All she does is touch my forehead for four seconds and tell me that I'm looking pale and that I should have soup for lunch. I don't argue.

I bury myself under the covers and prepare to wait it out.

I hear the click of the front door as Mum leaves for work. My house is silent. My street is silent. My heartbeat booms in my blanket cocoon.

I think about the argument Camilla and I had on the phone last week: whether the *Ewok Adventure* movies are works of unrecognized genius and whether they should be included in the official *Star Wars* universe or not. I think about her dwarf doing that stupid dance in front of my night elf. I think about the first time I took her to the Astor, when it was just the two of us, how her face lit up as her eyes roamed over the ancient stairs and old movie posters. I think about when she went away, about my stupid, dumb-arse brain refusing to accept that I was miserable with missing her. I think about her curled against me in the red booth, her long hair brushing my arm, her lilac perfume and vanilla shampoo—

This. Is. Not. Helping.

I also realize that—when a guy's goal is to block out thoughts of the voice and face and lips of a girl for whom said guy is aching—bed is probably the stupidest place to be.

I leap out and pace instead.

A distraction. I need a distraction.

I take the stairs two at a time and skid into the living room. I face my DVD collection. And I realize, with an approaching sense of horror, that my go-to favorite movies are now effectively useless. I can't watch *Halloween* because Camilla and I have watched it together three times, and I can't watch *Alien* because I gave it to her to watch it over the Easter long weekend and then spent two hours on the phone with her talking about the screenplay. I can't watch *Battlestar Galactica* because she is a fan and has an opinion on every episode and also because she bought me an Asian Adama. Then there is *Star Wars*—

I can no longer watch *Star Wars*.

I am not sure my life could get any more disastrous. I spin around in a circle, panic burning through my insides.

I bolt back upstairs and collapse on my knees in front of my TV shelves. Right at the bottom of my red bookshelf is a dusty DVD set of the *Andromeda* series that I've only watched once, and only because it was last year's birthday present from Adrian. I yank it out and blow off the dust. There are at least three days' worth of episodes here. And it has zero connection to Camilla Carter. It will have to do.

I grab a blanket from my bed and almost fall down the stairs with the DVDs in hand. I guess breaking my neck could be considered a viable fallback plan.

I make a giant pot of bitter black coffee that looks like an oil slick. I set the house phone to silent. And then I huddle under a blanket in my living room and prepare to sweat Camilla Carter out of my system.

Three days.

I *will* get over this.

Three days.

Piece of cake.

✳

I almost make it, too.

Actually, I am completely and totally lying. I make it to one o'clock in the afternoon and then I grab my mobile. I can't help it.

This is due to the fact that in between *Andromeda* episodes, I spent thirty-three minutes going over the calendar in my school diary to try to find the last time I went a day without speaking to her. I approach this as methodically as I can, marking each Camilla day with a blue "X" across the date. I realize that in six months, apart from a few torturous days while she was away, I have not gone one single goddamned day without talking to her.

I turn on my phone and wait for the network to connect. The phone beeps. I have four missed calls and a message from her. My stomach lurches when I see Camilla's name appear on my screen. Her message reads:

You ok? Answer your phone or I'm gonna think you have something fatal.

I also have two missed calls and a message from Mike:

Call me. Adrian told everyone u have gastro. Explosive diarrhea.

Of course he did. I turn off my phone and go back to bed. Time seems to stop.

But I can't get my brain to shut the hell up. It's chanting at me, like some demonic creature hell-bent on driving me insane. It is chanting:

Camilla. Camilla. Camilla.

Why did it have to be *her*?

Of all the people in the universe who my stupid goddamned hormones or whatever could have chosen to have a chemical reaction to—why Camilla?

I pull the blankets up to my eyeballs. Do I really need to answer that question?

I tug the blankets over my head and give up trying to eradicate her face from my brain.

I fall asleep with the sound of her voice echoing in my head, and a feeling in my chest like someone is scooping my heart out with a spoon.

✳

I wake up and immediately regret it. It is still light outside. I have not miraculously been beamed onto an alien spacecraft. My first thought is, as always, about her. I can actually hear goddamned bells ringing.

Oh. I think someone is ringing my doorbell. I drag myself downstairs and open the door.

Allison is standing there. "Hey. Are you okay?"

"Um, just a bit…off. What are you doing here?"

"You weren't answering your phone and everyone was worried. Camilla had to fly to Adelaide, but she made me check on you. By the way, Mike says to turn on your phone. He's stuck in detention. His lab partner exploded a test tube. They both got kept in for detention."

"Camilla…went to Adelaide?"

Allison steps into the foyer. "Yeah. You knew that? One of her dad's friends from London is there."

"Oh. Did…she say when she'll be back?"

Allison looks at me closely. "Sunday. Late. Why?"

I swallow. "Nothing. No reason. Nothing. What are you doing here?"

Allison frowns. "Do you have a fever?"

"Maybe," I murmur.

She shuffles into the hallway and touches my forehead with her fingertips. "You should probably be in bed then."

I drag myself into the living room and collapse onto the couch. Allison follows me cautiously.

"Yeah, probably. Maybe I'll just go back there."

"Okay, well then, I guess I'll go home. Even though you kinda do look like you're dying." She sits down next to me. "Maybe you should change out of your pajamas?"

"Why? Why must we put on clothes if we have no intention of facing the world? Why can't we just live in pajamas?"

Allison chuckles. "Why do we have to wear clothes at all in that case? Maybe loincloths or whatever would be enough?"

I grunt. "Some of us can't pull off the loincloth thing."

"You underestimate yourself, Sam," she says lightly.

I turn my head and realize that she is uncomfortably close. But before I can move anywhere she leans in a bit toward me, and I think it might just be to check my temperature again, but somehow I lose either a moment of time or space or possibly both, because the next second her lips are attached to mine and I am kissing her. Maybe she is kissing me. I'm not really sure how to tell.

It's weird. It's softer than I imagined it would be. I have to move my head so I don't bump into her nose, and then the only thing I can think is that someone else's nose is, like, right against mine, which was not what I was planning on dealing with when I got up this morning.

She moves around a bit, and I don't know if it's deliberate but now my hands are resting on her hips. Her tongue feels like it's looking for something inside my mouth, and I almost want to stop her and ask what it is, but then I think that might be a bit rude, so I don't do anything but continue kissing her while wondering if I should be doing something else with my hands other than keeping them stationary on her hipbones like I'm holding a handrail on the bus.

Part of me is finding the whole situation curious. My brain feels strangely detached from my lips, but my body is reacting as though it actually likes the situation it's got itself into. But then I open my eyes a little bit, and I see Allison's face in front of me. My lips are still moving, but my brain, and the rest of me, completely seizes up.

How did this happen?

Why am I kissing Allison?

I move backward, quickly, and she wobbles a bit before she opens her eyes. My breathing is all over the place; it takes at least eleven seconds to realign all the bits of me that the kissing had sent bouncing in different directions.

"Jeez, wow. Was that...okay?" Allison says.

I move backward again. She grimaces. Her face turns crimson.

"Um...I mean, yeah, it was cool, but weird, but I don't think...Allison, I'm not sure that was the best idea."

Allison pauses. Her eyes do that thing where they seem to go really far away. "It was...cool. But. Weird," she says quietly.

I don't know why she's speaking so slowly, or why her face suddenly looks like Mr. Nicholas's that time in class when Justin Zigoni superglued Victor Cho's English homework to his hair while he slept.

"Cool. But. Weird?" she repeats.

"Um, I mean. Maybe that wasn't the best choice of words—"

Allison leaps up from the couch. "You think! Oh my god, Sam, I can't believe you just—argh! This is *sooooo* embarrassing! You. Are. A. *Moron*!"

I think she expects me to argue with her. I do not believe my moronicity is in any way up for debate. I am slightly curious, however, as to what level my self-loathing will sink to today. Meanwhile, my legs are engaging in a heated argument with my brain about the various merits of standing up versus remaining seated, and I'm staring at the buttons on Allison's shirt in the vague hope that they grow mouths and tell me what to do.

I think I may have been silent for a few seconds too long. Because the next thing my brain registers is the furious slamming of my front door. My house is silent again.

My lips feel warm, and a tiny bit bruised or something.

I don't understand this kissing business.

✳

I spend Saturday curled in the fetal position on my bedroom floor with my face pressed against the blank page of a notebook. I have heard a theory that trauma is supposedly good fuel for artistic expression, but the only screenplay ideas that come to mind involve a clueless moronic loser being slowly devoured by various supernatural creatures.

I'm incapable of speaking to anyone till midday, at which time I call Mike and confess the entire Allison episode. Mike is silent for what seems like hours.

"So. How was it?" he says eventually. There is a definite tone in his voice.

"Bizarre," is the only response I can make.

Mike grunts. "I bet." He sounds disproportionately annoyed with me. I don't have the energy to question why. I hang up and assume my position on the floor.

I don't hear from Camilla until Sunday afternoon. I know I had big plans to avoid her, but the fact that she hasn't checked in with me is disconcerting. My stomach does that freakish leaping thing when I see her name on my phone. And then it does something else entirely.

Her message reads:

> *Hope you're feeling better. Just wanted to say I think it's really cool about you and Allie. I understand if it's a bit weird now, you and me hanging out so much, and it's cool that you need to spend more time with her. Hey—congrats! C*

I stare at her message.

I stare at it for approximately one whole minute.

The realization hits me in a place that is not my functioning cerebral cortex. It starts in my kneecaps and works its way up into my esophagus. It is a combination of tightening and compressing and squeezing. It is what I imagine the blonde chick in every horror movie feels when the masked psycho appears out of the shadows with the kitchen knife or hook or chainsaw or ice pick in hand.

Camilla knows.

Camilla knows I kissed Allison.

Camilla thinks that Allison and I are—

I call her. I don't know what else to do.

She doesn't answer the first time. She doesn't answer the second time I speed-dial her number. The third time the phone almost rings out before she picks up.

"Hey, Sam!" she says brightly. "How are you?"

I clear my throat. It feels like it has been fused shut. I don't understand the purpose of my palms starting to sweat when I hear Camilla's voice. What possible evolutionary purpose could clammy palms serve? I can probably google it. Possibly not at this second, though.

I clear my throat again. "Hi. I got your message—"

"Hey, yeah," she says breathlessly. "Really, I think it's cool, I mean, you know I think Allie's awesome, and—"

"But it's not...did she tell you...Camilla, how did—"

"Oh, Adrian texted me. Sam, hey, I think it's great! Did I say that?"

"Yeah, but—"

"Hey, listen," she says quickly. She almost sounds like she's running. "I have to go. I'm just about to step into a restaurant. Having lunch with my godfather. Did I mention that my godfather is here from London? Well, he is, and we're having lunch. Now. And then I'm on a plane home, so, hey, I guess I'll see you at school tomorrow?"

"Camilla—"

"Sam, I gotta go. Talk later! Bye!" She hangs up.

I stare at my phone for what feels like four hours.

Camilla knows. For some unknown, godforsaken reason, Allison told Adrian. And Adrian told Camilla.

Adrian Radley—the stupid, short, troll-faced, hairy, imbecilic, dumb-arse arsehat.

Radley is a dead man.

✳

I show up on his doorstep, not really remembering how my feet managed to transport me here. I think there may have been a bus involved. When Adrian opens the door, I am momentarily surprised to see him in front of me, even though I believe I have been leaning on his doorbell for several minutes beforehand.

He frowns. "Dude, your T-shirt's inside out."

"Yeah? So's yours!"

Adrian looks down at his hoodie. I am dimly aware that I sound unhinged, but my voice is coming from a great distance away and my brain is floating in a haze of red mist and wrath.

"Adrian, what the hell did you tell Camilla?"

"About what?"

My mouth is incapable of speech for six seconds. "About the scientific formula for rubber. What do you think? About me and Allison!"

"I told her what happened, but—"

"Adrian, *Jesus*! What goddamned business is it of yours? And how did you even find out?"

His eyes widen. "Because Al called me. She sounded really upset. She wasn't making a whole lotta sense, and you weren't answering your phone—I thought Camilla could talk to her—"

"You *thought*? Since when did that misfiring lump of gray matter in your giant fat head ever produce a coherent thought, Adrian?"

"Sam, what—why are you so pissed? So what if Camilla knows?"

I am not sure whose voice comes out of my mouth when I do, eventually, speak. Some distant part of my brain is telling me that I need to stop, now. Unfortunately that part of my brain doesn't seem to be controlling my mouth, or much of anything else.

"Radley, listen carefully. Do not come near me. Do not speak to me, or look at me, or breathe anywhere that I might be remotely downwind of. Get out of my face!"

"But...you're at my house," he says quietly.

"Yeah, well, consider this the last time!"

I turn around and barrel down his front path. I hear him calling out behind me. I have no idea what he is saying, but it seems to involve my name, and it sounds pleading and confused. I refuse to allow any part of me to feel bad, or sorry, or guilty, even though I think all three might be trying to worm their way into my consciousness.

All I can think is that Camilla knows I kissed Allison. Camilla is going to think I'm a moron and a loser. She's going to think I'm as stupid and shallow as those guys at school.

Camilla is going to think that I don't care about her.

Adrian grabs my sleeve. I spin around. I am unsure exactly what happens next. My hands are bunched into fists at my side; only suddenly they are not at my side anymore. I think I just meant to shrug off his arm. I'm pretty sure that this is the case. It's not my fault he comes up to my armpit. All I know is that there's red in front of my eyes when I turn around, and then the knuckles on my right hand feel like they have exploded.

"Jesus Christ, that hurt!" I clutch my fist to my chest.

Adrian stares at me through one wide, bewildered eye. His hands are clasped over the other half of his face. The eye that is looking at me fills with tears.

"You hit me," he says. His voice is so quiet I almost don't hear him.

"Adrian, wait—"

"No, really," he says, tears spilling down his cheeks. "I'm sorry my face got in the way of your fist!" He takes a couple of shaky steps backward. "I can't believe you hit me, Sam!"

He turns and runs into his house, leaving me beside his mum's lavender bushes, clutching my hand and feeling

225

like a massive tool draped in a colossal blanket of suck.

Did I actually just hit Adrian? My possibly broken fist would seem to suggest yes.

The red fury vanishes. All I feel is numb.

My feet somehow carry me home. I consider doing something useful there. I consider trying to write. I consider calling Mike. After eight minutes I give up on the idea of doing anything, and I curl up on the floor again instead.

I don't know what is happening to my life.

And the only person I want to talk to is the one person who can't help me.

15

What is happening to my life?

As above.

16

The Undiscovered Country

Back in my other life—the Before-Camilla-Carter life—the feelings that used to accompany Monday mornings were dread, mixed with doom and salted with misery. I'd almost forgotten what BCC life felt like, until I wake up to my screaming alarm on Monday with my stomach knotted into a pretzel of despair. I feel as if I'm moving through sludge as I shower and dress and drag my arse out of the house.

The first person I see is Mike. He is hovering near the school gates, his arms crossed tightly. His expression remains blank when he sees me. But beneath the blankness, I detect a world of fury.

"Hey," I say quietly.

"That's all you have to say? Have you seen Radley's face?"

I flinch. "I don't know what happened. I didn't mean to do it. At least, I don't think I did."

"And Allison?"

"Yeah. Same deal," I mumble.

Mike scowls. "Dude, seriously, what the frak? You're acting insane."

"I'm acting insane?" I echo. That recently familiar red haze seems to descend over my eyeballs.

"Yeah. You are."

"*I'm* acting insane? This is what you're saying, Mike? You are saying that I, Sam, am acting strange? That *I* am being weird?"

Mike's eyes narrow. "What's that supposed to mean?"

"It's supposed to mean that I may be experiencing an off moment, but you, Mike, have been acting like a complete goddamned psycho all year!"

I think I might be yelling. Several people stop and stare eagerly in our direction. I draw upon whatever tiny part of my brain is still capable of rational thought and I lower my voice. "It means I have been putting up with your crap and weirdness for months, and now that I am experiencing a tiny bit of a situation—"

"A situation? You punched Adrian in the face!"

I don't really have a response for that.

"And forget about kissing Allison," he growls. "You're allowed to kiss whoever the hell you like, cos apparently you're perfectly equipped to handle randomly kissing your friends—"

"Save it, *Michael*," I hiss. "You are the last person I need that kind of advice from."

Mike takes a step backward. "What is *that* supposed to mean?"

"Dude—figure it out!"

I storm past him. My hands are shaking. My knees are shaking. I have never, not once in the nine years we have been friends, yelled at Mike. And Mike has sure as hell never raised his voice at me.

Granted, I have never punched or kissed any of our mutual friends either. I am not sure whether it's the yelling or the punching or the kissing that's most disturbing.

I walk through the corridors in a fog. People wave and say hi. I think I respond with some sort of head gesture. I retrieve books from my locker and aim myself at my English classroom. And then, as if someone has turned a giant fan on the pollution-filled cavity that is my brain, the fog clears.

Because I see Camilla. She's wearing her favorite yellow dress and the cowboy boots that she bought from a market we went to a few months ago. She is engaged in an intense conversation with Victor Cho. She must see me from the corner of her eye, because she turns around. My heart starts to hammer in my eardrums when I see her face. I wonder if anyone else in the corridor can hear it?

"Hey, Sam," she says cheerfully. Victor scuttles into the classroom. Camilla clutches her books to her chest and looks up at me with a smile. But it's not her normal smile, the cheeky, warm one that, regardless of my mood, always makes me smile back. It's the polite smile she reserves for random hangers-on, for waiters and ticket inspectors on the train. Jesus. I even know how many different smiles she has. Her smile makes my stomach sink into my toes.

"How...are you?" I manage to say.

"Ugh, well, the chess club is trying to organize their end-of-year party, only they want to have it in the rec room, which isn't really a party—more like an average chess club meeting with party hats. So I'm trying to sort something. Oh, and I have extra volleyball training this afternoon, cos apparently we really, really suck." She glances at her watch. "*And* I promised Victor I'd help him with this assignment. I don't think poetry is his thing."

She slips into the classroom before I can respond. I duck behind her quickly.

Allison is sitting three rows back from our usual spot. She completely blanks me. She waves at Camilla. Camilla waves back at her. It seems a little overly enthusiastic to me.

"I'm going to give Victor a hand. I'll see you later!"

Camilla scuttles into the seat next to Victor Cho. He looks momentarily more startled than usual. Justin Zigoni peers at them, and at Allison, and at me. His face works itself into that expression he gets whenever he has to multiply more than single-digit numbers in his head.

Camilla doesn't look at me.

Allison doesn't look at me.

Mike skulks into the classroom and takes the seat next to the door.

Mike doesn't look at me.

I might actually be one small step away from sinking into a black pit of despair so bottomless that not even a colossal mining earthmover will be able to dig me out.

I have no idea what happens in that class. All I know is I can't bring myself to face anyone today. I make a bee-line for Alessandro's office as soon as the bell rings.

No one comes looking for me.

I make it to biology without seeing anyone of significance. Veronica sits at my station and tries to talk to me about the sound system they're organizing for the Spring Dance and the after party at Annie Curtis's house. I nod my head every time her mouth stops moving. I don't say anything, but I'm fairly certain Veronica doesn't notice, or care. I am as interested in the sound system they are organizing for the Spring Dance as I am in twelfth-century Latvian cave painting, or learning how to crochet.

When the bell rings for lunch I bolt out of the lab before I realize I have no idea where I should be going. I wander vaguely in the direction of the dining hall, my eyes drifting around the corridors. I can't even kid myself that I'm not looking for her. Fate clearly hates my guts, though, because it is not Camilla that I see, but Adrian.

Or at least, I see three-quarters of his normal face, and one eye that is swollen and blue and looks like it belongs to a native from *Avatar*. When Adrian sees me, he turns around and takes off in the opposite direction.

I hide in the bathroom for the rest of the lunch break.

Monday afternoon, I am alone in Alessandro's office. No one else shows up or texts to say they're not showing up. I stare at Alessandro's screensaver for two hours—a rotating schematic of the Millennium Falcon—and then I walk home and go to bed. I manage a couple of hours of broken sleep that is filled with dreams of punching a hobbit and being choked to death by strings of blue flowers.

Tuesday is no better. I pick up my phone approximately thirteen times before I leave the house, alternating between Mike's, Adrian's, Allison's, and Camilla's numbers. I end up calling no one; when it comes down to it, I have nothing to say to any of them. I stare at Camilla's number with my finger hovering over the dial button, before deciding that the most appropriate thing to do is avoid everyone from now until I graduate. I manage this successfully until lunch, when I emerge from the bathrooms to see Adrian and Allison having an angry, whispered conversation in the corridor. They don't notice me. Camilla and Mike are nowhere in sight.

I hide in the toilets for the rest of the lunch break.

By Wednesday, my misery has morphed into some sort of manifest, physical entity; my legs feel shattered and my

233

hands seem to have developed a will of their own, because they flop about my body without any apparent purpose or intent. Alessandro takes one look at my face in the morning and puts a special request in with the office to obtain my services for half the day. He sits me in front of his computer and sticks on the remake of *The Amityville Horror*. He doesn't ask me anything, but he does clasp me on the shoulder and tell me that he's sure Adrian deserved it. I grunt, which Alessandro seems to interpret as agreement.

I am late to history in the afternoon. Allison and Adrian are sitting in opposite corners of the room. Camilla is sitting next to Jackie Nguyen. Mike is sitting in the front row.

I slink into a seat near the door without making eye contact with anyone, and I all but run home as soon as the final bell rings. I turn off my phone and go to bed, pulling the blankets over my head and clutching Allison's Freddy Krueger doll in the hope that it develops a consciousness and stabs me to death in my sleep.

Thursday, I decide I simply cannot face school. When Mum comes into my room and I am still in bed, I don't even have the energy to make something up. I tug the blankets up to my chin and tell her I need a day off. She sits on the edge of my bed and stares at me for approximately thirteen seconds.

"So…I haven't seen Camilla at all this week," she says carefully.

I pull the blankets up to my nose. "Guess not," I whisper.

Mum plants a lingering kiss on my forehead and then leaves me alone.

As soon as the house is quiet, I change my mind. I can't spend the day here, alone, thinking about my messed-up life and my misfiring head.

I grab yesterday's jeans and T-shirt from the floor. I'm halfway down the street before I realize I have neither showered nor brushed my teeth, that I have left my phone at home and that I have no idea where I am going. I decide that—the current state of my life being what it is—showering and teeth-brushing are irrelevant, and wandering the streets aimlessly in a haze of my own filth is probably acceptable.

My feet somehow find their way to Jasper's doorstep. His bass guitarist, Ethan, opens the blue door, squinting at me as though he hasn't seen the sun in days. Ethan has a giant stain on the front of his Annabel Lees T-shirt, and a shadow of uneven stubble across his chin. "Sam? What the hell, man. It's not even ten yet."

"Hey, Ethan. Did I wake you?"

He yawns. "Yeah. Gig last night. Maybe it was this morning. What day is it?" He rubs his eyes and then peers at me closely. "You look like boiled arse. What's up?"

I stand frozen in the doorway, suddenly not at all sure what I'm doing here. I feel like I can't breathe, like the musty, coffee-and-cigarette-filled air from inside the house is tightening my vocal cords into a lump—

"There's this girl—" I manage to choke.

Ethan nods decisively. He hustles me into the Blue Delilah.

Ethan appears to have been sleeping on one of the velour couches, judging by the person-shaped depression in the cushions. Their drummer, Kel, is slumped against the bar. He's clutching a steaming mug in one hand and his head in the other. Ethan grabs a pool cue from the table and bangs it against the ceiling a couple of times, causing Kel to spray a volley of swear words in his direction. A moment later Jasper all but falls down the stairs, looking pissed off and half asleep.

"Someone better be on fire," he growls.

"We have a girl situation," Ethan says. He points at me. Kel stands with a groan.

Jasper sighs. "Sam. Dude. Bad?"

I swallow a couple of times before I trust myself to speak. "Yeah. I think so."

There are murmurs from all three guys that sound vaguely sympathetic.

Apparently, there are protocols for this situation. Kel sticks on some music that's so full of despair I wouldn't be surprised if the guy who wrote it dropped dead after the last chord was played. I consider adopting my fetal position on the floor. I decide that I do not need to be adding a fetid-carpet skin disease to my list of problems, and I curl into a ball in an orange armchair instead.

Ethan asks me if I want to talk about it. I shake my head. I don't even know where I would start. The guys therefore seem to feel it necessary to chronicle the most traumatic episodes of their various love lives. Jasper strums random chords on a guitar while he tells me about his first girlfriend who ran off with a Belgian keyboard player while they were on tour in Europe. He stops partway through his story to jot down some lyrics.

Ethan gives me a rundown of his boyfriend history; his very own top five all-time greatest stories of misery and heartache. I am not sure what I am supposed to take from these stories, other than to never continue dating anyone who steals your guitar on the first date. I believe I could have drawn this conclusion all on my own.

Jasper gives me a beer. It tastes like warm bottled foot odor. I choke down a couple of sips because it's the polite thing to do. Eventually their conversation drifts into non-relationship-related territory, and I sit in silence and let the music and voices and cigarette fog float around me.

When I can no longer handle the songs of agony and longing, I drag myself to my feet.

Jasper clasps me on the shoulder as he walks me to the door. "Remember, pain passes," he says solemnly. "But it will continue to be a giant pile of steaming gorilla shit until then. Ride it out. Use the pain. Just don't do anything rash like showing up on her lawn at three in the morning with a guitar, cos birds get freaked out by that stuff. Right, Kel?"

Kel grunts and says nothing.

I thank them for the beer as I shuffle out the door.

The sun is high in a perfect, clear sky. I may feel like a giant pile of steaming gorilla shit, but I am also suddenly starving. I think about heading home. I decide I am in no way ready to face my real life yet. So I jump on a tram and head into the city.

Mexican Lando greets me like an old friend. He pulls up a stool at the bar for me and gestures for a waitress to take my order. The music is that upbeat Latin stuff that has people shouting at random moments. I'm not sure this music is any better for my mood than the depressive stuff at Jasper's. Lando leans over the bar with a grimy dishcloth in hand and asks me if everything is all right. I think I may have seen something like this in a movie before, but I can't seem to remember which one it was. I wait for my tacos and Coke, and then give him the bullet-point version of the mess that is my life. When I finish, Lando nods sagely. He tells me that there are plenty more butterflies in the aviary, whatever that means, and he tells me something about women being like elephants, which is an analogy I'm not sure even he understands. I must be looking either pretty blank or really pathetic, because he gives me a free taco and tries to make me do a tequila shot. I decline politely.

As always, Mexican food makes me feel a bit better, but I face the afternoon on the crowded city street no closer to having a clue about anything.

I consider hiding out at Minotaur.

I consider drowning myself in crap coffee at Schwartzman's.

I consider sitting in the darkness of a cinema and losing myself in a movie.

I have no idea what time it is, but I'm guessing school will be over soon. I think about my friends, in the classes I know they'll be in. I wonder if anyone has noticed I'm not there. I wonder how much they all despise me now.

I jump on another tram. I don't even know how I know it's the right one, but I seem to have stored this knowledge away without my conscious brain realizing it. I'm doing that a lot lately. I even know the stop that I need to jump off at.

I sit on the floor in the foyer of the apartment building for an indeterminate amount of time. My eyes are closed until I hear my name.

"Sam?"

I haul myself to my feet. "Hi, Dad."

Dad clears his throat. "Your mum told me you were staying home today."

"Yeah. Wait—you speak to her?"

Dad frowns. "Of course."

We shuffle uncomfortably for several seconds until Dad waves his keys at the elevator. "Coming up?"

"Um, sure."

Dad's apartment is more cluttered than I remember. It's actually more chaotic than I ever remember his stuff being. I see a bike propped up against the narrow hallway wall. I have a sudden flash of him in bike shorts, and then immediately wish I could rinse my brain out.

Dad dumps his keys on the laundry-covered dining table. "Coffee?"

I sit on the edge of his La-Z-Boy. "Can I have tea?"

"Since when do you drink tea?"

"Since...a while."

Dad grunts and disappears into the kitchenette. His tea is too milky and weak and it's in a mug that has a picture of a monitor lizard on the side, but I drink it without comment. Dad sits tentatively on his threadbare couch. "So. Is everything all right?"

I shrug. I don't really have anything I want to share.

Dad clicks on the TV. We stare blankly at the screen, but every now and again, from the corner of my eye, I can see him glancing at me. Eventually he clears his throat again.

"You know, Sam...I'm not exactly good at this either. I think I can probably say...I'm bloody hopeless at this stuff."

"Stuff?" I mumble.

Dad is silent as he ponders the TV. "You know, at college…when I met your mum…I couldn't eat properly for weeks. I lost eight kilos. She thought I had some sort of disorder."

I feel the heat creeping up my face. I don't know if he is expecting a response. I don't know what he thinks he knows, or what Mum has told him, or what he has guessed. I don't know what I am doing here, or what answers I am hoping to find.

"I'm tired of not knowing things," I mumble.

Dad chuckles. "Yeah? Get used to it."

I look at his face. His blue-gray eyes—the exact same eyes as mine—peer back at me thoughtfully. "Really, Dad? That's your great advice?"

He shrugs. "No one knows anything. Anyone who tells you they do…is full of bollocks."

I choke on a mouthful of tea. Dad turns back to the TV with a grin.

We watch the last fourteen minutes of *Deadliest Catch*, then I stand with a sudden burst of resolve.

I may know virtually nothing. But I think I know where I need to go.

＊

I remember the first time I met Allison. It was lunchtime on my third day of year seven and by then I'd realized that BLS was not the awesome adventureland I'd been promised. Justin and a bunch of knobs-in-training had decided that Adrian and his prized Digimon card collection were the most ridicule-worthy things in the universe. Apparently, early-onset puberty was enough to elevate Zigoni to leader of the A-group. I still don't really understand how we ended up on the other side. But eleven minutes of torment later, Adrian was almost in tears and Justin was circling us like a vulture over carrion. When the bell went, Justin shoved past us, and standing behind him—there she was. This fragile-looking blonde person who was so small that for a moment I thought someone had brought their little sister to school for show-and-tell.

Allison frowned at Justin's retreating back. And then she marched right up to Adrian and mumbled, "Have you seen the *Digimon* TV series? My brother just bought season two on DVD. I think it's awesome."

She gave us a half grimace, half grin, and Adrian forgot all about crying. I was grateful there was another person on the planet who, if not on the same wavelength as Adrian, was at least on a tunable frequency. From that lunchtime on, she was part of our group.

When I show up at her house, Allison opens the door and immediately tries to close it in my face. Without thinking, I stick my foot in her doorway. I discover this move only works in films. My foot hurts like hell. "Allison, wait. Can I talk to you?"

"Why? Do you want to kiss me again and then tell me

how weird I am at it?" Her cheeks turn pink, but she crosses her arms and glares at me. Her red pixie hair is slicked to the side with some shiny hair stuff. She's wearing one of her oversized anime T-shirts and black tights. It strikes me that she wouldn't look out of place at Jasper's, maybe with a bass guitar in her hand.

I take a deep breath. "Allison, please? Can we just talk?"

Allison glowers at me. And then she stomps into her house, but she leaves the door open. I bolt behind her before she has a chance to change her mind. She throws herself onto a white couch in her living room and glares at me again. I hover in front of her, feeling like I'm on stage without a script or a clue.

"Allison...I shouldn't have said those things to you. It wasn't what I meant at all. I was just really freaked. By lots of things. By pretty much everything. I'm not even sure how it happened—not that it was your fault or anything. You're...the last person in the world I'd want to hurt."

I swallow a couple of times. When I finally manage to look at her face, the angry mask has slipped a little bit.

She shakes her head. "Sam, you know I hadn't actually kissed anyone before. Ever."

"Um. Me neither."

"I wasn't just planning on kissing someone random. But I did sort of want to. Just for practice. And, well..." She sighs. "You weren't random. You're, you know—

243

you're *Sam*. If I think about it, I guess it was pretty... weird."

She looks up at me. I test out a fraction of a half smile. It doesn't get me thrown out of her house. She sighs again and gestures to the seat next to her, and I all but collapse into it.

"Allison, I'm really, unbelievably sorry. All I meant was it was weird that it was you. Not that the kissing bit was weird. Or, Jesus, that you are weird. And, you know, it wasn't bad or anything like that. It was cool. I think I might have said that. Allison, can I please stop talking now?"

She looks sideways at me. And then she giggles. "Okay, Sam. Relax. If you're worried I've been hiding some secret thing for you all these years, please don't. It wasn't like that. I mean—" She gives me a sheepish smile. "I'd be lying if I said I've *never* thought about it. You're... cute, and you're not gay, and you're not, well, Adrian. I've never felt...invisible around you. But I'm not sure you're really my type. Although I'm not sure I *know* my type. I guess...I don't really know what I'm doing either."

I grin. "Yeah. I'm hearing that a lot lately."

She sinks back into the couch cushions and looks at me curiously. I don't know why, but her face seems different from how I remember it. Less soft around the edges. Like someone has adjusted the focus.

"Hey, Allison?"

"Yes?"

"Will you still go to the dance with me?"

She shrugs. "Well, at this point it's you or Alessandro. So sure."

"Cool. I think it'll be fun."

She raises an eyebrow.

"Okay, so I think it will probably be the equivalent of a colonoscopy with a rusty garden implement, but hey—I hear there will be cake."

"Cake is important. I think the committee might be having some dramas, though. I detected panic after Camilla missed their meeting today."

"She did?"

"I thought you would've spoken to her? She was home sick today as well."

"Camilla is sick?"

"Yeah. She has the flu. She sounded pretty bad on the phone. Not that I spoke to her for long. She's been…busy this week." She grimaces.

I stand up. "Allison—are we all right?"

She gives me her familiar lopsided smile. "Yeah, Sam. I think we'll be fine." She glances at her watch. "I should go, though. Nate and I are going to see *Ju-on* at the West-garth. Have you seen it?"

"I've seen the remake. I didn't love it."

"I can't believe you're the movie guy and you haven't seen the Japanese version."

I shake my head. "I don't think there is enough time in the universe to catalogue the stuff I haven't seen, Allison."

Allison seems to consider this. "Do you...want to come?"

"Well, I can't tonight. But—another time?"

She smiles. "Sure. That sounds good, Sam."

Allison walks me to the door. Her arm brushes mine a couple of times, but strangely, it doesn't feel all that weird or uncomfortable.

I step into the evening light and spin around to face her.

Allison leans against her doorframe. "Hey, Sam? You know, you're a really good kisser. I mean, like, *really* good. Like you've been practicing or something."

"I...am? Thanks. I guess?" My face starts to burn.

She nods. "Not that I have anything to compare it to, but it wasn't as gross as I expected. Not at all."

It takes me a few seconds to figure out that she is teasing. "Thank you, Allison. Your feedback is greatly appreciated."

She waves at me. "See you tomorrow."

I leave her house feeling a million years older and a billion times more tired than I have ever felt in my life. I feel the pull of my dark bedroom, my movies and my screenplays, and my bed. I can all but hear them calling me home.

But I turn around, and I walk the other way.

17

The Miyagi epiphany

I hear her shuffling on the other side of the door. I also hear a couple of rapid sneezes before the door is flung open.

She's draped in a thick wool blanket. She's wearing Snoopy pajamas and mismatched socks. Her hair is bunched behind her head in a messy bun-thing, and her cheeks are pink and flushed. But Camilla is beautiful. Even feverish and Snoopy-clad, with a big toe sticking out of a hole in one of her socks, she still looks *so* beautiful. My stomach seems to fold in half.

"Sam? What are you doing here?" she croaks.

"You look awful," I reply.

She sniffles. "Thanks. That's great. Did you come here just to tell me that? Or would you like to punch me in the face as well?"

"Not really. I came to see if you were okay."

She shuffles backward into her living room and flops

onto the leather couch. A wastebasket overflowing with tissues is on the floor in front of her. She's paused whatever she was watching; a guy standing up in a boat is frozen on her TV.

"Where's your dad?"

"Gone," she says from somewhere under the blanket. "Brisbane till Tuesday."

"You're here alone? Do you have medicine? Have you eaten?"

An arm flies out from under the blanket. She points to a bag of caramel popcorn on the floor. Then she sits up and wraps the blanket tightly around her. And she starts to cry. She buries her face in a handful of tissues, and my chest feels like it's being squashed in a woodwork vice.

"Jesus, don't cry." Suddenly I'm sitting on the couch beside her. "Camilla, hey…"

She shakes her head, her face obscured by tissues. "I'm sorry! I'm such a baby when I'm sick and…it's horrible being alone, and I'm so tired of it, and I'm almost out of tissues…and I don't even like caramel popcorn…and you're mad with me, and Mike's mad with you, and Adrian won't say anything about his face, and I don't know what's going on, and—"

She buries her face in her blanket. My arms, seemingly without any connection to my brain, find their way around her. "Camilla, it's okay. Please don't cry."

I have no idea what to do, so I rub her back a little

bit, like Mum used to do when I was five. Camilla's arms wiggle their way out and loop around my middle in a tangle of pajamas and blanket. She's warm and clammy, and I know I should probably be thinking about germs and getting her a hot water bottle and aspirin, but all I can think is that never in my almost seventeen years have I wanted someone so badly that their sneeziness and fever-ishness and tears aren't even a small deterrent. The sneezi-ness was sort of my last hope.

I rest my chin on her shoulder. The soft skin of her neck is suddenly inches from my lips. She's hugging me back tightly; I can feel her hands on my back, my T-shirt bunched in her fingers. And she smells like *Camilla*. I squeeze my eyes shut. The intestine-shredding thing does another lap through my insides.

"I'm sorry, Sam," she mumbles. "I know I'm being an idiot. I just feel like crap. And I hate not knowing what I've done to make you mad."

"Camilla, I'm not mad," I manage to say. "Why would you think that?"

She shakes her head. "We haven't spoken all week. I thought I must have done something—"

"Camilla, I am not, and have never been, mad with you. I swear. I've just had stuff going on...in my head."

"With Allison?"

"Yes—*noooo*. Sort of. I mean—it's all been so messy."

She untangles herself from me a little bit and wipes her

face with a wad of tissues. "You know, Sam, Allie is really great. I don't think it's weird that you would hook up. I meant it when I said that you'd be good together."

I ignore the abject misery-punch that statement delivers to my stomach. She may not be at all concerned who my lips are attached to, but I still need her to know the truth.

"Camilla, it wasn't like that at all. It was just a temporary, insane lapse or something. I think I had a fever...I may have been delirious. I don't even know how it happened but it didn't mean anything. I don't want to mess up stuff between anyone. I mean, I don't want it to change anything. Things are great just as they are. Or at least, they were. You know what I mean. I just...don't want anything to change."

"Nothing?"

She's kind of leaning against me a little, her arms against my rib cage. If I move my hand just the tiniest bit from the place where it is resting on her shoulder, I could touch her tear-stained cheek. My throat closes up. "No," I say. "I don't want anything to change."

Camilla tugs her blanket tightly around her. She nods. And then she takes a giant breath. "Sam, you...you guys are the best friends I've ever had. I don't want anything to change that either. I'm so tired of everything changing around me all the time."

"Camilla, I'm going to fix everything. I promise. At least, I'm going to try."

She wipes her face again with rapidly disintegrating tissues. "You know, Sam…I've never been anywhere that's felt so…solid. I don't think I realized how much I wanted that till I moved here. Out of all the places I've lived, this is the one that's felt the most like home. I just wanted you to know that."

I have no idea what to say to her. I wonder if I'll ever be able to speak to her again without my hands and knees feeling lost and weak. I hand her a bunch of tissues instead.

"I'm really glad you moved here too." It seems like the only reasonable thing to say.

She smiles tiredly. "And sorry for being such a baby. I become a horrible whimpering five-year-old when I'm sick."

I grab her phone from the coffee table. "Noted."

"What are you doing?"

"You can't stay here. You're coming home with me. Mum'll freak if she knows you're alone when you're sick."

"I…are you sure?"

I stare at her. She grins through her tears. "I should get changed then."

"Bollocks. Keep your pajamas on. Mum's going to make you go straight to bed anyway. Just go grab whatever else you need."

I stand up and help her to her feet. She unwraps her blanket and drops it onto the couch, and she takes a step toward me. She leans forward. And then she sniffs at my T-shirt.

"You smell like cigarettes and...fajitas?"

"Yeah. I've had a weird day."

"Really? Wanna tell me about it?"

I laugh. I think it might sound slightly strangled. "Camilla—not even a little bit."

✳

I change out of my feral depression clothes. I shower and brush my teeth, put on clean track pants and an old T-shirt, and then I stare at my face in the bathroom mirror until Mum taps on the door and asks if I've drowned.

I knock on the door of the spare bedroom and stick my head inside.

Camilla is buried in a pile of pillows, her loose hair spilling over them in a shiny waterfall. Her face glows in the dim light from the bedside lamp. She waves me in.

"Hey. You were right about your mum. I think she might have been a *M*A*S*H* nurse in a previous life." Her voice is still croaky, but her cheeks are less clammy-looking now.

I close the door behind me. "Well, I think Mum pretty much wants to adopt you. Are you feeling better?"

She smiles. "Yeah. Less feverish. Embarrassed for being such a baby. Julie is the best."

"Cool. Um...I brought this for you." I slink over to the bed with my laptop in hand. "I rescued it from your

DVD player while you were grabbing your stuff. *The Karate Kid?*"

She takes the disc from me with a sheepish grin. "You know I have a sad fetish for 80s movies when I'm blue. When I was little, *The Karate Kid* was always my go-to flu movie."

"I might have seen it. I don't really remember it, though."

"Sammy—shameful!" She pats the bed beside her. "I think I'm past the contagious stage, anyway."

Considering my current Camilla situation, sharing the same bed as her is probably as smart as swimming with a live toaster. I should leave her alone to rest.

So, of course, I haul myself on top of the blankets. I stick on the DVD and balance the laptop between us. The opening credits roll.

Camilla snuggles into the pillows. "This movie is unquestionably brilliant," she whispers. "You just need to get past the bad soundtrack. And the sketchy 80s hair."

I sink beside her and stare at the laptop in silence. I'm not really aware of much that's happening on screen. For the first time in my life, I feel like losing myself in a movie is impossible. I feel a thousand light years away from the place I started out this morning. I feel warped, and tilted, and so completely tired of the chaos in my head.

"Hey, Camilla?"

"Mmm?"

"Do you think you'll stay here after you finish school?"

She tugs the blankets up to her chin. "Assuming Dad lasts that long? I don't know. I might go back to London. Or maybe I'll go someplace new. Argentina sounds nice."

Of course. It's inevitable that, sooner or later, she'll go away again. She's spent most of her life in cool places. BLS is just a pit stop. The thought makes me feel unbelievably sad.

"You'll apply for that music course somewhere, I guess?"

"Well, if I can figure out a way past the whole debilitating stage fright thing. There are some great courses in London. Maybe I'll go back to New York. Or Berlin would be cool."

"Berlin...," I echo.

"Maybe. I might move there and adopt that dachshund I've always wanted. I'll call him Ben. He'll wear a bandana around his neck and sleep in my guitar case."

"You've given that way too much thought."

She chuckles. "Probably." She is silent for a long time. "The Sydney Conservatorium has a really amazing music composition course," she says eventually.

"Sydney?"

She looks at me through sleepy eyes. "I think I might like Sydney," she says quietly. "I might like Amsterdam as well. I don't know yet... Why, Sam?"

I shrug. I don't trust myself to say anything.

She closes her eyes. On my laptop, the weedy guy is getting his arse kicked at the beach as he tries to impress the blonde cheerleader chick. This movie really does have the worst soundtrack ever. I keep my eyes resolutely on the screen. I think I can feel her heartbeat.

"Sam?" she says eventually.

"Yes?"

"Can I please read your screenplays?"

"Okay. Tomorrow. But I'm warning you—they really, seriously, suck."

"Sammy—I really, seriously, doubt that."

I don't look at her. I can't. But I hear the rhythm of her breathing become steady and slow.

I watch the rest of the movie while she sleeps. I watch the frankly implausible scene where the geriatric Japanese guy takes on the gang of karate bullies and kicks all their arses. I watch the weedy guy slowly evolve into a karate champion with nothing more than some house painting and a sunset training montage. I watch the final scene where he fights his way through a series of identical-looking bad guys to win the championship and the blonde girl, as the evil Cobra Kai instructor-guy scowls in the background. Guess the evil Cobra Kai instructor-guy has never seen a Hollywood movie; bad guys in black uniforms never, ever win.

The movie ends. The credits roll. I stare at the screen.

I am an idiot.

I am a complete and total arse-faced moron.

How did I not think of this sooner?

I click through the DVD scene selection and I watch the ending again. The eyes of the Cobra Kai instructor-guy seem to bore into me from the laptop.

I switch off the movie. I pull my computer closer and open up a chat window. I type a message:

"Hey. Need to talk. Meet me at the park tomorrow before school?"

I wait for thirty-four seconds. The message comes back more clipped than I was expecting. Though I don't know why I expected anything else.

"Okay. Sure. Tomorrow."

I close the chat window and shut my laptop, a plan worming its way into my brain. In the midst of all this mess, maybe there is one thing I can get to the bottom of. I think I know what I need to do.

And I think I know something else as well. I think maybe Camilla Carter was only ever supposed to be part of my life for a passing moment. Maybe that moment is passing now.

But I've been kidding myself that this thing I feel for her is just a crush. No matter what I'd heard or read or seen in a movie—no one ever said it was supposed to suck so badly.

There is a solution, though. I think I've known it all along.

I will let Camilla fade from my life. I will shelve this insanity and store away the memory of her in the hope that one day it'll be distant enough to be useful for a screenplay. Maybe one about a cyborg or something. Everything is useful. I think someone told me that once.

I will not lie here and watch her sleep. It is, objectively, not helpful.

I will not stay here and look at her lips. I will not think torturous things that make my chest deflate like someone is sucking the air out of my lungs.

I will not stare at her face. Not for too much longer anyway.

18

Why kicking people in the shins
is sometimes the best solution

I get to the park early, but Adrian is already waiting. He leaps off the swings when he sees me, and he crosses his arms and scowls. It's Radley's attempt at looking hard-arsed. The effect is sort of diminished by the orange Mario Bros T-shirt clinging to the belly protruding over the top of his cargo pants. He looks like a mango with a head of curly hair on top. As always, I'm torn between wanting to scowl back and sort of wanting to hug him, and also wanting to punch him in the face again. I drop my sports bag onto the ground.

"Hey," I say. I glance at his eye. It's less *Avatar* blue and more C3PO yellow now. Guilt does yet another lap through my insides.

"Hey," he says. His eyes are focused on the ground.

I clear my throat. "Adrian, look, man—I wanted to say I'm sorry. I didn't mean to hit you. I was having an... insane day. But I'm really, really sorry."

He glances up at me. "You were so angry. I've never seen you that pissed before."

"Yeah. I know. As I said, insane day."

"You going to tell me why? Cos I still don't know what I did—"

"Can I not? Can I just say that I'm dealing with it, and that it won't happen again, and that I give you one free shot at punching me in the face? I can put it in writing if you want. A punch-in-the-face IOU. I'll duck down and everything."

Adrian grins. "Seriously, Sam. You have a pretty mad-arse fist. I mean, I would've thought you'd punch like a girl, but dude—your right hook is insane!"

"Ah, thanks?"

He nods. "No probs."

I look at his eye again. "Did it hurt a lot?"

He shrugs. "Only for a bit. 'Sides, chicks seem to like it. You have no idea how many girls have asked me about my face this week. I had to tell them that I got jumped by three guys, but still. Annie Curtis sat next to me in legal. Dude, she touched my arm! It was awesome."

"Well, I guess then—glad I could be of help?"

"Yeah. Though you had me seriously worried. And now Mike seems pissed off with me as well. He told me that I'm a dumb-arse, only he wouldn't clarify. I have no idea which part of my dumb-arseness he's talking about."

"I don't know what that means. But that's what I wanted to talk to you about. Mike. This whole situation with him. I think I made a bad call earlier this year. Things haven't been right with him for ages, and I should've never let it go. I'm just hoping it's not too late to do something now."

Adrian brightens. "You wanna have, like, an intervention? I saw one of those on *Law & Order* once."

"Actually—sort of. Yeah. An intervention is probably not too far off."

I explain my plan to Adrian. A slow, excited Adrian-smile blooms across his hamster face. "Sam—that is the best idea you've had all year."

"Yeah? Because I'm going to need your help."

He nods decisively. "Just point me in the direction."

"So then...we're cool?"

Adrian punches me in the arm. "Yeah. Course. Always. As long as you promise you're not gonna try and kiss me or anything. Just in case you were planning on working your way through the group."

I close my eyes. "Radley, I can safely say that if I ever try to kiss you, you have my permission to remove my head with whatever sharp instrument is within your reach. Or blunt instrument. Or just kill me with your bare hands, because clearly I have been possessed by a demonic spirit that is the harbinger of the apocalypse."

Adrian grins. "Sure thing, Sam. Good to know. Even

if Al did say you were an excellent kisser. Gotta admit, I'm a little bit curious—"

"Adrian—do I need to punch you in the face again?"

"Nah. I'm all right, Sam."

He looks up at me with a cheesy smile. I try to keep the grin from spreading across my face. I'm not successful.

We stand in silence for approximately thirteen seconds. And when an appropriate interval of time has passed, we turn and walk to school together.

＊

I find Mike before class. He accepts that Adrian, Allison, and I are now okay with a grunt. Mike still looks pissed at all three of us. I have no idea why. I decide that I don't care. I babble aimlessly about my new Rob Zombie box set and ignore the annoyed-blank looks that Mike shoots me.

I grab my phone approximately eighteen times to call or text Camilla, because that's what I would normally do in this sort of situation. But every time I click on her number, I remember that things can't be the same between us anymore. I remember that I need to untangle myself from her, for my own sanity. I know she's probably still curled under the blanket on my couch in her faded Nick Cave T-shirt and track pants, my red notebooks piled on the coffee table in front of her, exactly as she was when I left her this morning. The inadvertent daydream of curling up alongside her with my arms around her made me walk down the wrong corridor and almost miss the first bell.

So I check in at lunchtime with a brief text, and then I turn my phone off. It seems like the healthiest thing to do. I pour all my mental energy into the Mike project instead.

I also track down Allison and explain my plan. She is silent for a long time. "Sam. Are you sure that's a good idea?"

"No. But it's the best one I have."

"Yeah, but—seriously? Okay, so I'm a girl and we believe in boring things like, I dunno, talking about stuff, but—"

"Allison, I know Mike. He isn't going to talk to me without a serious shove. So—I'm going to shove. He might not care about his own self-preservation, but I have to believe he cares about mine. This is the only way to get his attention. Trust me."

"Um, I trust you. Trust is not what I'm worried about."

"Jesus. Thanks for the vote of confidence."

She grimaces. "I never thought I'd say this, but Sam— I think you've seen too many movies."

I face the rest of the day with rapidly increasing anxiety, steadily perspiring palms, and an escalating sense of doom.

The final bell rings. My intestines and I have a moment

of panic. Then I decide—to hell with everything. I'll face my fate like a man. Or at least, the closest approximation of one that I am able to manufacture on short notice.

✳

I've lost count of the number of times I've watched Mike do these things. Somehow, Mike can pull off wearing white pajamas and screaming stuff that sounds like Japanese swear words while punching a plank of wood, and not look like a giant, raging tool. I do not think that I am so fortunate.

The main dojo of Yu Kan-do It Karate is warm and stuffy and smells like pickled armpit. I try not to look at myself in the mirror as the class fills. And I try really hard not to think about what is possibly lying in store.

Travis Azumi enters with a sharp bow. Everyone scatters into lines and stands at attention. Travis faces the class—all six-foot-something of him, with his perfect hair and his black uniform and his chin-arse. He considers me for two brief seconds. Our conversation from eleven minutes ago floats back into my consciousness:

"You want to trial a class?"

"Yeah."

"This is a fighting class. It's full contact."

"Yeah. I know."

"Haven't I seen you here before?"

"Um, no."

"Have you done any karate before?"

"No."

At this juncture there was a somewhat scornful pause. "You seriously think you can handle a fighting class?"

"Yeah. I want to trial a class. And I want it to be this one."

I glance at the doorway. Apart from a few white belt observers kneeling at the edge of the dojo, the doorway is empty.

The class begins. I take a moment to question the wisdom of this plan. I take another moment to question the wisdom of entrusting Adrian with a key segment of this plan. I decide that, all things considered, it is probably too late to change the plan now.

So I yell. I throw my hands around and hope that I don't dislocate a shoulder. I squat into something called a horse-riding stance and I thrust my elbows forward in time to Travis's shouting, wondering when exactly a horse-riding stance is going to be called for in combat, and if anyone ever has the presence of mind to drop into one and then elbow someone else in the chin. I try to follow Travis's barking, throwing my legs out in a vague guess at a roundhouse kick. I catch a glimpse of myself in a mirror. I appear to be moving like someone is tasering my testicles. I give up trying to figure out the logic behind the bowing, and simply bend at random intervals, hoping it's in the right direction. My lungs feel like they're imploding. Every part of my body feels like it's trying to run, screaming, from every other part of my body.

And then, apparently, the warm-up is over.

Travis bellows something and the class dashes to the perimeters of the room. Everyone kneels and faces the center of the dojo with their fists on their hips.

I collapse onto my knees in a corner. Either lack of oxygen has given me the eyesight of the Fly, or there are now four identical Travis Azumis standing in the middle of the room.

Travis runs his eyes over the class. He yells something that at least one person understands, cos a brown belt with a giant eye tattooed on the back of his head leaps to his feet and stands at attention in the center of the room. Then Travis glances around again, and he shouts something else. For a moment, I think it must be a complex Japanese command of some kind.

Then I realize that he is, in fact, shouting my name.

I stand on wobbly legs and hobble onto the mat. I face the brown belt, because I figure if it's a choice between him and Travis, the tattoo-head with the mouth guard that has the front teeth blackened out seems like the marginally more sensible choice.

"Sam!"

I focus my watery eyes in the direction of the frantic yell. Mike and Adrian are standing in the dojo doorway.

Adrian waves. "Hey, dude—sorry we're late. Took a while to convince him I wasn't joking."

Mike's face is bewildered. "Sam, what the hell?"

Several people turn and stare. A couple of guys wave at Mike. Travis Azumi's face becomes stone-like. "Guests sit at the back of the room," he says coolly. "And shoes aren't allowed on the mats."

Mike stares at Travis. Travis stares back. Then Mike kicks off his trainers, bows quickly and sprints into line at the side of the dojo. Adrian follows with a solemn series of bows to all four corners of the room.

Travis barks something, and the tattoo-headed brown belt jumps into a fighting stance. I raise my hands, trying to remember which part of my fist my thumb is supposed to be on. Then tattoo-head kicks me in the ribs and I end up across the other side of the room in the lap of an amused-looking black belt chick.

My lungs have apparently decided to go home without me. I curl into a ball on the floor and pray that tattoo-head doesn't kick me in the face after I pass out.

"One point," Travis says. He sounds almost bored.

Someone appears at my side. I don't need to open my eyes to know who it is.

"Get off the mats," Travis growls at him.

"What are you gonna do?" Mike snaps. "Give me push-ups?"

A wave of hushed murmurs rockets around the room.

Mike grabs my arm. "Sam, what the hell are you doing?" he hisses in my ear.

"I...am...sparring," I gasp. "I thought that...was... obvious."

Mike glowers. "Do you wanna die? You know what these guys do to smart-arsed newbies? They will *kill* you. What are you trying to prove?"

I drag myself to my knees. "You ready to tell me what's going on with you?" I manage to pant.

For all of six seconds, Mike looks confused. Then, I see realization dawn. His face becomes twisted. "Sam, it's got nothing to do with you—"

"Okay then." I shove his hands away and stagger to my feet.

Tattoo-head is standing with his legs braced apart, staring at the back wall of the dojo like whoever is holding his remote has pressed the pause button. I shelve the part of my consciousness that is screaming at me to run, and I haul my moronic arse in front of him again.

Travis barks. I raise my fists. I feel, rather than see, Mike scuttle to the side of the room. I hear Adrian cheer. I pray that now is the time my dormant superpowers choose to make an appearance. Then the brown belt does a spinning back kick that lands on my forehead, and the next thing I am aware of is the fluorescent lights on the ceiling. My brain feels like it is leaking out of my ears.

Mike and Adrian scramble to my side.

"Two points," Travis says. Above me, his hand is raised in tattoo-head's direction. Perhaps there is confusion over whom this point belongs to. I find myself hoping only that I don't wet myself as I die.

I don't know if my best friend has ever been subjected to a radioactive spider bite. But Mike shoves his hands under my armpits and drags me bodily out of the dojo. I make zero contribution to these events.

Mike dumps me in the corridor. I fold myself in half and try to remember how this breathing business works.

"Sit up," Mike hisses.

"Yeah…okay," I gasp. "Just give me a moment to retrieve my lungs from my intestines—"

"Jesus, you are a knob!" He shoves my shoulders back, grabbing my hands and placing them, not at all gently, onto my head. "You're squashing your lungs. Breathe. Slowly!"

I close my eyes and take a couple of giant gulps of air.

"And open your eyes—you're gonna get dizzy."

I force my eyes open. Sure enough, the entire corridor spins in a not-at-all-pretty kaleidoscope. Mike and Adrian grab at my arms as I sway sideways. I wait for my vision to clear, and then I glance at Mike.

Mike's face is twisted into an expression I've never seen on him. He looks sad, and scared, and defeated. "Sam, okay. You've proven your point."

"What point is that, Mike?" I wheeze.

"That I'm a coward and a loser—I get it! You think I don't know that?"

"I never said you were...a loser. I definitely never said...you were a coward. I just want to know what's wrong."

Adrian gives Mike his best look of school-counselor concern. "Dude, we're just freaked. Talk to us."

Mike's gaze ping-pongs between us. "So, Sam's gonna get pulverized cos, what, you guys don't think I can deal with my own crap? Sam, I can't believe you thought this would work."

"Right. Because you're capable of getting your arse kicked but I'm not?"

"Uh—yeah! Dude, do you even remember taking PE? Pretty sure twisting your ankle on a soccer ball that one time doesn't count."

Adrian laughs. Mike and I both glare at him. He wrestles his expression back into submission.

"Mike...are you going to talk?"

Mike glowers at the corridor wall.

"Fine. Then this is on you." I somehow make it to my feet, and I stagger back into the dojo, remembering just in time to bow before I collapse into line. Several people look at me with a combination of pity and disdain.

Mike and Adrian bolt into the room again. Mike drops onto the floor behind me. "Sam, seriously. Enough."

Travis Azumi barks another command. In the center

269

of the room, two sweating black belts bow curtly at each other and then dash back into line.

Travis looks at me, then Mike. His mouth does this almost imperceptible smirk-thing. He points at me and gestures to the center of the room. Apparently, I don't even warrant a Japanese shout now.

"Sam, don't do this—"

I ignore Mike. I stand and limp onto the mat. Perhaps the self-preservation sector of my brain has shut down in disgust—but I don't take my eyes off Travis Azumi. He raises an eyebrow at me. I narrow my eyes at him. I think he almost looks surprised. Then he yells something else, and a black belt the size of a smallish truck leaps up in front of me.

Oh well. At least this should be quick.

I do the bowing motions and then I raise my fists. I wait, not entirely sure what's supposed to come next. Then the black belt punches me in the stomach, and I resume what is becoming my signature position on the floor.

"One point," Travis says blankly.

Mike stands and pushes his way through the line. "Okay, enough. Just stop."

"You're going to tell me what's going on?" I gasp.

"Yeah. Fine. You win. Just...let's get out of here. Please?"

I glance up at the black belt. He glares down at me. Mike squares his shoulders and scowls at him. The black belt looks hurriedly away. Travis smirks. I stare at his chin-arse for seven seconds while I wait for the sensible part of my brain to kick in. Unfortunately, the sensible part of my brain appears to have gone home with my lungs.

I think about my top five all-time greatest movie heroes. I'm not sure any of them have ever been in a comparable situation. At least, not without a chainsaw or flamethrower. But I think I know what all of them would do right now.

I haul myself to my feet. "I can't go. I have to finish. Just this one."

"Sam, are you *crazy*?"

"Mike, I have to."

Mike stares at me. He forces his face into its customary blank mask. But for the first time in ages, I know exactly what's going on behind it. He shakes his head and then grabs my hands. "Your arms are flapping around like frakking baby birds." He shoves my elbows down by my sides and pulls my fists forward. "Use your elbows to cover your ribs. Keep your hands up. And Jesus, at least try and block one goddamned punch!"

"Block?"

Mike rolls his eyes and makes a sweeping downwards motion with his hands.

Oh, right. I knew I should have paid more attention to *The Karate Kid*.

I hobble back in front of the black belt, who I think looks momentarily impressed.

I think there should be some logic to all of this that I might figure out, eventually. I'm sure that if I studied and worked at it and examined it from every angle—if I devoted my spare time and brainpower to it—I could figure out the logic. There is always logic and order. There has to be.

I think about all the things that have spun out of my control lately.

I think about Camilla.

A sound comes from someplace that doesn't seem to be my lungs or vocal cords. I yell, and I wind my fist backward as I launch myself at the black belt with every bit of power and muscle and energy that I possess.

I wake up on my arse in the changing room with an icepack on my face and my two best friends peering down at me with a mixture of concern and fury.

All things considered, a not-entirely-surprising outcome to this day.

19

Awkward revelations
[that apparently were fairly obvious]

The floor of the changing room smells only slightly better than the dojo: less armpit, more fungal cream and a thousand cans of deodorant. I try to sit up. I fail miserably.

"How did I get here?"

Mike is squatting next to me. "Gavin helped me carry you."

"Gavin?"

"The black belt whose foot your face got in the way of."

"Ah, Gavin. Remind me to thank him later."

Adrian crouches on my other side. "Dude, you should've seen it. It was like watching Gandalf bring down the Balrog. One moment you were standing, and then, *bam!* On your arse. It was—"

Mike scowls. "Radley, give Sam and me a minute."

"But I—"

"Adrian, I need to talk to Sam. Alone."

Adrian glances between us. He looks hurt for all of four seconds before he shrugs and disappears from the room.

Mike sits on the cold floor beside me. "I'll buy him a burger later. He'll get over it." He sighs. "So. How trashed are you?"

I give my toes an experimental wiggle. Pain cascades from my extremities to my eyebrows. On the upside, I can still move my toes, so I don't think I've suffered any permanent neurological damage. Under the icepack, my jaw feels—well, pretty much like it's received a roundhouse kick from a giant black belt.

"I am awesome. Really, really great. I see now how much fun this is. Dunno how you've gone almost a whole year without it."

"Sam, you are a knob. This was your best plan? Seriously, dude—what plans did you reject?"

I laugh. Everything hurts.

Mike lifts the icepack and frowns at my face. "So which movie inspired this piece of brilliance?"

I attempt a scowl. "Not everything in my life is inspired by a movie, Michael."

Mike stares at me.

"*Karate Kid.*"

"Course." Mike clears his throat. He shakes his head.

He takes off his glasses and massages the bridge of his nose. "You've really been…worried?"

I manage to turn my head, but the rest of me refuses to budge. Mike is focusing somewhere on my feet. "Yeah. I have. We all have. Look, I know we haven't really talked about it. The whole, you know, you liking guys thing. But it's okay. If you and this Travis guy, or whatever…I mean, if you're thinking I'm gonna get all judgey—"

Mike's brow furrows. "Sam—English?"

"Well, just that, I know it's probably weird for you… being into someone…a guy or whatever…especially one that seems like a giant tool, but—"

Mike stands in one sudden motion. He looks like he's not entirely sure which way to move next. "You think I like…Travis Azumi? Like, *like* like him? You think Travis and I—"

Mike closes his eyes. He is silent for approximately eight seconds. When he eventually speaks, it is a barely audible growl forced out through clenched teeth.

"Sam. Listen carefully. I do not like Travis Azumi. Not *like* like. Not in *any other way* like. Travis Azumi is, quite probably, the biggest knob-head to ever walk the face of this planet. Or any planet. Travis Azumi. Is. An. Arsehole."

"You…are you sure?"

Mike snorts. "I am goddamned one hundred per cent positive of his arseholeness."

"Then, I don't understand. Why did you quit?"

Mike slumps against the lockers. I manage, somehow, to pull myself into a sitting position, despite the determined protest from my entire body. I hold the icepack in place and move my jaw carefully beneath it. Miraculously, my jaw is still attached to my face.

"Mike, come on. It's me. I've watched you play Peter Pan on stage, remember? Green tights and all. It can't get worse than that. Just tell me."

Mike laughs tiredly. "Self-Esteem through Drama. Man, that sucked arse."

"Don't change the subject. Talk."

Mike sinks to the floor beside me. He takes the icepack from my hands and he peers at my face again. "You're gonna bruise. Lucky he didn't knock out a tooth."

"I'll live. Stop deflecting."

Mike closes his eyes. "Sam, look—this is the only thing I've ever been good at. Face it. I suck at pretty much everything else. I get that you don't notice. You coast through school and you're gonna be a famous movie guy some day—but I have to bust my arse to get anything close to decent grades. I can't do anything else. I'm not good at anything else. I don't even know if I want to do law, not that I have much shot of getting in anyway. I have no idea what I want to do. I know it sounds dumb, but…karate is the one thing I've always been good at."

"So…?"

He grimaces. His face looks like someone is jabbing him with a bayonet.

"Mike?"

He shakes his head.

"What?"

Mike buries his face in his hands. "I failed my second dan test," he whispers.

It takes me a moment to sort through the karate-belt knowledge in my head. "Wait—you took your second dan test? When? And why didn't you tell us? We always come and watch you."

"Beginning of the year. And I would have told you. But then Azumi showed up."

"And?"

"And he hated me. From day one. I dunno why. Maybe cos around here, it's no secret that I like guys. Maybe cos the first time we met, I kicked him in the face. Who knows?"

I try to process this information with the seriousness it obviously deserves. I try to remind myself how important it is to my best friend. How this stuff has sent Mike on a downward spiral of gloom that has lasted almost an entire year. But then I think about how freaked I've been, all the explanations that have been running through my head, all the worst-case scenarios I've been contemplating—

And I lose it.

I laugh. My rib cage feels like it is being squashed in a giant nutcracker. My jaw hurts. My stomach hurts. The cuticles of my fingernails hurt.

I laugh. I believe tears may be streaming down my face, but my face is frozen under an icepack so I'm not sure. "You kicked him in the face?"

Mike grins sheepishly. "Yeah. There was blood. I think he was pissed. But Sam, he's my senior. He's in charge. I had a bad feeling from the second he showed up. I knew he had it in for me. And I was right."

With some effort, I rein in my laughter. "Okay, so he's a massive tower of suck. My guess is because you're the only black belt here who would've been a threat. You're awesome. You know that. But I don't understand why you couldn't just go someplace else? I know you've been here forever, but it's not like this is the only karate school in Melbourne."

Mike sighs. "Yeah. I know that. Thing is, Sam—what if he isn't just a massive homophobic tool? What if he's right? What if I deserved to fail? I trained as hard as I could. What if that's not enough? If I stuffed this up, the one thing that I've always aced—then how do I know I haven't just been fluking it all these years? How do I know—"

"Mike. Seriously? You can't. You don't. No one knows anything."

Mike is silent. "That's all you got?"

I grin. "Yeah. Pretty much."

Mike leans back against the lockers. He closes his eyes. And he starts to laugh. "Dude. That was the worst inspirational speech ever."

"Well, I'm saving the truly awesome stuff for my movies. But so...this doesn't have anything to do with a guy?"

Mike rolls his eyes. "Believe it or not, I am doing okay with that. Actually...sort of more than okay." His face takes on this goofy lopsided smirk-thing that I've never actually seen before.

"What does that mean?"

Mike shrugs. The goofy smirk-thing doesn't quite disappear, though.

"Mike, are you...is there someone...?"

"Maybe. It's new, but I think...yeah."

I try to keep the disbelief from my voice, but I'm pretty sure I am unsuccessful. "Who?"

Mike looks sideways at me again. "Noah?"

"Who's—hang on. The guitarist? From Camilla's gig?"

Mike grins. "Yeah. He's...cool. We've hung out a couple of times this week. He's nice. Really nice. Kind of like me, but not at all like me. It's weird. Good weird."

"But Mike—*how*?"

Mike shrugs. "I liked him. So I asked. Not all of us are as hopeless as you."

"What is *that* supposed to mean?"

Mike spins around to face me. He shakes his head tiredly. "Samuel. You're probably the smartest person I know. You know…I love you, in a completely non-gay way. But you are also a frakking retard."

"What did I do?"

"That's kind of the point." Mike crosses his arms. "Maybe no one else can see past the whole Tin Man thing, but I can. I've been keeping my mouth shut for months, but you are losing your mind and I'm on my way to developing a brain hemorrhage."

"I don't know what you're—"

"You. Camilla. The fact that your eyes pretty much turn into googly hearts every time you look at her."

I stare at Mike. He stares back at me. He raises an eyebrow and I know, in an instant, that there is no point arguing. "You…know?"

"Yeah. It's been painful to watch."

I sink onto my back again. It feels slightly dramatic, but also the most appropriate thing I can think to do. "Do you think she knows?" I whisper.

Mike snorts. "Doubtful. You aren't exactly Mr. Open Book. You forget, though—I know you. And I can't watch you make yourself this miserable anymore. What hurts you hurts me and all that. Believe me, it's the only thing that's stopped me from punching you in the face for being so hopeless. I've done everything I can. But dude, the kissing-Allison episode was, like, a last-straw moment. I'm out."

"Hang on—what do you mean, you've done everything you can?"

Mike groans. "Sam, come *on!* I left you alone with her *every* Friday. D'you know how hard it was to get Adrian out of your house? I avoided being anywhere when there was a chance you two could be alone. It's not my fault you're useless."

"Mike, why the hell didn't you just *say* something?"

Mike laughs. "Dude. I've known you for half my life. And when it comes to sticking your neck out of your comfort zone, you are as skittish as a frakking baby gazelle. I was sort of relying on you to figure it out on your own. You know, without your brain exploding first. Guess that was too much to hope for."

"So *that's* why you haven't been hanging out with me as much?"

"Well, yeah. I thought that was obvious. And it would've been, if you weren't such a moron. The Camilla thing, and, you know, all this stuff too. Trying to get a handle on school and…figure out my life and stuff. It's been a weird year."

I struggle to my feet, my legs jelly-like beneath me. Mike stands up and grabs my arm, steering me to a bench in the middle of the room. I sit, transferring the icepack from my bruised face to my battered ribs.

"So. You thought about actually talking to her?" he says.

"I can't! Mike, it's *Camilla*. Why would she give a rat's that I'm…I'm…"

"Crazy about her?" He shrugs. "Maybe cos you're her friend, and she's your friend? Maybe she might actually want to know that you have feelings for her? Maybe you should let her decide how she wants to deal with it?"

The idea of having that conversation with Camilla fills me with the kind of mortification reserved for naked-in-public dreams and parent sex-talks. Where would I even start? What would I say? How would she react? Camilla isn't harsh. I know exactly how she would deal with it—try to be nice and then run as far as she could. It would be awkward and horrible and I'd have to move to Bolivia just so I didn't have to look at her every day and know that I messed things up so badly.

"Mike, I can't. It's not like that. It's different."

"Different how?"

"Different cos…Camilla's supposed to move to New York or Paris or Berlin. She's supposed to just pass through."

"According to who?"

"According to all laws of the known universe. I've seen this movie, Mike. And I know how it ends. Camilla is supposed to ride out of town on the back of a motorcycle with that muscled cop dude with the giant gun and the mustache, and I'm supposed to be the comic-relief convenience store clerk who gets his face chainsawed off as he's cowering behind a dumpster."

"Jesus, Sam—"

"But Mike, it's okay. Really. I'm dealing with it. I just need to let this weirdness run its course."

"I…are you sure?"

I focus on my feet. "Yeah. I am. Camilla is my friend. And I can't do anything to wreck that, Mike. For as long as she's here…she can't not be my friend. I just need to deal with the other stuff and move on."

Beside me, Mike stands. He holds out his hand. I consider staying right here in the changing room for the foreseeable future. And then I grab his arm and let him pull me to my feet.

"Sam, whatever you've decided—stop torturing yourself. Cos I really don't want to have any more of these moments with you in the bathroom. It's kinda girly."

I laugh. I think it sounds worn and tired. "Okay. But same goes for you. You need to promise me something. Actually, two somethings."

"Which are?" he says carefully.

"One—that you'll let me help you with whatever school stuff you're freaking out over. There's no point having a nerd for a best friend if you don't take advantage. And two—that you'll come back here. You'll start training again, and you will kick Travis Azumi's arse. Otherwise I will be forced to do it myself, and dude, seriously, I'm not built for arse-kicking anyone. I actually enjoy all my ribs right where they are."

Mike takes a deep breath. He shakes his head, and he looks at me with his customary Mike-mask. But beneath the blankness, I know that he is grinning.

✳

In the movies, the hero's triumphant return is, as a rule, a cause for celebration. There are carnivals or fanfares of some kind. Mead is poured, or at the very least there is a keg. Typically a band will be playing, made up of various aliens, dwarves, or non-specific grateful townsfolk.

I am not sure if any of my movie heroes have had to suffer the indignity of being dumped onto their mother's floral couch while their friends bury them under kitchen towels of ice and bags of peas and one sad-looking frozen chicken breast.

Camilla is kneeling on the floor near my head. And she is scowling. "Really. This is what I'm reduced to? Swooning in a sickbed waiting for my menfolk to return from battle? I'm just glad your mother is out."

She frowns and touches my jaw. Her fingers are fever-warm but feather-light. Beneath them, my face aches.

"Sammy, tell me you at least conquered the monster?"

Maybe I am still concussed; maybe the self-preservation part of my brain is still pissed with me. But I reach up, for just a moment, and I wind a strand of her long hair around my fingers. She looks at me with those wide, kind eyes, and my chest feels exactly like someone has punched it again. I am not sure I'll ever understand how her eyes can do that.

I run her hair between my fingers for four seconds. And then I let go.

"I think so. Pretty sure it's been conquered."

She looks at me for the longest moment. And then she nods and moves away.

Allison sits gingerly on the edge of the couch and adjusts an icepack over my forehead. She grimaces. "Promise me that is the last time I'll ever have to use the phrase *Sam is going to fight* in a conversation."

"Yeah. I'm surprised saying that out loud once didn't cause a crack in the space-time continuum," Adrian says, dissolving into snorts at his own hilariousness.

Mike leans over the back of the couch and gives my ribs an experimental jab. I wince. "Can we all agree—if anyone has a concern that relates to me, please, for the love of all that is good—do not enter my karate school. Or any karate school. Anywhere. Ever."

"Sam?" Camilla says from her perch on the piano seat.

"Yeah, okay, fine. Consider that the last time I get kicked in the face for any of you."

My friends buzz around me, poking at my bruises and recounting my arse-kicking in painful and embellished detail. I close my eyes as the babble of four familiar voices drifts around me—the four people who I would choose first as allies in the event of a zombie or asteroid or alien apocalypse.

I have kissed one, obsessed over one, punched one in the face, and been punched, repeatedly, for another.

I am not sure if I will ever understand anything. My guess is probably not. But right here, for just this brief moment, I decide that really, I couldn't care less.

20

A sort of dance scene
with fifty billion Marilyn Monroes

I am not sure if having your face almost broken counts as a rite of passage. I suspect it's probably a rite of passage only for a certain sort of people, like pirates, or Klingons. All I know is once my bruises heal, everything returns to normal. And yet, nothing is really the same.

I throw myself headfirst into school. Or at least, I try to. It suddenly feels like every spare moment of my life is filled with commitments: serving as a rent-a-crowd in various dingy bars and band rooms for The Annabel Lees or for Noah and James, or tutoring Mike, or getting a crash course in Japanese horror movies from Allison. Some of the movies are cool, although I think their screenplays might lose something in translation. Juggling my parents also proves to be a pain in the arse, since their social lives have exploded as well. My father actually has a spoken-word recital. Turns out he's been writing for years. Mike and I trek out to hear him in a Brunswick café. Dad's stuff sort of makes me want to surgically remove my eardrums, it's so arse-numbingly awful. But he seems happy. I guess I am not the person to judge.

After some prodding, Camilla does show me her writing. I can read enough music to know that her songs aren't just simple piano tunes; her compositions are incredible and layered. Her lyrics are amazing. It's weird, because I've never been much good with poetry, but even her obscure stuff sort of makes sense to me.

Camilla is working hard to conquer her pathological stage fright, even letting herself be dragged up with a guitar at one of Noah and James's gigs. Despite her being pale and shaky, it turned out to be a great set. She's still too freaked to let Henry hear her music, but I have faith she'll conquer that too. She really is going to be brilliant some day.

Camilla is also busier than ever; the dance committee goes into overdrive, and the volleyball team unexpectedly makes it into the C-division semifinals. We still spend a bit of time on Warcraft. But apart from hanging out with everyone else, the two of us spend less and less time alone together. I know this is the sensible course of action. But every now and then I'm struck with this raw, dull ache— a sort of sadness, or nostalgia. Every now and then, if I allow my mental focus to slip, I catch myself looking at her face and forgetting how to breathe. I guess these things take time to fade completely. I think this is probably normal. I don't allow myself time to contemplate it.

Before I am ready for it, October arrives on my doorstep, bringing with it a blast of unseasonable hot weather, the beginnings of exam panic, a last-minute outbreak of Spring Dance dramas, and also, my seventeenth birthday.

My friends organize a surprise after-hours party for me at Schwartzman's. Given Adrian is involved, this turns out to be one of the worst surprises in history. Still, I pretend to be astonished when I walk through the doors to find the café decked out in red streamers and balloons, and a cake in the shape of a blood-dripping axe that Allison has made. The tables have even been moved to create a dance floor, something for which I have zero use but that everyone else seems to like.

I am, however, genuinely blown away by the turnout. Jasper and Ethan and a bunch of their housemates are there, and James and Noah, who, it turns out, know Jasper's guys from the pub circuit. Alessandro shows up in a brand-new Korn T-shirt, which is pretty much his equivalent of black-tie. Veronica and Annie and a few other guys from school make an appearance, looking somewhat intimidated by the shambolic musicians. Inexplicably, a couple of the old Schwartzman's regulars are also there, though possibly only because they have melded to the Formica booths.

Allison gives me a Michael Myers doll to match the Freddy Krueger one she gave me last year, and a new edition of the Robert McKee screenwriting book to replace my battered copy. Adrian gives me a Batman card filled with Kino vouchers. Mike and Noah give me a subscription to *Fangoria* magazine, which is one of the most awesome presents ever.

Since Noah became the official sixth member of our group, I've been trying to define the slightly weird feeling I get whenever I see him and Mike together. Noah is cool, and interesting in an understated, mumbly way. He also has his very own goofy grin-thing whenever he's around Mike. He can spend hours chatting to Camilla about music that no one else has heard of, but never seems to run out of things to talk to Mike about, even if the only band Mike really knows is Foals. I am not sure if I will ever get used to my best friend being someone's boyfriend. But when I open their joint present, I realize what the weird feeling is. I am kind of envious of them.

Camilla spends the night rushing around in a blood-red vintage dress that matches my balloons. She fills people's drinks, skips songs on her iPod playlist, and makes sure everyone knows everyone else. She introduces Noah to the guys from school as Mike's boyfriend with no elaboration, and if Veronica and the others are fazed, they don't show it.

Maybe it's the looming reality of our final year of high school, or maybe after five years, they've simply run out of material. Whatever the reason, lately it feels like even the A-group can't be bothered heaping crap on anyone. It renders Bowen Lakes Secondary oddly calm.

Camilla eventually grabs me for half a minute to give me her present. "Sam, so basically I scoured the earth for the perfect thing, but since I couldn't get hold of a functioning lightsaber, this was my next best option. Hope you like."

She hands me a flat black box. Inside is a copy of the official *Star Wars* illustrated screenplay. "Open it," she says excitedly.

So I do. On the first page is a messy black mark. It takes me a moment to figure out that it is a signature. It takes me another eight seconds to realize whose signature it is.

"It is...you got me...it's signed by *George Lucas?*"

"Uh-huh. Amazing what you can find on eBay."

"Camilla! It's awesome, really, I can't believe...but, Jesus, this must have cost you a fortune?"

"Nah. Besides, that look on your face was worth it. Hey, remind me to get your autograph on something. Might be worth more than George's someday."

I laugh. "Doubtful."

"Sam, I'm serious. You're a really great writer. Okay, so you might need to refine some of your ideas, but you know that. And knowing what you need to work on is going to make your great stuff amazing."

"Yeah, thanks, Yoda."

She nudges my shoulder. "Shut up. By the way, I'm still waiting to read the new one."

"I'm still stuck on that bit where my cyborg and pitch-fork killer cross paths. It's sounding—I dunno. A bit lame.

You'll see what I mean. I think you have an ear for dialogue. Your notes on my other scripts were great."

She shrugs. "It's probably a music thing. But sure. E-mail it to me? I'm away with Dad this weekend."

"Sure. I'll e-mail."

She smiles at me. I smile back. It feels a little strange on my face.

From the corner of my eye, I see Allison signaling to me. Ethan and Kel are scouring the diner for a cigarette lighter. I think I am supposed to cut my cake now. I wave back.

"I should go before someone tries to light the candles with a toaster. But hey, Camilla? Thanks again. For the awesome present. And the party. And...everything."

She gives me her customary salute before bolting away to break up an argument between Adrian and Alessandro.

✳

My post-birthday universe is filled with exam prep and the obligatory end-of-year chaos. Still, I feel somewhat unprepared when conversations start shifting to people's summer vacation plans.

Camilla is spending Christmas in Singapore with her mum. It'll be strange not having her around, but I think I have enough scheduled to keep me busy. Allison and I are going to attempt a week-long sit-in at the Moonlight Cinema in the Botanical Gardens. I've asked Ethan to give me bass guitar lessons, cos I think bass might be more my thing. Noah and James have a bunch of gigs booked, which I am duty-bound to be at.

And then there is my screenplay. I'm hoping this is the one that doesn't end up in the back of my closet. I think my cyborg character is cool. But I still have this nagging feeling that it's missing something. Maybe I'll figure out what it is over the summer.

Of course, all of these things suddenly become background noise. School and exams become irrelevant. Because November rolls around. And with it comes the Friday of the Spring Dance.

Our teachers collectively recognize the futility of attempting a full day of classes, so we are dismissed at midday. Allison disappears to the hairdresser with Veronica and Annie, and James collects Mike from the school gates in his rusty Datsun, since Mike is getting ready at Noah's. Adrian has his long-awaited appointment with the old man barber near the station, which he faces with all the enthusiasm of a tooth extraction.

I am, however, co-opted by the decorating committee to hang string lights in the corridors near the gym. Apparently, there isn't a single other person who can reach the roof.

"It's the curse of the tall and manly, Sam," Camilla says as she runs past my ladder with an armful of crepe paper. She's wearing a yellow summer dress, her hair pulled into a messy ponytail that swings frantically behind her.

"Manly?" I call out.

"Oh, right—maybe just the tall then," she calls back with a wink as she disappears inside the gym.

As soon as my manly tallness is no longer required, I am booted out of the school. Evidently, the decorations are wrapped in a level of secrecy rarely seen outside the national security service. I am not sure how much crepe paper and string lights will be able to transform the BLS gym. But I figure it's safer for my health if I don't question the decorating committee.

I go home and try to work on my screenplay. I try to study. I try to watch *Simple Men* for the sixth time. I try to talk to Mum as she runs out the door for a spa weekend with Aunt Jenny and their friends. I am unsuccessful at all of the above.

I am not sure when, or how, this insanity infested me as well. But I think I might be experiencing something that is possibly, maybe, semi-adjacent to excitement.

And then it is 6:24 P.M. and I am standing at the entrance to Bowen Lakes Secondary School in an authentic *Star Wars* Stormtrooper outfit. It is way too hot, and chafes in unexpected places. I feel like a bit of an arse.

But at the same time, I feel just a little bit awesome.

Allison is standing on my left, and Mike and Noah on my right. Adrian gives the limo driver instructions on where to pick us up for the eightieth time, and then slams the door and shuffles to Allison's other side.

Two Marilyn Monroes and a King Kong scurry into the school with excited waves in our direction. But somehow, silently, the five of us seem to recognize that this moment requires a brief, reflective pause. It's cheesy and completely movie-inspired. But it still feels totally right.

I glance down at Allison. She grins at me. The corsage I bought for her is a little big on her wrists, but I'm glad that I went with the advice of the florist-lady. The pink orchid looks like it was made for her costume.

She is wearing tight black pants that end just below her knees, and a matching black jersey. Her pixie hair is no longer red, but sculpted into chocolate-brown waves. Mum has made me watch the original *Sabrina*, like, three times now. Apart from her blue-green eyes, Allison can actually pull off Audrey Hepburn. I can't believe I haven't noticed this before.

Mike and Noah stand side-by-side in their matching suit-and-fedora-hat combos. Mike hikes his stuffed horse head under one arm, adjusts his glasses, and then takes Noah's hand. Neither of them can really pass for *Godfather* gangsters. But regardless, they look great together.

Adrian shuffles forward and turns around to face us. My laughter echoes through the insides of my helmet, again. I can't help it.

Adrian has finally shaved off his troll fuzz, and is as baby-faced as he was when he was twelve. Of course, I know this only in theory. Because Adrian is concealed within an honest-to-god Ewok costume.

Adrian has been tossing up costume ideas for months now. But when he threw open his front door—once I managed to stop laughing—his only explanation was:

"Meh. I thought about going as James Dean or someone. But dude, seriously—can you really see it?"

Ewok-Adrian takes a few backward steps toward the school. "Come on, guys. I don't want to spend the entire night hanging out here like losers!"

I yank off my Stormtrooper helmet and balance it under one arm. Allison threads her arm through my other one. And somehow, we collectively amble in Adrian's wake.

Music pounds inside the building and we walk through the familiar corridors, past our English classroom and our battered lockers and our glitter-encrusted notice boards.

The hallway to the gym is hidden beneath a thick red carpet. Movie posters on art-room easels stand behind ropes that line the corridor on either side. Pretty sure they're the same red ropes used for wrangling junior students into vaccinations, but whatever. The string lights I hung earlier flicker in a canopy over the dark ceiling. At the end of the red carpet, the gym doors are guarded by two giant cardboard Oscars, in front of which are a couple of smiling dance committee members with press passes and cameras in hand. The effect is as lame as anything. But at the same time—if I narrow my eyes and blur them a little bit—I can almost imagine we are somewhere other than here. I can almost, just about, see the glamour in the dreary school corridor.

Three Marilyn Monroes walk past. They coo over our costumes before draping themselves around the Oscars as their pictures are snapped.

"Jesus," Mike murmurs. "Was there only one actress in Old Hollywood?"

Allison grins. "I think it might have something to do with the undies-baring dress. You know there's going to be some 'accidental' flashing tonight."

Adrian giggles. "Can I just say—best costume party theme ever."

I don't have a chance to respond, because a shrieking blur grabs me by the arms and slams me into a wall. I drop my Stormtrooper helmet and blaster as I experience a brief but vivid flashback to the last five years of my life.

"Sammy! Dude, I swear I knew that was you! I did!"

Justin Zigoni's beer breath gusts across my face. He is dressed, I think, as a *Planet of the Apes* ape, although his costume is missing an ear and his wig is on backward.

"Um, that might be because I'm wearing my face?"

Justin dissolves into snorts. "Dude, you are so fecking smart! Seriously, you're gonna be, like, a doctor, or nuclear physics doctor or, like, accountant. You are!"

He trips over his own feet as he stumbles backward. His eyes blur over Mike and Noah. They land on Allison with a start. "Hey, hello Angela," he purrs. "Nice...pants. Hey, maybe you wanna dance later?"

Allison grimaces. "I'm not sure if my dance card has room for a drunken idiot, but I'll let you know."

"Hey, cool," Justin says with a wave.

There is a chorus of thunderous shouting from somewhere down the corridor. Justin pumps his hands in the air, and then bolts down the red carpet and body-slams a Charlie Chaplin into the floor.

"And there goes the plague of our existence," mutters Mike.

I adjust my costume and collect my stuff from the ground. "Is it just me or is there something strangely unsatisfying about knowing your arch nemesis is going to end the night vomiting on his own shoes before passing out in the bushes?"

Noah is still staring in Justin's wake. "Dude does seem a little...highly strung?"

"Yeah," I say. "There are stories. We'll fill you in sometime."

Mike shoots me a grin.

We stand in front of an Oscar while a beaming Michelle Argus snaps our pictures. An assortment of gangsters, a couple of vampires, a disheveled Wolfman, and a steady stream of Marilyns pass by. People wave and stop for photos, and there is an awful lot of excited shrieking even though everyone has seen everyone else only hours before. It is chaos. I am not sure if it is supposed to be anything else.

Allison slips her arm through mine again. I allow us to remain joined at the elbows for four seconds, before I slide my hand down and link my fingers through hers. It feels like the right thing to do. Allison squeezes my hand back. And then we step inside.

I don't know if I will ever make it to Hollywood. Maybe I will. Or maybe I am destined for a career writing scripts for crap TV soap operas. But when we walk through the gym doors, and my eyes land on the giant Hollywood sign on a painted backdrop of hills and palm trees and lights—for a split second, I forget where I am. For the briefest moment, I can see myself walking into the premiere of my own movie. It is, unquestionably, a very cool feeling.

"Holy crap," Adrian whispers.

"Wow. Did the decorating committee actually get any homework done this year?" Allison says.

Star-shaped beams circle the floor from a lighting rig on the roof. Round tables drip with red and silver cloth, candles and giant cardboard film reels and clapperboards. There is an old-fashioned snack bar set up at one end of the gym; I can see Sharni Vane in an unwieldy-looking Scarlett O'Hara costume handing out striped boxes of popcorn, like they serve at the Astor. The gym screens are broadcasting a black and white movie; it takes me all of three seconds to figure out that it is the 1940s version of *King of the Zombies*. It is a sucky movie. But it still looks cool up on the screens.

Noah whistles. "My school does streamers and jugs of punch. I usually give our formals a miss. This is…intense."

Adrian flips back his Ewok head. His curls have been neatly cropped. His face is smooth. He still looks like the same exact Adrian. I am, bizarrely, relieved.

"And they managed to get rid of the smell of BO," Adrian says. "How awesome is that!"

We walk along the edge of the dance floor. Music from the very un-Old Hollywood DJ pounds through my legs.

The center of the basketball court is covered by an array of PVC stars, stuck down in no particular pattern. I walk over to the closest star. Victor Cho's name has been stenciled on the top in bold gold letters.

"Everyone has one. We triple-checked." Annie Curtis pushes her way through the crowd. She is wrapped in a layer of plastic, her dark curls shoved underneath a short blonde wig. A knife handle in a bloody pool is glued to the plastic on her front.

"*Psycho!*" Adrian shouts.

She giggles. "Damn straight. I *so* wanted to be Janet Leigh the first time I saw that movie. Until she got serial-killed, I mean." She looks Adrian up and down with a wide smile. "You look so cute! Hey, thanks again for the ticket. I can't believe I forgot that committee members still had to buy one."

Adrian yanks his Ewok head back on and performs some sort of 1970s disco spin. Annie laughs. She grabs Adrian by the paw and drags him onto the dance floor.

It will never cease to amaze me how many people are capable of appreciating Adrian Radley. I think it's a mystery that is destined to remain unsolved.

Mike and Noah and their horse head disappear to find drinks. Allison tugs at my hand. I realize that my fingers are still knotted together with hers. "You wanna dance, Sam?" She grins.

I roll my eyes. "Maybe later, Allison. When the Cylons take over. But you go. I'll find you in a bit."

Allison twirls in her Audrey Hepburn heels and bounds away toward Veronica Singh's *Wizard of Oz* Dorothy.

I watch her go. My eyes drift aimlessly around the noisy room.

"Well? Does it gain your stamp of approval? You know the opinion of the original movie guy is the only one that really matters."

I turn around. In the dimly spinning starlight, I'm not entirely sure that I'm seeing what I think I'm seeing.

The voice is coming from what I assume, at first glance, is a giant worm, or a caterpillar carcass. It takes me five full seconds to figure out who—or rather, what—it is.

"Jesus. You came as goddamned Jabba the Hutt."

Camilla flicks back her Jabba head with a giggle. "Uh-huh. I tossed up a thousand different glamazon costumes, but then I found this on ThinkGeek and I couldn't resist." She spins around awkwardly, her Jabba tail swishing behind her. Her wavy hair is scooped up behind her neck. She looks a little flushed under the costume. I burst out laughing.

She grins. "And you, Sam, look great! How does it feel being an Imperial henchman?"

"Awesome. I am ready to crush all uprisings with my mindless conformity and surprisingly crap aim."

She laughs. "And so...?" She sweeps her arm around. "Whaddaya think?"

"I think your superpowers are clearly unlimited. This looks amazing. I'm not wishing even a little bit for the gym to be invaded by homicidal telepaths."

"And not a hint of glitter in sight. Don't say I never do anything for you, Sam."

"I would never say anything like that, Camilla. I know exactly how much you've done."

She looks at me curiously. I give her Jabba arm a nudge. "I just mean that...it's been a really interesting year. Mostly. Partly, well, just bizarre. But really great, too. And I know I have you to thank." I chuckle. I think I might be sounding a bit lame. I give her arm another nudge. "So—thank you, Camilla."

She smiles at me. "Sam, for what it's worth—you are welcome."

Alistair McIlroy dashes over, his crumpled *Blue Hawaii* Elvis shirt flapping beneath a pink ukulele. He gives me a sheepish wave and then whispers something frantic in Camilla's ear.

"Ugh. I gotta go, Sam. Apparently some members of the music committee missed the no-ABBA directive. I've already heard *Dancing Queen*, like, twelve times. If I don't speak to the DJ you might actually get your wish to see a dance-scene homicide."

"Okay. We'll catch up later."

She waves and shimmies away. I walk away from the dance floor, and I find my friends again.

The Spring Dance is an endless, shambolic night. Camilla is rushed off her feet with organizational dramas, but periodically appears to round us up for photos. I am fairly certain that Mike, Noah and I look like wax figures in most of them, but Allison, Adrian and Camilla never seem to run out of ridiculous poses and alternative ways of fitting six heads into a single shot. Other people also seem to feel the intense need to capture a billion photos of people doing fascinating things, like drinking and standing. I have no idea why I need to be frozen in so many people's memories. But when the screens change to a slide show of photos that were taken in front of the Oscars and it pauses, briefly, on a shot of me and my friends crammed tightly together, I am a little bit glad. I guess I can see the purpose in keeping some small fragments of time preserved.

I float around with Adrian as speeches are made and costume awards handed out. Then Mr. Nicholas drags Mrs. Chow and some other teachers onto the dance floor. I'm pretty sure that Mrs. Chow would rather be home doing Sudoku. Her varicose veins attempting to do the Time Warp is not something I need to see again in this lifetime.

Mike and Noah are co-opted by Veronica and Brie to help hand out the Hollywood-themed party bags. They accept the task stoically, but I make a hasty excuse and bolt.

Adrian is back on the dance floor, his Ewok head flapping behind him as he gyrates in a semispasmodic state with Annie. Annie appears to have lost her knife, but not her enthusiasm. Adrian catches my eye and gives me a wave; I half wave back as he spins on his hairy feet and swings Annie into a surprisingly coordinated backward dip.

I peer through the crowds as I walk along the edge of the dance floor. Justin Zigoni is attempting some kind of Latin dance move with Michelle Argus. He actually looks like he's trying to secure her in a headlock. Michelle does not look at all impressed. I can't help but laugh. Despite everything, Justin is—and I suspect will remain— a giant knob. But somehow, I don't think this is my problem anymore.

I find an empty table in a corner and sneak into a chair.

I watch the spinning lights and PVC stars that are slowly becoming grimy under a hundred pairs of feet. I think about the weirdness of the last year, and about the strangeness possibly to come. I'm pretty sure I'll be ready for it, whatever it is. At the very least, I hope I can expect more material for my screenplays.

Everything is useful. I really do believe that this is the truth.

A shadow falls across my table. "There you are. Why are you hiding? I've been looking for you for ages."

I slip off my helmet. "You have?"

"Sam, look, I know your philosophy on dancing. But it's the end of the year, and I'm not leaving until you dance with me at least once."

Camilla is standing in front of me, her hands on her Jabba hips. She gives me that look of hers, the wide-eyed innocent one that I swear is some form of Jedi mind trick. She holds out her hand.

I do not dance. I feel this has been made abundantly clear.

But all things considered—maybe I could make an exception, just this once. I don't know why, but stumbling through my first and final dance with Camilla Carter seems strangely fitting.

I reach up, and I take her hand. Her fingers close around mine. I glance at the crowded dance floor. I am not sure I can talk my legs into functioning.

"Camilla…"

The music is too loud. My voice gets lost.

She leans down over the table. "Listen, Sammy, you know what I'll have to do if you don't stand up, don't you?"

"What?"

"You. Here. Sitting in a corner all by your lonesome. You're going to make me be incredibly cheesy. You know what I'm going to have to say."

"Camilla…"

She leans a little closer. "Nobody. Puts. Baby…"

"Camilla, I'm sort of, a little bit…"

"Sam, are you *really* going to make me finish that line?"

"…a little bit completely in love with you."

Objectively, I know the world continues to spin. The music hasn't stopped. People haven't frozen in place. There is nothing to mark that everything has changed.

Except I glance at her face. Her face is white.

"What did you say?" she whispers.

I let go of her hand and I stand up. It seems like the right thing to do. But I can't look at her; I can't bring myself to process the horror I know I would find on her face. So I focus somewhere on the candlelight instead.

"I said that I am in love with you. I've tried not to be, I really have, but it's just useless. I know you don't feel the same way about me, but I had to tell you because…well,

306

you're all I think about. All the time. I miss you every second that you're not with me...and I know you won't want to be around me anymore, but, Camilla...you're one of the best friends I've ever had. You're smart and amazing and weird and probably the most beautiful person I've ever seen...and before I met you, all I wanted was just to fast-forward through everything. But, really, I think my life was just paused, or something. You...made me press play. You made everything move. And no matter where you go, or whatever you feel about me...I will love you forever for that. That's all I wanted to say. I'm going to go now."

I turn around and walk away.

She doesn't follow me.

She doesn't call out my name and chase after me in the rain. It isn't even raining. The sky doesn't even have the decency to provide me with a good movie cliché.

I walk home, change into my Superman T-shirt and track pants, and I crawl into bed. I decide that I'm fairly safe here until the aliens take over, or the earth is sucked into a wormhole, or I develop age dementia and Camilla Carter is finally erased from my memory—whichever comes first. I pull the blankets over my head and curl into a ball.

Time stops.

I feel like I might actually be dying. I allow my consciousness to float far away from my body.

I am not dying. Objectively, I know this. But this thing

that I'm feeling is physical, and tangible. From far away, I remember that I have heard about this feeling.

I feel like my heart is broken.

Time stops.

I wake up to a pounding in my head, which I realize after nine seconds is actually pounding at my front door. I stick a hand out of my blanket and grab my silent mobile from the nightstand.

It's almost midnight. I have twelve missed calls from Mike.

I do not want to speak to Mike. I don't want to speak to anyone, ever again, unless they can wind back time.

I pull the blankets over my head again. The pounding doesn't go away. If anything, it settles down into a steady rhythm, as persistent and annoying as a dripping tap.

I fly out of bed and storm down the stairs. Suddenly, I'm convinced I know exactly whose fault this is. Mike, with his stupid abs and his awesome boyfriend. Maybe punching Mike in the face will fix everything.

I throw open my front door.

Of course it isn't Mike.

She's changed out of her costume. She's wearing her yellow dress again. Her hair is loose. She looks perfect.

Actually, she looks angry. Really, really mad.

"Hi," I manage to say.

"Sam," she barks back.

"You're mad at me."

"Yes, I'm mad at you, you big tool!"

I nod. I can't bring my body to do anything, or my mouth to say anything. I feel empty, and exhausted, and I just need her to go away and take her face with her.

"I'm sorry," I mumble.

"You're not even going to ask why I'm pissed off?"

"Because some giant arseface thought you might want to know how he felt?"

Camilla steps into the light of the doorway. Her eyes are wild. "Argh—no! Because you say those things to me and then you *disappear*? You tell me you love me and then leave me standing in the middle of the school gym in a stupid goddamned Jabba the Hutt costume surrounded by spiked punch and teachers and fifty billion Marilyn Monroes?"

"I didn't know what else to do," I whisper.

"Huh, well, that's just the story of your life, isn't it?"

I close my eyes. I deserve this. I deserve to have my heart ripped open and mashed all over the fake Grecian columns for being an idiot, and a loser, and for not being smart enough to realize that she would never, ever, want me. "I'm sorry, I shouldn't have said those things—"

"Sam! Would you please, for one moment, pull your head out of your giant arse?"

With my eyes squeezed closed, I hear her take a deep breath. "Sam—I liked you from the first moment I met you! I made you invite me to your house for a study group, even though—you know what—I'm pretty good at study-ing on my own! When I went away, you were the only person I wanted to talk to! You were the first person I needed to see when I got back! I *sang* in front of you, and I've never let anyone see that part of me before! You are the person...I feel like I've run halfway around the world to find! I thought that was pretty obvious! Apart from throwing myself naked at you while holding a giant sign that says, *Samuel, I am completely in love with you too*, I don't know what else to do!"

My eyes seem to have welded themselves shut. I can't bring myself to face the world again and realize that I didn't just hear what I think she just said.

I open my eyes. Her hazel ones are staring back at me. They are wide and bright. Objectively, they are great eyes. But un-objectively—they might just be the best eyes in the universe.

"Camilla. You're talking with exclamations."

"Yeah, well, tough," she growls.

"But why *me*?"

"Because, idiot, you...are funny and smart and you have a giant heart that you can't even pretend to hide. And you love your friends and your mum, and you held my hand and made me sing when I was so scared I thought I was going to die. I knew you understood, right from the beginning, this thing inside, the stuff in your head that you need to make real. You *get* that." She takes a step toward me. And then she jabs me in the chest. Her voice wobbles. "And you wear stupid Superman pajamas without any irony, and your face lights up when you talk about the movies you love."

Two fat tears spill down her cheeks. I can feel them because somehow I have moved toward her, and my hands are touching her face, and she is not moving away.

"And...you protect my dwarf. You always have her back. And you have a dimple when you smile that's so cute I almost died the first time I saw it. And when I heard about you and Allie I spent two days lying on the floor listening to *Songbird* on repeat cos I couldn't bring myself to do anything else...and...and...when I first met you I thought you looked a bit like Luke Skywalker. From the first movie, before his face went all sketchy, and—"

I am aware that she is not speaking anymore.

I am not aware of anything else.

Because I am kissing her. And she is kissing me back.

I still don't understand kissing. It's just lips on lips. But somehow I feel it in my stomach and lungs, in my fingers and in my feet, in my skin and toenails and in the things between my blood cells that I can never remember the name of. I can't feel the ground beneath me. I can't feel anything other than her; her lips, and her face beneath my hands, and her body crushed so tightly against me that the thud of her heartbeat seems to echo through my rib cage.

311

I think I would give up movies for this feeling.

Camilla's lips stir beneath mine. I think she might be smiling. She pulls away a tiny bit, but her arms stay wrapped tightly around me. And unless the zombie hordes invade my front porch, there is nothing on earth that's going to make me let go of her either.

"Sammy," she says breathlessly. Her forehead creases into a frown.

"Camilla? Are…you still angry with me?"

She seems to consider this for several seconds. "Yes," she says decisively.

"But why?"

She grins. "Well, we could have been doing this a long time ago, if you were quicker on your feet. But I guess I'll get over it."

I think about this for a moment as my hands circle around to the small of her back. It feels like there's a place there that was made especially for them. My lips brush her forehead, and her nose, and this one spot on her cheek that I've wanted to kiss for forever. My head is filled with fog and my skin feels like it's buzzing, but my lips seem to know exactly what they are doing.

"You know, you could have said something," I mumble.

"What, throw myself at you when—by all objective measures—you had zero interest? I have my pride, Sam.

And I was so sure you'd freak out if you knew how I felt. Guess I wasn't...brave enough to take that chance." She wraps her arms tighter around my middle. "It's possible, Sammy, that when it comes down to it—I'm as big a wuss as you are."

"Millie, I thought we established a long time ago that I'm pretty much useless. But I can't believe you didn't know...that it wasn't obvious..."

"What?" she says. Her smile disappears, and she looks up at me with her serious-Camilla eyes.

I brush the hair away from her face. My fingers trail over her skin, over the soft, perfect curve of her lips. My heart feels like it's trying to beat its way out of my chest, like that cartoon skunk whose name I've forgotten.

"I can't believe you couldn't see that I was crazy in love with you."

Camilla closes her eyes. But that beautiful smile is back. "Say that again," she says. "It might be the single greatest thing I've heard all year."

She touches my face with her guitar-calloused fingers, and then she rests her forehead against mine.

And I have no more words. I don't think I need them.

My lips touch hers. Maybe it's the other way around. Really, it's impossible to tell.

I'm thinking about the top five all-time greatest movie kisses. I can't believe I haven't made that list.

And I'm thinking about a screenplay I want to write. I have a hunch it'll be the first good movie I've ever written.

This one will be about a girl.

I don't know how I ever tried to write my story without her.

THE END

Acknowledgments

This novel may not have made it past the first draft without the carrot-and-stick encouragement of my friend and writing partner, Sophie Splatt. Thank you Sophie for your support, enthusiasm, endless supply of beverages, and for tirelessly admonishing my drone of self-doubt.

Thanks to my amazing writing group—Ilka Tampke, Jacinda Woodhead, Benjamin Laird, Simon Mitchell, Jo Horsburgh, and Sally Rippin—for your always-thoughtful feedback and surprisingly tasty vegan snacks. Sally, your "matchmaking" skills will not be forgotten!

Thank you to my first reader, Phoebe Norris, for laughing in all the right spots; my first publishing bosses, Maryann Ballantyne and Andrew Kelly, for teaching me about structure; and to Yollette Franklin for the crash course in World of Warcraft—my dwarf never made it past level twelve, so any WoW mistakes are purely my own.

To my wonderful fairy-god-folks at Hardie Grant Egmont— Karri Hedge for finding me in the pile, and Marisa Pintado, kick-arse editor and fellow nerd, for your unwavering belief in Sam and Camilla; I will be eternally grateful that my manuscript landed on your desk.

To the Melbourne Horror Film Society, whose poster at Thousand Pound Bend inspired the voice that became Sam's; you guys do good work.

And finally, the staff at the beautiful Astor Theatre for never calling security on the strange person photographing their carpet and walls; I hope to be catching *The Evil Dead* there for many years to come.